Kate Cann lives in Twickenham, right by the river Thames, with her family and dog. She loves long, intense conversations, running, reading, gardening, walking and white wine. She edited teenage fiction before rather arrogantly thinking she could do better, and writing it.

Have you read the other books in this trilogy?

Moving Out
Moving In

And look out for other books by Kate Cann:

Leaving Poppy

Footloose
Fiesta
Escape

Diving In
In the Deep End
Sink or Swim

www.katecann.com

Moving On

Kate Cann

SCHOLASTIC

To Nell, with love

Scholastic Children's Books,
Euston House, 24 Eversholt Street,
London, NW1 1DB, UK
a division of Scholastic Ltd
London ~ New York ~ Toronto ~ Sydney ~ Auckland
Mexico City ~ New Delhi ~ Hong Kong

First published as *Speeding* in the UK by Scholastic Ltd, 2002
This edition published by Scholastic Ltd, 2006

10 digit ISBN 0 439 95033 3
13 digit ISBN 978 0439 95033 6

Printed by Nørhaven Paperback A/S, Denmark

10 9 8 7 6 5 4 3 2 1

Papers used by Scholastic Children's Books are made from wood grown in
sustainable forests.

Chapter 1

Bonny doesn't trust me. She doesn't trust me an inch. She's looking at me across the pub-garden table and her face is all amazed and gorgeous and open, but it's like it's waiting to be hurt, like she thinks I'm suddenly going to get up and walk away.

Speak to her, Steele, you bonehead. Tell her how you feel. Tell her it's her you want after all. Tell her you were stupid not to realize it before. Tell her you hope, you *really* hope, she still wants you. Ask her. *Speak to her.*

I take a nervous swig of my beer, smirk like rigor mortis has just set in, and open my mouth.

Nothing comes out. . .

Shit, I can't! I'm sort of *fossilized* with embarrassment, and fear, and shock, and God knows what else. Half an hour ago we met up again by chance after a whole summer apart. And she tried to get away from me, but I chased after her and grabbed her and kissed her. And now I can't even speak to her.

If this was a film, it would've stopped at that kiss, wouldn't it. The clasp, the grasp, the oh–my–God–I've–found–you–again–and–I'll–never–let–you–go–again, *doof*, *doof*, *doof*, crashing finale music, screen blanks out. A film would let me off the hook. It wouldn't show me sitting across from her at a beer-stained table, gaping like a fish, wondering what the hell to say to her now.

Feeling so much I can't say a damn thing.

"I like your hair," I mutter.

"What?"

"Shorter. I like it."

"Oh. Right. Thanks."

"It's gone all bleached in the sun," I croak.

"Those are streaks."

"Oh."

"I had them put in."

"Oh."

"But I'm glad you thought they were the sun."

Silence. Bonny's face is floating in the heat haze. I turn away, watch the canal move sluggishly past on the other side of the low pub wall, then I look back at her, all tanned and fabulous from her holiday in Spain. Inside my head I threaten myself with violent self-induced death, then I count to three, reach across the table, get hold of her hand and mutter, "I've thought about you all summer."

"Yeah?" she mutters back. Her hand's shaking in mine. Or is it my hand shaking?

"I thought about what you said — you know, that day you moved out of the flat. And . . . and. . ."

. . .and I choke up. *Shit, I choke up.* I've thought about that day just about every day since, that day she told me she was crazy about me, so crazy she couldn't carry on living side by side as my flatmate any more. And I just stood there like a moron, saying nothing, and let her walk out and go and live with her dad.

And now I'm sitting here like a moron saying nothing. I don't know how to begin to talk about it. It's just too damn important to talk about, that's the problem.

Abruptly, Bonny drains her glass, so I finish my beer and she stands up, so I stand up too, and she mumbles, "Shall we go for a walk?" and I say, "Yeah" and we troop out of the pub garden miles away from holding hands.

Jesus, what a loser I am. What an inadequate. I bet she hates me now. I could kiss her, why can't I talk to her? Maybe that's the problem. Maybe that kiss spoiled everything. Maybe now I've started fancying her back, it won't work. Maybe we could only talk like we used to, all the time, open and free about anything and everything, when I didn't want her like this.

Because I do. I really want her. I keep thinking about that kiss, how good it was, how great it felt to hold her.

* * *

Like we're under a spell, we wander along the canal towpath towards the old Victorian wool mills and the flat we used to share. We stand and gaze across at its great arched windows burning in the late sun. "Nick still not charging you rent?" she murmurs.

"No," I say. "And I've gotta keep it that way. I can hardly afford food, let alone rent. I keep topping up his guilt about me."

"What, about the ad account falling through?"

"Yeah – I tell him he's shattered my confidence for good."

"Some hope of that. You're brilliant and you know it." She smiles at me, and for the first time in a long time our eyes meet. "You're still working for him, aren't you?"

"Yeah – storyboards. It's OK – fall out of bed, stagger down half asleep, draw a load of daft cartoons. It's money for jam, honestly. Well – it gets boring. But Nick pays me a good rate. Gotta save up so I don't starve next term."

"He's great, isn't he?"

"Yeah – and his missis."

There's a silence, and I know that like me she's thinking of the time they let her move into the flat, too, when she was fleeing from her hideous, vampire mother. She's thinking of the time we had there together. It feels awkward again, and I'm racking my brains for something to talk about when she suddenly says, "I'd love to see Petal again. How's he been?"

Petal – or Pitbull as I call him – is the huge mean ginger tom Bonny introduced into the flat to sort out a rat problem we had. "He's fine," I say. "Murderous as ever. Brings in chewed-up pigeons now he's running out of rats, leaves them on my bed."

Bonny laughs. "He really *loves* you."

"Yeah, well, that kind of love I can do without. Want to come up and see him now?"

She kind of twitches anxiously when I say that, like she's got to prepare herself for being up there with me again, facing all the feelings she had in the place. Unless she's feeling them right now. I hope she is.

"Yeah – in a minute," she says. "Let's just sit down for a bit, eh?"

We perch on one of the skinny benches they've spaced along the canal edge. The heat has dried up half the water, left cracked craters of mud with lush waterside weeds growing up. The sun's low in the sky now and it's kind of steamy, sleazy, sexy – apart from the gnats zooming around.

I'm so aware of her beside me I'm burning up. I gaze down at the mud like it's going to help me out.

"Look at the canal bank," says Bonny. "Isn't it weird?"

"Yeah. A couple of days ago, I came down here and drew it." Bonny glances up at me, smiling. She always loved me drawing, which could possibly be why I mentioned it. "I made it dead sinister, like a

5

swamp," I say. "I did it all grey and black, and the plants toxic-green."

"Can I see it?"

"Sure."

She stares back at the cracked mud. "Don't you fancy squishing your toes in that?"

"*No*, Bonny, I don't. And if *you* do you can forget about coming up to the flat to see Pitbull. It's pristine-clean."

She laughs, and it's such a gorgeous warm sound I edge closer to her on the bench, and then *hallelujah* she leans her head against my shoulder. I'm so pleased I forget to breathe for about five minutes. I rub my cheek against her hair, inhale its fabulous, citrusy, Bonny smell. "*Pristine*," she scoffs. "I bet it's a tip now I'm not there clearing it up."

"You suggesting you were the only one who cleared the place up?"

"I'm not suggesting! I'm saying! Come on, Rich – I remember you insisting toilets were self-cleaning . . . and that if you left fat on the cooker long enough it got burned away. . ."

"I did not," I say, into her hair. "Anyway, Andy and I – we've really got it sorted. We've got a cleaning rota stuck up on the fridge."

She lifts her head up from my shoulder, looks at me. "Andy?"

"He moved in, I told you. After you—"

"Left."

"Yeah. He's got your old room."

I wonder if that makes her sad. I kind of want it to.

"I don't believe you, about the rota," she says.

"OK, I lied. But he is tidier than me. And he knows about Mr Muscle Kitchen Cleaner and stuff."

"Mr Muscle. Wow."

"Yeah. We felt it suited us, seeing us we're so macho and everything. Seriously, Bonny, it's class now. Come up and see for yourself."

"In a minute," she says, and she nestles her head back down on my shoulder. "I love it here."

I give a kind of sigh of pleasure, rub my cheek against her gleamy hair. We're talking again. It's going to be OK, it's going to be fine. It's so good being this close to her.

The angle I am, I can't help but look straight down her top. I feel a bit crass, seeing as I'm still shaking with the shock and pleasure of finding her again, but I just seem to find myself doing it. Bonny's got fantastic tits. I thought that from the first time I met her, even though she used to wear these matronly shirts, no doubt prescribed as slimming by her evil mother. There's this gorgeous bit of baby-blue bra showing, and I can't help it, I start to think how fantastic it would be to unhook it and slide my hands under her top and—

"Rich?"

Guiltily, I snap my eyes middle distance. "Yeah?"

"Do you want to do something tonight?"

"With you, you mean? Definitely. What d'you wanna do – go out and eat or something?"

"But I want to be outside, and everywhere outside'll be packed in this weather. . ."

"OK. We'll get some grub, go up to the flat, climb down the fire escape, eat out on the balcony."

She gives this kind of squeal of pleasure. "The balcony – I'd forgotten about it! Have you been going there?"

"*Going* there?" I enthuse. "I practically *live* there. Me and Pitbull fight over the best sunbathing bits. I eat there, I *drink* there – it's fantastic sitting up there over the canal with a beer in your hand. . . When the sun goes down it's magic, the rooftops glow like they've just been transmutated—"

"Trans *what?*"

"– the *clouds* look like the Second Coming – in fact it's one hell of a religious experience up there, Bonny, I'm thinking of forming a cult."

She's looking at me all fondly. "I'd forgotten what an idiot you are. Come on, let's go." And she gets to her feet.

I stand up too, grinning, and she says, "Do we need to get food?"

"Er . . . yes. Unless you want stale bread and half a tin of baked beans that's been in the fridge for about a month. . ."

"Oh, *Rich!*"

"I was going food shopping! I was going shopping when I met you!"

Bonny reaches out, takes my hand all natural, fantastic. "We can get stuff," she says. "Come on, let's *go*." And she starts towing me back towards the town.

"What d'you want to eat?" she asks.

"Steak," I say, which is what I normally say when offered a choice of food. "We could grill it, pretend it's a barbie. . ."

Bonny stops, looks at me. "D'you want a barbie?"

"Yeah, but –"

"I remember you saying you could get one down the fire escape. Only Daddy's just chucked one out – one of those little ones that look like a kettle-drum. He's got this state of the art one now, with gas and a proper spit. . ."

"He would."

"Rich, don't be like that – he *likes* you! Look – why don't I go and get the old one now? No one would mind – Ellie dumped it out in the garage, she thought it was dangerous for the twins. You get the food, I'll get the barbie and some fuel and nick a bottle of wine. . ."

"But you live miles away – how're you going to carry all that over on the bus?"

She looks at me, like she's wondering how I'll react. Then she says, "Well – I've got a car now."

Chapter 2

"*Don't* start on me Rich. Just *don't*. I know you think I'm obscenely rich."

"Did I say anything?"

"You don't need to. Your face says it for you. Look, if my dad wants to buy me a car 'cos he feels guilty about all the shit I had to put up with because of Mum, I'm not going to say no, am I?"

"No," I admit. I'm floored, I can't help it. I'm wondering why she wants anything to do with a pauper like me. "When did you learn to drive?"

"Daddy gave me open-ended lessons for my seventeenth birthday."

"He would."

"Oh, *stop it!* Stop saying *he would*."

"Sorry. It's just – your dad's so . . . *loaded*. Never mind. Tell me about your driving lessons."

She looks at me, a bit arch, then she says, "*Well* – I've been learning on and off for about eight months now. More *off* than on when things were bad with Mum, and – and I didn't keep them up when I – you know—"

"Lived with me. No, you didn't. I'd've noticed."

"But when I moved in with Daddy, he made me step them up to two a week, and Ellie was great, she came out driving with me, and . . . I passed first time."

"Brilliant," I say, trying not to sound too jealous. Driving lessons, a car – it's so out of my financial sphere it's extra-terrestrial. "And *Daddy* bought you a car soon as you passed, did he?"

She looks down. "Yes. And if you say *he would* again, I'm going to whack you one."

Inside, I jump. I risk it. I put my arms straight round her, hug her to me. "I'm teasing, dummo. You can't help being a posh rich bitch, can you."

She jabs me hard in the chest, but not so hard I let go. "No. Any more than you can help being a rude skint *yob*."

We stand and look at each other, smiling, faces close, really liking each other. I'm as turned on as anything. I want to keep my arms round her, but I don't, I let them kind of fall back to my side and say, "*So*. What kind of car is it? Merc? BMW? *Jaguar?*"

"Oh, *come on*, Rich, it's not a big deal! It's just useful, right?"

"Right," I say.

"Come with me while I pick it up, and you can see it," she says. We start walking along again and she adds, "I'll give you a lift to the supermarket."

Her car's a little blue Polo, a couple of years old. She swings into it all self-consciously, and I get into the passenger seat beside her. Then we both buckle up and she starts the engine and checks behind her in the rear-view mirror. And we drive off. I have to admit it, she's smooth, she's good, not showing off in the slightest. I don't tell her this, of course.

Sheer envy aside, I'm not sure how I'm going to handle this new, super-assured, independent, car-owning Bonny, if you want the truth. It's like she's moved out into the fast lane and left me behind. Don't get me wrong, I like it, I admire it. But I kind of feel nostalgic for the old Bonny too. The old Bonny was a hell of a lot easier to impress.

"OK if I drop you off here, Rich?" she asks, and without waiting for an answer she pulls over at the kerb. Then she kind of fumbles in the leather shoulder bag she's dumped in the well between us and says, "Look, let's go halves on this food—"

"*No*," I say, louder than I mean to. "Nick's just paid me a wad for a load of storyboards I did last week."

"I'm so *glad* you're still working for Nick!" she says, then she goes all flustered and mutters, "See you back at the flat, OK?"

"Sure. Don't be long, OK?" I mutter back. Everything's gone all awkward again. I get out, missing the chance to plant a kiss on her, and she drives off.

Minefield. Why do new relationships have to be such a bloody complicated *minefield*?

Calm down, Rich. Chill. It'll be fine. Later, on the balcony, after some wine, when it's dark, we'll *really* talk.

I've got to tell her I've changed. She's got to tell me she hasn't.

I tour the supermarket, looking for the cheapest food. The constant battle to make money last – once I've earned it in the first place – is a major theme in my life. And this amazing meeting-up with Bonny, far from sending it out of my head, adds weight to it, because I hate it that she's flush with cash and I'm not. Bonny always used to be adamant that that doesn't matter. The first row we ever had, right after she'd moved into the flat, she went on about how I was hung up about money, how it just wasn't all that important in life. And I liked what she said, although I thought then – like I think now – that it's easy to talk like that when you're loaded.

There's a saying about money and sex – if you're getting enough, you don't think about them much. If you're not getting enough, you think about them all the time. Well, I'm living proof of that saying. My mind's always full of both. And the queasy suspicion that the two are tied up together.

I hang over the meat chillers wondering whether I can afford to get rump steak, and realize with a jolt that it was during that first row that I started to get turned on to Bonny. I remember thinking how she'd changed, come alive somehow. I wanted to draw her, get her down while she looked all fired up. But I was too dense to work out what was happening. Just because she wasn't the type of girl I normally went for.

I pick up the rump, then some beer and floury, crusty bread, and a bit of salad so Bonny's impressed I've taken on board her nagging about eating a balanced diet. Then I pay, head back to the wool mill, let myself in through the big glass doors, and ride up to the top floor in the clanking old wrought-iron lift.

Great. Andy's not in, and the place isn't too much of a tip. I stand and look at the off-key art display I've been steadily sticking up around the walls of the main room as I've drawn like a madman all summer. I move the sinister canal-swamp one I promised to show Bonny to a better position. Will she think I'm showing off, all these pictures plastered up everywhere? I'm gonna take them down. No, I'm not. She loves my work.

I shove the food in the fridge, clear the half-a-sink of dirty plates and mugs that Andy's thoughtfully left for me, then I head into my box-sized bedroom. I shove the clothes lying around into the wall-cupboard, shake out the duvet and pull it over the bed. This is not, I tell myself, because I seriously think Bonny's going to allow me to haul her in here, it's just better to Be Prepared, isn't it? Ten thousand boy scouts can't be wrong. Not that boy scouts ever get laid. Stop it, stop it. Why am I so nervous?

The intercom on the wall buzzes; I jump. Bonny's voice crackles, "It's me!"

I press the button to let her in, go out on to the landing to meet her, and she steps out of the lift looking gorgeous and absolutely laden with barbecue and bags. "You gave your keys back to Nick, did you?" I say.

She shrugs, says, "Well, I didn't want to just let myself in, did I?" Then we fuss about, making a big deal of me taking the barbie off her and shifting it into the flat to cover up the awkwardness we feel.

And then she spots my art display. "Oh – God," she says. "Oh – *God*. They're *brilliant*." And she races over to them, hands clasped in front of her, impressed as all hell. She studies them, one by one, ignoring me like she's forgotten I'm here. She's biting her lip and she's totally absorbed. I love it that she likes them so much. Who wouldn't?

After a long few minutes, she's had time to see them all, and go back to the ones she likes best for a second look. Then it's like she comes to, and she's embarrassed for letting them absorb her so much.

She says, "They're really great, Rich, honestly," but she can't look at me.

All diplomatic, I change the subject, and say, "I don't know where the mog is. Off murdering some small innocent creature I s'pose."

Bonny grins. "Petal!" she calls. "*Pe – tal!*"

"He only answers to Pitbull now. Seriously, Bonny, don't screw up his hard-man image, calling him Petal. The rats would really take the piss out of him if they knew."

"I thought he'd eaten all the rats?" she laughs. Then she rummages in one of the bags and comes out with one of those crazy luxury pots of cat food.

"Oh, Jesus, Bonny! Only sad old crones buy that stuff."

"Oh, shut up."

"*Pussykins will love you more if you treat her to Mangled Blackbird in Puked-Up Vole Sauce!*"

"Shut *up*! I just wanted to get him a treat! Petal! OK – *Pit-bull!*"

And the mog himself suddenly swaggers round the door of Andy's room, where he's doubtless been curled up in his favourite spot – Andy's pillow. He spots Bonny, canters, mewing, over to her side and weaves round her legs purring like a steam-engine. "Look at that," I grumble. "You lousy traitor, Pitbull. Who's looked after you all summer, eh, you ungrateful little git?"

"Have you missed me, baby?" Bonny's cooing.

"*Have* you?" She pulls the foil lid off the posh cat food and puts it down on the floor. Pitbull rams his snout into the pot, gobs up a great mouthful, looks up at me with a withering sneer like he's saying maybe if I bought him decent food for once he'd like me better, and rams his nose back in the pot again.

"He seems very hungry," says Bonny, all critical.

"Yeah, well, I usually feed him about this time. Depending on the number of bits of corpses I find in the flat. Look – are we going to stand here and watch him slurp up the last mouthful? I'm hungry too, you know!"

Bonny laughs, and I toe-end Pitbull out of the way and pick up the barbecue. I'm quite grateful to him, though. He's helped us break the ice. God, I'm looking forward to when there won't be any ice left between me and Bonny to be broken. It's weird, some of the time it's just like back before she walked out, just mates, all jokey and relaxed, but this other thing keeps coming in too now, this new thing, making us awkward, stiff.

Stiff, Rich – yeah, great. Very Freudian.

"OK," I say, all masculine and efficient. "I'll get the barbecue down on to the balcony, get it lit up."

"It comes apart," says Bonny. "Maybe if you took it down bit by bit. . ."

"Andy's got this territorial-army type backpack," I say. "I bet it would fit in that."

Five minutes later, we've rammed the barbie bit

by bit into Andy's enormous backpack and I'm swinging out on to the fire-escape like some action hero with it strapped hugely to my back. Bonny's hanging out over the edge all gratifyingly anxious, telling me to go carefully, and I'm going as impressively fast as I can.

Down I climb, past Abacus's office window, then down to the second floor where the iron ladder stops at the balcony. I tip the barbie out of the backpack, then I climb the ladder again to get the coal.

Bonny's disappeared by the time I make it back to the flat. "I'm in the kitchen," she calls. "You got *salad*!"

"Yeah, well, you can drop the surprised voice, Bonny. I'm dead healthy in my eating habits now."

"*Yeah?* What's this Pot Noodle doing on the shelf then?"

"That's Andy's. Pass us the grub, I'll take it down with the coal."

Bonny hurries over to me clutching loads of goodies including a big packet of luxury-looking choccy biscuits that I decide not to comment on. She's so *sweet*. Just for a minute I want to drop everything, I want to get hold of her and hug her, but I don't, I cram it all in the backpack and set off down the ladder again. "I'll light the barbie, then I'll come back for you and the salad," I call up.

It doesn't take me long to reassemble the barbecue, despite engineering not exactly being my strong point. I set it in front of the big glass doors that lead out from the deserted second floor, then I tip some coal in its grate and risk burning off my hair by using far more lighter fuel that I think you're s'posed to to ignite it. I open the wine and put it on the ground with the glasses and the bread in its bag. Then I knock the cap off a beer, take a long pull, and look around me.

It's pretty bloody amazingly romantic, if you want the truth. Like Juliet's balcony, all flagstones and sexy balustrades. Only I'm not going to be down below like Romeo, spouting up poetry; I'm going to be right up here with my girl, cooking steaks. It's kind of a shame Pitbull uses the two stone urns either side of the balcony doors as toilets, 'cos there's a definite whiff of catshit floating over. Still, the steaks'll over-power that, won't they. And maybe later we can plant the urns up with night-scented flowers, and we can come here in the sensual dark and. . . What we need is a blanket. A blanket on the ground.

"Ri-*ich!*"

"Yeah?" I shout back.

"It's all ready!"

"Great – I'm coming." I sling the backpack back on and swarm up the ladder. And there's Bonny standing at the top, arms full of two plates and a bowl, with a huge tartan rug wrapped round her. So she had the same idea about the blanket, did she?

"You look like Rob Roy," I smirk.

And she goes pink and says, "I just thought we needed something to . . . you know. *Sit* on."

Chapter 3

Thirty minutes on and the steaks are sizzling succulently on the grid, and we're sitting side by side on the thick tartan rug drinking beer and wine and watching the setting sun set fire to the canal. It was a bit awkward at first as we waited for the coal to heat up, and I had this thought that we should've gone to a restaurant or a pub to eat, so we could hide behind lots of other people making a noise, but after a drink or two we both relaxed and started chatting. And then a whole crowd of noisy kids went along by the canal, dropping hamburger cartons, and I made these ghostly wails over the edge and Bonny shrieked "*Stop dropping rubbish!*" and the kids all started swearing and looking round but we'd ducked down behind the balustrades then and they couldn't see us. And then one of the girls started picking up the cartons, looking really spooked. This cracked us up, of course, and what with that and feeling all superior, 'cos we were having our own barbie and not takeaway crap, we end up all bonded and close.

"Stop picking at the bread, Rich," says Bonny, fondly. "There won't be any left."

"I'm starving."

"Well, have some salad." And she picks out a chunk of cucumber, and feeds it into my mouth. It still feels weird, doing these touchy things together, but I'm not about to stop her.

"D'you reckon they're ready yet? The steaks?"

She pokes at them as they sizzle. "How bloody do you like them?"

"If it means I get to eat now – bloody."

"OK. I want the smaller one, though – it's more cooked."

And soon we're chomping through these wonderful steaks, and Bonny makes me have some of her dad's expensive wine and laughs at me when I say I like the beer better. It's got really dark now. There's a moon like a nail clipping floating up above the rooftops, hardly shedding any light. Bonny says, "So, you sorted college, did you? You're back in for a second year?"

"Yup,' I say. "I just about caught up."

"You thought about uni or anything?"

"Nope. I just know I want a year out after A levels."

"Doing what?"

"Dunno. Travel."

There's a long pause, then she says, "What's up? You've gone all quiet," and I look at her, and then straight out before I can chicken out, I say, "It's 'cos I'm not interested in talking right now." Then I kind of twist round and put my hand on her shoulder. She doesn't back off, so I bring my mouth down to hers.

It's brilliant. It feels as great as the first kiss we ever had, that kiss we had just a few age-long hours ago, and then it gets better, much better. Ten seconds into it and I know she's really up for it, too. She wraps her arms round my back, digging her nails in just enough, pulling me up tight against her. We kiss and kiss, and it's so hot I find myself kind of automatically manoeuvring her backwards, and soon we're all stretched out on the rug. I'm up on one elbow over her, stroking down her neck, looking at her lovely open face, then I move in and kiss her again – and suddenly, without warning, she wriggles away from me and blurts out, "Do you *mean* this?"

"*What?*"

"Do you really want to kiss me or—"

"Course I bloody want to, Bonny! What – you think I'm *acting*?"

Shit, *shit*, why did I snap like that, why did I swear at her? She huddles up on the rug, arms round her knees, won't look at me. It's all gone horribly wrong. "What's up?" I wail.

"I just can't believe you," she hisses, into her

knees. "I can't believe you've changed this much. You never used to give me a second glance. You were all into *Portia*."

Portia. Portia my stunning, poisonous ex, who was around all the time Bonny was sharing the flat. I was waiting for her name to crop up again.

"I told you, Bonny, it's over. Well over. I haven't seen her all summer."

"Yeah, but if she crooked her finger at you again you'd go running. . ."

"She already has done. I told her to get stuffed. I told her she didn't do it for me any more."

"You said that?"

"Yup. She was all – *I have to make the choice between you and Tony*. You know, that poor sod she was two-timing me with. And I told her I'd made the choice for her." I can't help but sound a bit proud, when I say that. It was one of my nobler moments, telling Portia to sod off.

"I haven't regretted it once, Bonny. Yeah, she was all glitzy and flash and everything, but she was a real pain in the arse to spend time with. Whereas *you*. . ." I trail off and put my arm round her shoulders, try and tip her back on to the rug again. She's gone all wooden and rigid and rejecting, though. She reaches past me, picks up the bottle of wine, takes a great glug straight from the bottle. "Whereas I *what*?" she croaks.

Damn. I was hoping to show her, rather than have

to tell. "Look, Bonny," I start up, "you're *real*, OK? She was completely fake."

"She might be fake but she's fantastic looking."

"So are you."

"Not like her, I'm not."

"You are. You're the sort to . . . to *grow* on people."

Possible bad comment. Bonny seizes the wine again, takes another huge swig, won't look at me.

"Oh, come on, Bonny. Gimme a break. Yeah, Portia knocks you dead between the eyes, but that kind of palls on you when you're around her for too long, listening to her stupid yakky voice. Whereas *you* . . . it was the other way round with you. I got to really like you, and so I started really liking the way you look, too."

I'm pretty chuffed with this explanation. After I've said it, I realize it's true. Bonny's started to smile, liking it too. "And anyway, you've *changed*," I go on. "You know you've changed. Soon as you got away from your mum, you kind of came alive, didn't you? Not just wearing different clothes and stuff, just the whole way you are. You started laughing, for one thing. And smiling. You have got the most gorgeous sexy smile, Bonny, you have, seriously. It's all lopsided. Portia just used to look like she was baring her teeth at you when she smiled."

Bonny takes another slurp of wine – she damn nearly finishes the bottle off. Then, just as I think she might show me her smile again, she collapses back down on to her hunched-up knees and starts to cry.

"Bonny! What's up?" I put my arm round her shoulders, hug her to me, kiss her hair.

"I'm sorry!" she's sobbing. "Rich – oh, God, I'm really sorry! It's just – seeing you again, it's such a shock, I can't take it! I can't take what you've said – about missing me and stuff – I can't take it!"

I'm full of hope, full of fear. "Why not?" I croak.

"'Cos it's too *brilliant*, that's why not! It's . . . *everything* I've wanted! Brilliant things don't happen to me, I don't trust them. Oh . . . *shit*. I've been fine, I've been in control, I've been getting on with my life, all that stuff . . . but seeing *you*, you're just so fantastic, Rich, and I'm feeling everything I felt before, I can't *bear* it. . ."

I hug her tighter to me, rock her back and forward like a baby in a cradle. I feel like I could start crying too, with relief, emotion, everything. It's like she's cracked wide open, telling me everything I want to know.

"You're gonna run a mile now, aren't you?" she gasps out. "I wouldn't blame you."

I kiss her hair again. "I'm not going anywhere. I'm not."

"Even though I'm blubbing all over you. . ."

"Bonny, you can drench me in snot for all I care. Look, I—"

"What? *What?*"

OK, this is it, Steele. Say it. *Say it.*

I take a deep breath.

I open my mouth and let it come out.

"Ever since you walked out, Bonny, and said what you said about liking me . . . I've been kicking myself. I couldn't stop thinking about you. When I wasn't seeing you every day I realized how much I really, really like you. I've been *dying* to bump into you again."

"Yeah?" she whispers.

"Yeah. And then when I saw you today, it was like – why didn't I realize how gorgeous you were before? I mean – you've changed, yeah, you've got *more* gorgeous, but it's always been there. It's just I was too thick to see it back then. It was like Portia had put a sack over my head or something. Shit, I'm not making sense. Look – d'you want to come out with me, Bonny? Will you?"

Come out with me. I sound about as sophisticated as a fourteen year old. But it has this magical effect on Bonny. She puts her arms round my neck and starts crying, wonderfully, into the collar of my shirt. "Do you mean it?" she sobs.

"*Yes*, I mean it. I want us to be together. I want you to be my girlfriend."

"'Cos we can just be friends. You don't have to pretend you—"

"That I what? *Fancy* you? Bonny, trust me, I fancy you something wicked. God – look at you. When we were sitting on the bench by the canal? I was looking down your front. I couldn't stop myself."

She lets out this explosive laugh, then she says, "I hate them."

"What?"

"My boobs. I hate them. They're too big. You get men leering at you like you're some cheap stripper."

"That's not what they're thinking, trust me. They're thinking you're unbelievably sexy."

"Hah! Mum used to say I could always get them . . . you know . . . *surgically reduced*."

"*Wha-at?*" I'm so incensed I can hardly speak. "Cutting into your – that evil *cow*! Sorry, Bonny, that is the foulest thing I ever heard. It is, honest."

She's looking up at me, eyes wet, and she's really smiling now. "She used to say it was an option. If they made me unhappy."

"Yeah, and I bet they only made you unhappy in the first place 'cos of her attitude. With her obsession about looking like a fucking stick all the time. God, Bonny, I think you're gorgeous and if you even *think* about letting some psycho surgeon and his knife anywhere *near* you I'll chuck you over this edge here, OK? Into the canal. *OK?*"

"OK," she gurgles.

"Well?" I demand.

"Well, what?"

"Are you going to come out with me?"

"*Of course I am*," she breathes, then she twists round and I think she's going to kiss me but instead she says, "Oh, God, I'm *drunk*! How'm I gonna drive *home*?"

Chapter 4

Bonny's right, she's drunk as a skunk. All the wine she's been tipping down her throat in the last fifteen minutes is suddenly kicking in. "You're not," I say.

"Oh, I *am*!" she wails. "I'm *pissed*!"

"I'm not arguing with that, Bonny! I mean you're not driving home."

She's got her wristwatch about a millimetre away from her face, trying to focus. "S'not that late. Snorreven midnight. I can phone Daddy. Tell him I'm staying the night."

I can't believe she's said that, so open and easy. "Bonny – *look*. We don't have to rush things. We've only just got together again. We—" I break off then 'cos Bonny's collapsed back down on to her knees, only this time she's giggling, not crying.

"Rich-*ard*! You don't think I mean stay the night as in – *stay the night* – do you?"

There's no answer to that, apart from *yes*. I start laughing too, and Bonny laughs louder – she's gorgeous like this, all loony and soft. "The state I'm in I couldn't sleep with my *teddy bear*," she gurgles. "I couldn't sleep with my *rubber duck*! I couldn't sleep with Barbie, or Barbie's boyfriend Ken, or—"

I hug her harder. "Yeah, Bonny, *hilarious*. Spare me the list of your toys. I bet you've still got 'em, haven't you? Up on a shelf."

"No. In a trunk."

"OK. Look – what are we going to do?"

"I'll phone Daddy," she says. "I'll tell him I'm staying with you. He'll be fine. He'd sooner I did just about anything than drive when I'm drunk."

"Even stay with me?"

She nestles into my chest like she wants to burrow right into me. "Yes. Can I sleep in your room?"

"But you just said—"

"I just want to lie next to you, and you be there, OK?"

"OK."

"I can't believe this, Rich. You know – the way we've met up and everything."

"Me neither." There's a kind of awed silence, as we both contemplate what's happened tonight. "How'm I gonna get you up that wonky ladder?" I whisper, finally.

* * *

Somehow, we manage it. I put my arms right round her, hold on to the railings on either side of her. She fits into me like we're one of those old Russian doll nests. And I try not to get too horny as, very slowly, we stumble up the ladder together. When one of her feet slips, I press against her, keeping her on the rung. We get to the top and I hoist her as gently as I can over the window opening, and then she's rolling over, giggling, safe on the floor of the flat.

"What about all the stuff?" she gasps. "The stuff on the balcony?"

"It'll be fine, till tomorrow. I'm not going down there again, not till it's light. Now come on, Bonny, you better call your old man, hadn't you."

"My phone – it's in my bag – over there."

I fetch the phone for her. It's real decent, one of the latest. Of course. She presses a couple of buttons, and I watch her compose her face as she waits to be answered.

"Ellie? Hi! Hi, it's me – sorry it's so late. . . Oh, were you? I'm sorry. Look – I've met up with an old friend. . . No, you never met him. Anyway, it's been great, but I've had too much to drink. . . Yeah, yeah, it's OK, I'm going to kip down at his place and come back in the morning. . . Will you? Thanks, Ellie."

She clicks the phone off and grins at me. "Ellie never asks loads of questions, not like Daddy does. She just wants to know I'm OK."

"It's really worked out with her, hasn't it?"

"Yeah. She's so exhausted all the time, running round after the twins. I just have to say I'll *bath* them for her and she just about *passes out* with gratefulness."

"Which she wouldn't do if she was your real mum."

"Right. Then she'd expect it. She'd—" We're interrupted by Bonny's phone playing an ominous, martial-type tune. "Daddy," she grimaces, and flicks the phone on again.

She listens for a few seconds, then she says, "It's Rich. I'm at Nick and Barb's flat. . . No he's *not*, Daddy, that's not fair. What? I'll be in my old room of course. . . Look, don't you trust me? I just didn't wanna drive when I'd had too much to drink, that's all. . . Yes. . . Yes. . . *Yes* . . . no. Daddy, *no* – you are *not* speaking to Rich, don't be so *bloody* patronizing –"

She's getting really worked up, slurring her words. I come over all he-man and protective and gesture to her to give me the phone. And she screws up her face, shuts her eyes, and shoves it at me.

"Hi," I say, in the deepest voice I can sink to, "it's Richard here."

Daddy's smooth businessman voice comes oiling efficiently down the line. "Richard. I'm a little concerned about my daughter. She sounds pretty drunk to me."

I laugh, all suave. "I'm afraid we've been celebrating meeting up again. . ."

"Of course, of course. Look – can I be frank?"

"Of course."

"I've never been completely clear about her reasons for moving out of your flat at the start of the summer. Don't get me wrong, I was delighted she did – it was wonderful to have my little girl living with me again. But – look, I'll come to the point. I understand from Barb that she had a bit of a *thing* about you. Now, I'm sure you're an honourable chap, Richard, and you wouldn't dream of taking advantage of a girl who was the worse for drink, but I'm also sure you can appreciate the concern I feel. . ."

This is excruciating. It's like being projected back to 1945. "Look, Mr –" I start, then I stop 'cos I realize I don't know his name. Bonny's got her mum's surname, Davies. I can hardly call him *Daddy*, can I? "Look – please don't worry – Bonny and I are good friends, that's all. . ."

"Even so, Richard, I think it would be better all round if I drove over and fetched her home now, don't you? Then I can drive her back in the morning to collect her car."

"But she's gone to bed already!" I fib desperately, my eyes locked into Bonny's. "She's gone into her old room and shut the door. She'll sleep it off, she'll be fine in the morning."

There's a long, long, disbelieving pause. Then Daddy says, "Very well. Thank you. I'll phone her in the morning, all right?"

"Not too early!" I say, all jesting, and then wish I hadn't. Daddy hangs up.

"*Jeeee*-sus!" I wheeze. "He's like someone out of the Mafia! Why didn't he save the phone bill and just say 'Toucha my daughter – I kill you'?"

Bonny laughs, shuffles across the floor towards me, puts her arms round my neck. "He's just very protective – he didn't have much to do with bringing me up, and it's like he's trying to cram it all into the time we've got together now."

"He was *tough*. I thought you said he liked me?"

"Well – it's relative. He likes you compared to that guy I got involved with over the summer."

"Who was some kind of axe-wielding psychopath. Don't tell me."

"I won't. Don't wanna think about him. Anyway, Rich – you *lied*. You lied loads. You told him we were just *friends*."

"Yeah, that was a huge porky," I say, and kiss her. Then I go, "You lied too. Do all girls lie that easily to their dads?"

"Yeah. Survival. Don't boys?"

"They just don't answer."

We fall silent, arms round each other, looking out of the huge arched windows at the black night. "I want to sleep here," she suddenly says. "I love these windows so much. And this is where your bed was when I moved in. I used to come and lie on it when you were out, and think about you."

It kind of overwhelms me, when she says that. It's the kind of thing I do. It's passionate, that's what it is, passionate and just a little bit obsessive. "You stay here," I say, "and I'll tow it in. You shall have your wish."

When I get back to the windows, dragging my mattress behind me, Bonny's curled up on the hard floor, asleep. Very, very gently I lift her, slide her on to my bed. Then I lie down beside her.

I feel like I stay awake for hours, just looking at her. She's beautiful. She moves about in her sleep, and once she mutters, "I can't, I can't. . ."

I think – this is different, deeper, to anything I've been in before. This relationship that's starting – it makes Portia and me look like a stupid strip–cartoon. And there's no going back, not after everything we've been through. That makes me feel scared, but I don't want to change anything. She's beautiful.

Chapter 5

Of course it's kind of different in the morning. Isn't it always? I can tell Bonny feels grim and skuzzy having slept in her clothes and not done the complicated nocturnal skin routine girls seem to go in for. I offer to lend her my toothbrush and she laughs, says, "Actually, Rich, I think I'm going to drive home now, get showered and stuff there."

I put my arms round her but she won't let our faces touch. She won't even look at me properly. "If I get home early," she says, "it kind of cancels out staying out all night."

A gust of wind with rain in it hits the window. "God," I groan, "what happened to the lovely heat we had yesterday?"

"Yeah," she says mournfully. "Autumn's on its way. How long before you've got to go back to college?"

"Not long enough. Don't wanna think about it."

"Me neither."

"I wish we'd got together at the start of the summer," I blurt out.

"*Do* you?" she says, and at last she looks at me. She's still lovely, even with her mascara all splodged round her eyes.

"Yes," I say. "When you coming back?"

This big, body-shaking sigh comes out of her, and she presses her face against my chest. "I can't believe it, Rich. I can't."

"You mean you can't trust it."

"Yes. No. Dunno."

"You will, Bonny. Honestly, you will. Meet me for lunch?"

"I can't. I promised to help out with the twins. Ellie wants to take them swimming and she can't do it on her own. Last time one of them was halfway up the steps to the high diving board before someone spotted him. . ."

"OK. This evening?"

"Yes. Early. Here or The Ship?"

"The Ship," I say, thinking that if she's this twitchy still it'll be easier to start off in a pub. "Now, can't I even make you a cuppa before you go?"

"No. Honestly, Rich – I'd sooner get off. I really want to get some clean clothes on and stuff. But can I. . ." She trails off.

"Course you can. What?"

She laughs. "Can I have one of your pictures? To take away with me?"

"Sure. Which one d'you want?"

She hesitates, then she says, "That one of the canal."

I know she wants this one 'cos it'll remind her of last night, when we were sitting there, all on the threshold of everything, and I feel really pleased. I fetch it for her, then I say, "OK. Seven o'clock at The Ship, yeah?" Then I put my hands either side of her face and make her kiss me goodbye.

Ten minutes after she's gone, I'm making tea and thinking I should shower and get down to Nick's office, because I need to get in as much work and bank up as much dosh as I can before college starts up again. Then Andy strolls yawning and scratching out of his bedroom. "Make one for me, mate," he goes. "Grruurgh, I feel like shit."

"Good party?"

"Great. A whole crowd of us got loaded up with cans, went down to that bit of wasteland by the canal – you know the bit by the old shoe factory? We got a fire going . . . trouble is that brought the feds down after us, didn't it. I pointed out that our fire was nothing like as big as the fire that gets lit in the exact same place for Bonfire Night by seriously responsible citizens in charge of vulnerable little kids, and one of the bastards took my name and address."

I shake my head sagely. "Never talk back to the feds, Andy, mate. Especially not when you're right. What time you get in?"

"About three, I think." Then he suddenly goes, "*He-ey!* You had Bonny here! You were out there –" he lurches over to the kitchen door, peers out into the main room. "Yeah! There's the bed! I remember – last night – I nearly fell over you – what you move the bed for? Hey! You an item now?"

"I hope so," I say, and I hand him his tea. We go and sit on the edge of my mattress, watch the sun trying to nose its way through the clouds. I fill him in with what happened with Bonny. He doesn't say much; in fact, he doesn't say anything.

"What's up?" I demand.

"What you mean?"

"Well – I'm telling you how chuffed I am we've got together at last, and you're not saying a bloody thing."

There's a pause, then Andy shrugs. "OK, it's great. If you feel like that, it's great. It's just –"

"What?"

"Well – from all you've told me about her, Rich, she's bringing one hell of a load of emotional baggage along with her."

Andy's mum's a therapist, and he's absorbed all this psychoanalytical jargon. It can really piss you off. "*Emotional baggage?*" I sneer. "You mean her suitcases keep bursting into tears?"

"Yeah, yeah, Rich. Funny man. I mean all that crap

she had, from her mother. That's not just gonna disappear just 'cos you're on the scene, is it?"

"But she got away from her mum. She hardly sees her now."

"Yeah, but it's damaged her. It's made her all insecure. . ."

"I think she's dealt with it. She's *changed*. She's changed so much."

"But it's still there inside her. It's bound to be."

"Bloody hell, Andy," I scoff. "You'll be on about her inner child next."

"OK, you sneer, mate," snaps Andy. "I'm only trying to give you a bit of advice. But since you *mention* her inner child, I wouldn't wanna be around when it flips out. *OK?*"

I shrug, look at my watch, mutter about needing to get downstairs to Abacus and needing a shower, and stomp off to the bathroom. I'm careful not to slam the door so I don't sound like I'm sulking, but I am. Sulking. Where does Andy get off, warning me like that about Bonny?

He's jealous, that's what it is. Obvious. He hasn't pulled practically all summer, only some slapper the other week at that club who kept jamming her tongue in his ear and then passed out on him. Nice. And now I get together with someone who's not only gorgeous but who's got a brain and I know I like 'cos she's already a friend – well. He's bound to be jealous, isn't he?

Chapter 6

I'm not a bit prepared for what's waiting for me half an hour later when I get downstairs to the bright, arty offices of Abacus Design. Instead of Nick's usual "what time d'you call this, I've been sat here for hours" routine, there's a load of smirking and suggestive laughter, and on my desk a huge, pink cardboard cut-out of two hearts skewered together with an arrow.

"All right, Richy boy!" crows Nick, all sing-song. "We know what you've been doing!"

"Yeah? How the hell d'you know that?"

Nick swings round on his long-suffering assistant, Camilla. "There, babe – as good as a confession. Not – *What you talking about?* But – *How d'you know?*"

Camilla smiles, says, "Ignore him, Rich. Have you

had breakfast? Only there's a bacon butty going begging over there on the tray. . ."

I'm over there like a shot. I don't like to see food going begging, even if I did have a mega-bowl of Andy's Krunchy Kornflakes before I came down.

"Like the hearts?" leers Nick. "Class, aren't they?"

"Yeah," I mumble, through a mouthful. "Real class. Who did 'em?"

"Me," smirks Nick. "Took me five minutes. 'Cos I'm a *professional*. You wanna keep them? Show them to Bonny?"

"All right, Nick – stop dicking about. How d'you know about me and Bonny?

"'Cos we had a very late phonecall last night. From a very anxious *Daddy*."

"Shit," I groan.

"How come she calls him Daddy still? What's he have to do to her? My kids call me Craphead."

"They do not. What did *Daddy* say?"

"Well – he'd just been talking to you, he said. On her mobile. And she was staying upstairs with you and he wanted to check out how *honourable* you were. Well, I didn't let you down, mate. I didn't say you were randy as a newly-turned werewolf. I said what an all-round, ex-boy-scout great guy you were. How you actually preferred DIY to sex. How if faced by the prospect of a bit of shelf erection or the other sort you'd go for shelves every time. How—"

"Christ, Nick – what are you *on*? It's ten o'clock in the *morning*!"

"Sorry, darling. I'm just a sucker for soap operas."

"Oh, great. So you think Bonny and me are a soap opera?"

"Yeah. One of those cheesy, intense, teenage-angst ones. And I'm on *tenterhooks* about what happens in the next episode."

"Nick – you're sick."

"Yup. Now the *wife* – she's even more excited about all this than me. Matchmaking being one of her chief interests in life. Daddy's under the illusion you're just-good-friends, but Barb suspects different. And since she reckons she matchmaked you and Bonny by letting her move into the flat an' all, she's absolutely *agog*. She wants you both to come round for a barbie tomorrow night."

I glare silently at Nick. I don't know what to say. Talk about going public before anything's exactly happened.

"Come on, mate, say yes," Nick rattles on. "You can't be booked up – no one is on a Thursday. And you know Barb's barbies are legendary. She'll get steaks the size of your thighs, garlic bread dripping in . . . garlic bread stuff, and salads like you've only ever fantasized about."

"I don't fantasize about salads, Nick."

"I bet you don't. You randy little ape. Anyway – you coming or not? Barb wants catering numbers."

I consider briefly. Potential excruciating embar-rassment to Bonny and me of appearing as new, dewy couple weighed against one of Barb's gut-filling hot steak and cold beer barbecues.

The barbecue wins. After all, we don't have to stay all night, do we? "Sure," I say. "I mean – I'll come. I can't answer for Bonny."

Nick turns on Camilla, who's trying to file a teeter-ing pile of papers about as tall as she is. "Hear that, babes? Isn't he sweet? Pretending he and Bonny aren't already joined at the hip. Joined somewhere, anyway. God! Young love, eh? Doncha *love* it?" Then without pausing to draw breath he spins back to me and says, "OK, Steele – are you going to hang around chewing the fat all day or are you going to get down to some *work* here?" And while I'm still gawping with indig-nation he dumps a pile of storyboards on my desk and says, "Zap these up. Add some colour. You're not paid by the hour here, you know – it's the *result*!"

Bonny turns up at The Ship at five minutes past seven that night, ten minutes after I've got there. I buy her a drink, and we sit down at the little table I've found in the corner.

We're kind of shy with each other. It's so weird, this switch from friends to – whatever we are now. She looks great, with her hair all shiny and floppy and this tight mauve top, but I bottle out of telling her she looks great. She tells me she got home this morning just as Daddy was phoning for the second time to find out if she'd returned.

"He really checks up on you, doesn't he?" I mutter. "Why didn't he just bell you on your mobile?"

"Oh, he's got wise to that. I could be answering it anywhere, couldn't I? I could tell him I was home and actually be. . ."

". . .in bed with me," I quip, and then wish I hadn't, 'cos Bonny goes red. "I got grilled by Nick this morning," I go on hastily, "seems like we're the new Big News." I tell her all about it, and pass on the invite to the barbie Thursday. She's quite keen. She really likes Nick and Barb, and I think (I hope) she likes the idea of us appearing somewhere as A Couple. "Nick really laid it on," I go on. "He's such a prat. He'd done this big love-hearts cut-out and put it on my desk."

Bonny looks all embarrassed again, but pleased, too. "Did you keep it?"

"Yeah. It's up at the flat."

"Why didn't you bring it to show me?"

"'Cos it's bloody enormous! It'd be like coming in here with a billboard under my arm. Come up and see it after this."

There's a pause, then she says, all kind of hurried and still not looking at me, "I can't, Rich. I promised Daddy I'd be back before nine – we're going out to eat."

Oh, *brilliant*. I glower at the table, and she goes on, "At the Italian near us. Just the two of us."

"Nice," I mutter.

"He really works at – you know – him and me having our own relationship, and not getting swallowed up by the twins and stuff."

"That's good," I say, but I don't mean it. I feel dead resentful, like the gate's come down on the end of our evening, like we can't go forward now.

"You don't mind, do you?" she goes on. "I thought it was a chance to – tell him about us. You know." She looks all flustered as she says that, confused, as though she's not really sure what "us" means. "You told him we were just friends, and, well, if we're going to be seeing more of each other. . ." We look across the table at each other, and she blurts out, "How d'you feel about coming round for a meal or something?"

"*Already?*"

"Yeah, yeah, I know it's soon—"

"I haven't even been out for a meal with you on your *own* yet!"

"It's just – when I tell him we're together, he'll get all hostile, I know he will. If he could meet you properly—"

"He has met me properly. That time when you'd just moved into the flat."

"I mean meet you now we're . . . you know. Together. Oh, *Rich* – don't look like that. All that time Mum was blocking him seeing me – it's made him paranoid. He's suspicious of any boy I hook up with—"

"Sure, but – *Jesus!* Does the meal have to be right away?"

"It's just – he'll be a pain until I fix it up. I know he will."

"He ought to back off a bit. Give you some space. I mean – I can understand why he's protective, but with *your* mother he should be grateful you're normal enough to *get* a boyfriend!"

A kind of dull thud and a long painful silence follows this. Bonny's looking down at the table – I can't see her face. *Shit!* It's Andy's fault – all that crap he was coming out with about Bonny's inner child must've got lodged in my brain. "Bonny," I whimper, "I didn't mean. . ."

Bonny looks up at me like she'd like to fry me with her stare. "That's what you think, is it, Rich?"

"Look—"

"That I ought to be grateful?"

"Look, I didn't say *you*—"

"OK, *Daddy.* That Daddy should be so grateful I can get someone, anyone, to go out with me, he should back off and just – just be *grateful*?"

"Oh, God. Look, Bonny – rewind, OK? Up to before I said that. Rewind and delete."

"Don't get all slick with me, Rich. You sound like a total prat."

"Yeah, well, OK. Maybe I am a total prat. Look – you know I think you're great. I think the fact you got away from your mum and made it on your own – that's great. It's made you stronger. And what I think is – your dad ought to see that too, and not go trying to wrap you in cottonwool and protect you all the time."

Bonny looks down again, and there's another long silence. Then she looks up at me again, but this time she's smiling. "You really think that?"

"Yes," I say, heaving a great, inner sigh of relief. "You know I do."

"He will. He will see it. He just needs time." She picks up her drink, finishes it, then she says, "And he needs to see you again, meet you properly."

I can't get out of it now, can I? Not now I've just managed to haul myself up the ladder from the rung marked "complete insensitive bastard" to the one marked "maybe not such a total shit after all".

"OK. So when's a good time to come for a meal?" I mutter.

"Sunday lunch would be great."

Oh, God, Sunday lunch. The slowest meal of the week. Daddy carving up the joint like he'd like to be carving up me. Sprouts, gravy, apple pie. Oh, God.

"Sure," I say. "That's fine."

Chapter 7

Bonny says she has to go soon after she's got me to agree to come to Sunday lunch with Daddy. She tells me she can give me a lift home, though, which makes me feel weird, kind of sappy, but I can't refuse, can I? She leaves the engine running when she stops the car in the derelict gravelly car park outside the flat, and we have this quick and not very satisfying snog, and when I try to move in for some more she checks her watch and says, "Rich, I have to go. I do. Daddy's got this thing about being punctual."

"Yeah? Well, I've got this *thing* about getting a proper goodnight kiss. . ."

She laughs, pushes me off. "Shall I pick you up tomorrow? For the barbecue?"

"OK," I say. I want to suggest meeting earlier, in

the day, but something stops me. "Seven o'clock again?"

I stand and watch her little Polo zoom efficiently out of the car park, and I don't feel a bit like going up to the flat. It's not even eight-thirty. I'm restless, kind of uneasy, kind of resentful still. I tell myself not to be so stupid. It's not Bonny's fault she's got an obsessive dad, is it? Although she could've suggested meeting me tomorrow in the day, couldn't she. Why didn't she? I didn't, 'cos I didn't want to push it. Suddenly it feels like I'm the keen one, she's the cool one.

Oh, sod it. If I can't be with Bonny then at least I can have another beer. I turn round, head out of the car park again, and go into the urinal cunningly disguised as a phone box at the end of the road.

"Chris? Yeah, it's me. Fancy a session at the Rose and Crown tonight?"

Chris is just about my best mate – we go way back, back to short trousers and farting competitions. I haven't seen much of him over the summer, though. He's in a serious and stormy relationship with the fiery and no-nonsense Natalie, and it takes up quite a bit of his time.

"Could do," he says. "Nat's here, though."

I like Nat, but I don't want her along tonight. She'll inhibit the male chat I'm gearing up for. "Can't you get away?"

There's a pause; I can hear the muffled sounds of Chris talking to Nat with his hand over the receiver.

Then he comes on all clear and says, "Yeah, mate, sure. See you at the Rose, half an hour or so?"

After that I phone Ollie, who's having a mid-week slump in front of the box. He says he's skint but he'll come if I buy him a beer, and he'll give Ryan a bell too.

I head towards town, hop on a bus more cheerful. My mates are all right.

Chris is already in the pub when I get there, calling over to me to get him another beer in. "Blimey, mate," I say as I join him. "How come you got away from the wife so easily?"

Chris smirks. "No problem. She's well under the thumb."

"Ha – Nat? Like hell she is."

"No, OK, she's not. What I did was, I told her you sounded well upset. I told her you were practically crying down the phone."

"You *what*?"

"I told her I had no idea what was wrong but clearly something was. And Nat – like most women – loves her bloke to show a touchy-feely side. As well as loyalty to his friends. So she said to come and meet you."

"Great. So what you going to tell her when she asks what was wrong with me?"

Chris shrugs, takes another mouthful of beer. "You'll think of something, mate."

We chew the fat for a while, and Chris tells me about his last blow-up with Natalie and how (he reckons) he got the better of her this time, which has to be a first. I'm waiting for the other two to arrive before I tell everyone about Bonny. Then Ollie and Ryan turn up, and we get in more beer and I spill my big news. And their reactions – unlike Andy blithering on about emotional baggage – are pretty satisfyingly positive.

"You shit," says Ryan. "I really fancied Bonny. I fancied her before you did."

"Well done, man," says Ollie. "She'll do you better than that bitch Portia."

"But I fancied her first!" bleats Ryan.

"Yeah, but she and Rich jell so well," says Chris. "Nat used to say how dense Rich was, not seeing it."

"Did she?" I ask, pleased. "Rude cow."

"So . . . are you like . . . *really* together now?" demands Ry. He means, of course, are we sleeping together. Ryan's got a virginal obsession with everyone else's sex lives.

"Bloody hell, give us time," I grunt. "I only met up with her again yesterday."

"That would give me time, man," smirks Ollie.

I tip some of Oll's beer on the table, and while he's swearing I say, "I hope we still jell. It's kind of weird, going with someone you've been mates with." I want to talk about the awkwardness there, the way we keep shifting, close and distant, but I don't know how to explain it.

"Saves time, doesn't it?" says Ryan. "I mean – you already know each other."

"Yeah, but it's different. Dunno. I want this to work, you know? She's special."

"And loaded," adds Chris.

"Yeah, well, that's one bit I'm not too happy with. She's a bit posh. Private school and all that. Calls her old man 'Daddy'."

"That's OK," pronounces Chris. "It's quite sexy if they're posh."

"As well as being useful," says the ever-practical Ollie. "If her old man's loaded."

"Yeah, well, I'm not so sure about that. It's like this – difference between us. She's got a car and everything."

"Wow, that's great, man!"

"Yeah, you say that, but it makes me feel weird. Being driven around and everything."

"It makes you feel inadequate, doesn't it," says Chris, going all third-pint philosophical. "I wouldn't worry about it, mate. Stands to reason it makes you feel a bit inadequate, her driving and you not."

"Yeah," chips in Ry. "It would make any bloke feel inadequate, if they're honest."

"Yeah," says Ollie. "It's kind of like you've swapped roles. Like you're the girl."

I'm not sure my mates are exactly helping here. I was looking for them to tell me how stupid it was to feel less of a man 'cos my girlfriend drove me about. Not have them tell me I'm a girl.

"God, you lot, you're really dated," I snap. "Nowadays – girls *drive*. I think it's crazy I feel weird about her having a car."

"No, it's not, Rich. It's natural. The bloke should drive."

"Your take on the sexes – it's straight out of the stone age!"

Chris shakes his head sagely. "Now you're being defensive. You feel like she's lopping your nuts off, so you're all defensive."

"*Crap!*" I squawk.

"No need to get so shrill, mate."

"Yeah," says Ollie. "Don't go getting so hysterical."

I leave the pub soon after that, claiming I've got a headache starting.

I work flat-out the next day down at Abacus, even though the sun's come out again. Everyone's impressed by the mounting pile of storyboards beside my desk; even Nick, when he gets back from a hard day's schmoozing with potential clients, comments on how much I've done. "Shame I just changed the work arrangements, though, darling," he says. "I've just decided to pay you by the hour, OK?"

I laugh loudly, to make it clear I know this is a joke, and carry on. I just feel like working, that's all. In the end Nick pays me and throws me out, tells me to go and get all gorgeous for the barbecue. "See you about seven," he leers. "You and your *girlfriend*."

Bonny's all on edge as she drives us over to the Hanrattys' house. She's not focused on me at all. I ask her how Daddy took the news of us being together now, and she goes all evasive and says, "Well, I didn't exactly tell him we were *together*. Just – you know – that I liked you and maybe we were going to get together."

"So do I still have to turn up for Sunday lunch?"

"Not if it's such a chore, no!"

"God, Bonny, what you so touchy for?"

"Sorry. I just feel strange. Going to the Hanrattys' and everything. I mean – I used to talk to Barb about you."

"*Yeah?* What did you used to say?"

"Never you mind. But it's strange."

I feel pretty strange too, if you want the truth. Fake, like I'm acting a part. I wish Bonny and I could have tonight alone together. "We could always cry off," I mumble.

"What? Are you kidding? They'd never forgive us." And she turns into their road.

At the front door there's a whole welcoming party: Barb looking all energetic in jeans and sleeveless top, Scarlett her daughter (ten) in a purple tiara and matching full-length dress, and the two lurchers weaving happily and bonily about. Barb beamingly hugs both of us, and then Scarlett solemnly copies her. It's like Bonny and I have announced our engagement or something. "Where's Nick and Freddie?" I ask, loudly.

"Nick's in the garden, making his usual big deal about getting the barbecue going," says Barb.

"And Freddie's getting undressed," says Scarlett, savagely.

"Ah," says Barb, gently. "Does that mean. . .?"

"I spent *hours* making that cloak!" Scarlett wails. "And he *won't wear it*."

"Cloak?" asks Bonny.

"Freddie's . . . got into magic tricks," explains Barb. "In fact – now, don't turn and run, you two – he's planning a magic show tonight."

And on cue, Freddie appears at the top of the stairs, wearing nothing but shorts and a pugnacious frown.

"*Fine*, Freddie," hisses Scarlett venomously. "If you want to look like someone ordinary and nothing like a magician, that's *fine*."

Freddie juts his lower lip out like a shelf. "It got in the way of my arms, Sca!"

"Oh, well, if you can't put up with that—"

"I couldn't do my *tricks*!"

"Oh, *so what*! No one will want to see your stupid tricks if you just look ordinary! They won't say, 'There's a fantastic magician doing fantastic magic tricks.' They'll say, 'There's a stupid little boy doing . . . *stupid little boy* tricks.' So *there*."

Barb, who's been making soothing maternal noises

throughout this exchange, breaks in with, "Why don't you wear it just to *appear* in, Freddie? To make your entrance? Then you could slip it off when you do your tricks."

There's a pregnant pause. Then Freddie goes, "*Yeah!*" and Scarlett squeals, "Come on, Freddie! I'll put some glitter in your hair, too!" and they race upstairs.

Barb looks smug. "Sometimes motherhood can be oddly rewarding," she murmurs. "Come on, you two, let's get you a drink."

We follow Barb through into the kitchen, where Bonny refuses a beer and has mineral water because she's driving. We're both kind of lurking vaguely, letting Barb do the chatting. She's circling like a jackal round the whole subject of me and Bonny being together, not actually going in for the kill yet. Then suddenly there's a roar from outside.

"*Barb!* You going to give me any *food* to cook out here or shall I just keep grilling my *arms*?" Bonny laughs, picks up the tray of kebabs lying ready and takes them outside.

And I'm left alone with Barb. She rounds on me, grinning hungrily, and says "*Well?*"

"Well, what? What about those steaks? Shall I take them out?"

"No, they're marinating. What about you and Bonny? I want the whole story – I want to know how you got together!"

"Barb, don't make a big deal of this! I mean – I know you know us both and everything, but –"

"*Know* you? You're my babies, my protégés, I *introduced* you, I've watched over you. . ."

"Look, just relax about this, OK, Barb? Me and Bonny being together, I mean."

"I *am* relaxed. Just eaten up with curiosity." She picks up a huge pair of shiny metal tongs and starts flipping the steaks over.

"Can I do that for you?"

"Rich – will you stop obsessing about the *steaks*! I want to know what *happened*."

"Nothing. I mean – not a lot. I mean – we met, and got together, and – you know. We'll see how it goes."

"*Riveting*," scoffs Barb. "Some boys just haven't got the knack of gossiping, have they."

"Look—"

"Oh, you're embarrassed, I know. Anyway, it's OK – I can get the whole story out of Bonny. I just want to say one thing."

"What?"

"Treat Bonny badly in any way and I'll barbecue your goolies." She waves the huge pair of shiny metal tongs at me, as if for emphasis.

I swallow. "Oh, that's nice," I whine. "I'm really going to feel relaxed and free with her now, aren't I?"

"I don't want you feeling relaxed and free. I want you feeling dedicated, loyal, attentive, worshipful. . ."

"You make me sound like a spaniel."

"A lot of men could learn a thing or two from dogs, Rich. Trust me."

Then Bonny comes back into the kitchen looking like someone's just smacked a wet towel across her face. "You might've *told* me Mum was gonna be here!" she wails.

Chapter 8

"Oh, *bugger*," groans Barb. "She must've come through the garden door."

"She did. Just as I was handing Nick the kebabs. She went into her full, *gushing*, loving mother act. For the benefit of everyone else."

"Oh, *Bonny*. She meant it for you too."

"No, she didn't. Last time we met she was ranting on about what an awful disappointment I was to her. Barb – why didn't you *tell* me she was coming?"

Barb looks defiant and guilty, both at the same time. "Oh, love – *look*. It was all very last minute. She was helping Nick prep this food ad, and he mentioned having to leave early for the barbecue, so then of course –"

"– she invited herself. You could've *phoned* me."

"And then you wouldn't've come, would you? And

I wanted you to come – I haven't seen you for ages. Look – you've left your mum's, Bonny, but you can't stop seeing her altogether."

"I know. It's just that I like to be in *control* of when I see her."

"Well, you can't always, can you? Life isn't like that." Barb puts her arm round Bonny and gives her shoulders a squeeze. She has this way of saying tough things in a kind way, a way that makes you not mind. "Come on, kid. It'll be fine. You've got your new man to protect you, after all."

Bonny looks over at me, panic-stricken. "Don't tell her we're seeing each other!" she squeals. "She'll be *disgusting!*"

"OK, OK, Bon," I say. "I'll be discreet."

"I mean it, Rich. Don't even give her a hint. We're just mates, all right?"

Just mates, I think sourly, as we leave the kitchen and head out to join the others. *Tell me about it.*

There's quite a gathering at the end of the garden. When the Hanrattys give one of their small parties, it generally grows into a large one. I recognize two or three workers from Abacus; Barb points out neighbours and nearby friends, and the parents of one of Freddie's mates. Nick's dancing about tending the barbecue like a priest at a sacrifice; he sees me and Bonny and his face lights up with sadistic glee. "A *ha!*" he booms. "The young lovers!" Barb knocks into him sharply with a salad bowl and jerks her head towards Tigger, and, with that telepathy very married couples get, he understands and – to Bonny's clear relief – buttons it.

Tigger hasn't heard a thing, though, because she's fully involved telling a poor dumpy blonde woman how much weight she's recently lost on a new diet from Scandinavia. "I mean, *yes*, it's hard to stick to," she's braying, "but I've always been blessed with strong will-power. And the results are so *fantastic* –" she indicates her torso with a flamboyant red-nailed hand – "that I'm *spurred* to continue. . ." She spins round to Bonny. "Darling! I was just telling June here about my new diet. I'll have to let you have a copy of it, sweetheart. It works on the principle of combining fats with pure fruit pulp, eating two hundred grams of simple protein within an hour of waking up, and avoiding complex *carbohydrates* after seven o'clock at night—"

"No, thanks, Mum," says Bonny, stony faced.

"Oh, now don't get all touchy with me, darling. I'm not saying you desperately need to lose weight. Just –" She breaks off, reaches out, adjusts the neck of Bonny's top. Bonny adjusts it back again, turns abruptly away. Tigger looks at me and raises her eyes skywards as though we're both in on the problem of Bonny's touchiness. Then she says: "Still with that fabulous girlfriend, Richy? Portia, wasn't it?"

"No – we finished it."

"Oh, what a *shame*! She was so *gorgeous*! And such style. So few young girls really know how to dress. . ." She shoots an acid glance at her daughter, who's helping herself pointedly to garlic bread, and turns back to the plump blonde.

There's not a lot for me to do. I sit down, I get fed, I listen to the lazy summer chat going on around me. Nick as usual is master of ceremonies; Tigger presides like some kind of perched vulture, radiating nastiness. Bonny's cut off from me. No communication going on at all. I keep looking over at her, lonely for her, but she won't look back. She's smiling and joining in but it all looks like an act, like the way I feel, like we're just taking part in some function. I'm getting seriously pissed off with it. The food's great, the beer's flowing, but it's no way enough.

Then Freddie rushes up to us all self-important, announces they're too busy *getting ready* to come down and eat, and takes three burgers back upstairs with him.

"What's happened to the magic show?" asks a woman. "Hugo was so excited, being allowed to be Freddie's assistant."

"I think Scarlett may still be making them up," says Barb, tentatively. "She mentioned glitter. . ."

"Making them *up*?" squawks the woman, and Nick says, "Polly, darling, you have to appreciate my daughter is going to grow up to be possibly the greatest make-up artist of *all time*. She needs victims to practise on. . ."

"But Hugo hates looking feminine. . ." quavers the woman – and it's here I have my brainwave. On how I can get Bonny on her own for a bit. Make contact with her again.

"Shall I go up and see?" I say, dumping my plate on the grass and standing up. "Rescue the boys from being turned into drag queens?"

Polly lets out a tiny squeak of anguish at the very thought, and Barb goes, "Oh, Rich, would you?"

"Sure. Come on, Bonny." Bonny looks hesitant, and I go on, "You know what Scarlett's like when she gets a mascara brush in her hand. I might need *you* to rescue *me*." Then I get hold of her hand, all macho, and pull her to her feet, and we head back together into the house.

"Don't you think this looks a bit rude?" she hisses.

"What?"

"Both of us going in—"

"Bonny, I don't give a toss what it looks like. I was sitting there thinking – what the hell are we doing here when we could be on our own together."

"You were the one who said we'd come!"

"I know. I know I did. I don't know why I did. It's just – Nick was making this big deal about it and it was easier to say yes. Like you said yes to your dad's *quality time*, and to Ellie wanting you to help out with the twins, and to me coming round to your place for lunch . . . it's bloody stupid, Bonny. We need some time *alone*."

We're in the kitchen now. She's heading for the hall but I put my arm round her and steer her towards a door at the side, towards what Barb calls the Futility Room, where the washing machine and the tumble-dryer and the dog beds are.

"Rich – what are you doing?" she squawks, but she sounds pleased, excited even, so I carry on. I pull her into the Futility Room and put my arms round her and kick the door shut behind us. "They'll wonder where we *are*," she says.

"So let 'em. It's crazy, the way we're acting. Letting everyone else stick their oars in. I wish no one else knew. About us."

"Why? Are you ashamed?"

"Oh, don't be so bloody stupid – course I'm not ashamed," I say, and I bring my mouth down to hers, and she reaches her arms round my neck and then we're into this deep kiss, this *great* kiss, like we recognize each other again. "It's *us* who ought to be talking about us getting together," I murmur, when we pause for breath. "Not your dad, or my mates, or Barb and Nick. . ."

"What've your mates said?"

"They think it's great. Ryan's jealous." I don't tell her about Andy and his psychobabble.

"My friends want to meet you."

"Oh, *Jesus*. You see? Other people all the time. You know what it reminds me of?"

"No," she laughs, liking me getting all worked up about it. "What?"

"My cousin's wedding."

"*What?*"

"Seriously. I got forced to be an usher, I had to wear a stupid suit and everything. I had to go to the rehearsals. The fuss – the *discussions* – it was unbelievable. It was like the stupid wedding was the reason for this couple being together, like their whole aim was to bring off this big show."

"Well, why is that like us?"

"Because – dunno. Because we've become a show. And what matters is being on our own."

She reaches up, hooks her arm round my neck, and kisses me again. Then she says, all intently, "I hate white weddings."

"Yeah?"

"Yeah. I hate those horrible *dresses*. All white flounces and off the shoulder, laced up like whalebone corsets. Part virgin, part stripper. Why can't women get married looking like who they *are*?"

I laugh, really liking her, liking what she said. "Maybe they want to get away from who they are?"

"Well, that's sad then, isn't it."

"Yes," I say, and we start kissing again.

"We ought to go upstairs," she whispers, after a bit. "We ought to check on the kids. . ." I nuzzle into her neck, and she presses herself into me, winds herself round me, and I start tracing down her body, amazed at how slim her waist is, how sexy the curve is out to her hips, desperate to touch her breasts, not letting myself, though, not yet.

"Tomorrow," I say, "have you got anything planned for tomorrow?"

"I said I'd go shopping with Liz."

"And are you going to?"

"No. I'm going to cancel. I'm going to spend the day with you."

"Thattagirl." She whacks me on the arm, and I say, "Ouch. What d'you want to do tomorrow?"

"Go out to the countryside. Make the most of the last of the summer."

"You're on," I say, and we start kissing again, and in the end it's me who says, "They'll be sending out a search party."

As if on cue, there's a bang on the door. Low down, like whoever's knocking is on their knees. "What the hell —" I mutter, and pull open the door. The lurchers are there, gazing at us with weary disapproval, one with a paw still raised.

"It's their bedroom," giggles Bonny. "We shut them out of their room." The two dogs stalk indignantly past us, head for their water bowls, and lap noisily.

"Sorry, guys," I say. "We were just using it for a bit."

Upstairs, in Scarlett's fairytale bedroom, there's a dramatic scene underway. Scarlett's in her element, putting the finishing touches to Freddie who has the face of a pantomime demon and an amazing cloak with all kinds of things tacked to it: plastic spiders, glittery earrings, forks, little dolls, toothbrushes. . .

But the real shock is Hugo.

"Oh *no*," breathes Bonny. "What's his mum gonna say?"

Hugo's crouched over the huge green hatbox that houses Scarlett's tiara collection. He's wearing a pink tutu, lots of lipstick and eyeshadow, spangly tights, and an enormous pair of gold stiletto shoes. He's picking up tiaras one after the other, gazing at them in awe and what could almost be desire.

"Have you chosen one yet?" raps out Scarlett. "For goodness' sake, hurry up!"

"Look at him," breathes Bonny, "he *likes* it!"

"Likes it? He *loves* it!"

"Rich, what're we gonna *do*?"

"Dunno. I thought I was *joking* about him being turned into a drag queen."

"But you said you'd *stop* her!"

"Stop Scarlett in the throes of a make-over frenzy – are you kidding? Like stopping a T Rex at feeding time."

Bonny reaches out, grips my hand, and we both start laughing. Scarlett's head snaps up. "Have you come to get us?" she demands. "We're nearly ready. Hugo – *choose* one!"

"Scarlett," I gurgle, "why have you made Hugo look like a girl?"

Scarlett throws me a pitying look, like she thinks I'm acting even thicker than usual. "He's a *magician's assistant*," she explains.

"But why couldn't he be a boy assistant?" asks Bonny.

"Don't be *silly*," responds Scarlett, scathingly. "You've seen magic shows, haven't you?"

"Yes," we both admit.

"Well then! You should know that magician's assistants are *always* glamorous girls with high heels."

We're silent. "*Aren't* they?" she demands.

"Yes," we parrot, faintly.

"I really wish I had some ostrich feathers, but a tiara will have to do. Now – could you tell the grown-ups we'll be down in three minutes?"

"Sure, Scarlett," I gulp. "We'll tell 'em." And I pull Bonny out of the door, along the landing.

"Shit, Rich," giggles Bonny. "Hugo's mum – and his *dad*—"

"Look – they've got to face the fact they've got a trainee tranny for a son. Not our problem."

"You can talk about trainee trannies! What about the time Scarlett made you up?"

"*Yeah?*" We reach the stairs, start jostling down them together. "And who egged her on, eh? Who *helped* her?"

"I've still got the photos I took," she sniggers. "Of you looking like a total queen."

"Oh, *great*. Planning on blackmailing me, are you?" I stop a step below her. Our faces are lined up perfectly.

"Maybe. Or I might need to take revenge. You remember I asked you out? That same day?"

"Yeah, I do." I lean closer.

"And you said no 'cos of *Portia*."

"And 'cos I was an idiot."

"This is true," she says, and kisses me. I put my hand on the back of her neck and kiss her back. And we're still all revved up and close from our session in the Futility Room, so it lasts, and it's great.

Then she says, "What are we going to do? The kids'll be ready in a minute."

"We'll bluff it out. We'll go down, and sit down and act like it's fine. . ."

"Or. . ."

"Or what, Bon?"

"We say thanks for the lovely nosh, and scarper before the shit hits the fan."

"You'd do that?" I demand, delighted.

"Would you?"

"Yeah, Bonny – great! Come on – let's do it."

We're halfway through the kitchen, at the door to the garden. "You," she says.

"What?"

"You tell 'em."

"It was your idea!"

Bonny mock-glares at me, then she sets her face

and marches resolutely up to the crowd of people by the barbecue. "The kids're just coming down," she announces. "And I'm really sorry, Barb, but we have to go."

"Already?" wails Barb.

"I'm *really* sorry – I didn't realize how late it had got! I promised Daddy we'd go and babysit, so he and Ellie can get out to the pub . . . the twins've been driving Ellie crazy recently and –"

"Oh, for *goodness*' sake," interjects Tigger venomously, "can't that woman even cope with her own children?"

"I understand," says Barb, hastily. "You go."

"Yes, Bonny, go and bail *her* out," shrills Tigger. "Go and babysit for your *stepmother*. Even though last week you were *far* too busy to go shopping with your *real* mother – "

"Go, you two," says Barb. "*Go!*"

Outside, Bonny unlocks her car and says, "Well, Mum was useful for once, being such a bitch. Barb felt so guilty she practically threw us out."

"Bit of an accomplished liar, aren't we, babe? First Daddy, now Barb. . ."

"Sod off."

"It's kind of scary, that's all."

"You'd lie if you had a family like mine."

"As long as you only lie to *them*, I don't care."

Bonny smiles at this – her man getting all

demanding – and we get in the car and drive off. "You reckon the shit's hit the fan yet?" I say.

"Probably. Poor Barb. We shouldn't've run out on her."

I put my hand on Bonny's leg. "She'll be OK. I just wish I could see all their faces when Hugo totters out in those heels. . ."

"We can always go back. . ."

"No way. Where d'you want to go? The balcony?"

She grins, speeds up a little.

Chapter 9

I let Bonny into the flat and the first thing she spots, propped against the wall, is Nick's big bold pink cardboard cut-out of two hearts. "Oh, shit," she gasps, half delighted, half appalled. "Did everyone at Abacus see that?"

"Yes. *And* Nick was grilling me about you, in front of everyone. *And* Barb was interrogating me in the kitchen, when you'd gone out. She practically had the rubber hose and bright lights out. And she told me she'd do me hard if I didn't treat you right."

Bonny laughs. "Come on, let's get down to the balcony."

"I just remembered," I say. "I haven't exactly cleared up since the last time."

"By *haven't exactly* — you mean you haven't touched it?"

"That's it."

She groans, and I go into the kitchen and come out with a bottle of Coke I noticed Andy bringing home earlier. "We'll swill out the glasses," I say. "They'll be OK."

Everything's just as we left it when we get down there – the barbecue, the rug, Andy's backpack, the steak plates scoured to within an inch of their lives by Pitbull, who's taken up comfortable residence on the rug in the last slice of evening sun. "Shift, Pitbull," I say, toe-ending him. He flops back down again and ignores me.

Bonny wanders over to the balustrade as I pour out the Coke. "You're right," she says.

"Course I am. What about?"

"You know – what you were on about tonight, at Nick and Barb's. About everyone shoving their oars in, getting in the way of us being together. The thing is – I was kind of glad for it in a way. I think."

"Bonny – am I supposed to be following this?"

"Last night – I could've got out of having supper with Daddy. Or the barbecue – you weren't that keen, I could've said no."

"So why didn't you?"

"I was – I dunno, *hiding* behind it all. 'Cos I was. . ." She takes in a big breath, shrugs. "Scared."

"Oh, *Bonny* –" I come up behind her, put my arms round her waist. "I don't know what horror stories you've been hearing about me, but they're lies, honest, most of 'em anyway —"

"You're laughing at me, aren't you."

"Well, what you got to be *scared* of?"

"Of fucking everything up."

"What d'you mean?"

"Of spoiling this when I've . . . I've *wanted* it so much —"

I hug her closer. "Are you saying you're scared to start it? Start *us*?"

She sighs. "Yes."

"Well, that's daft, isn't it."

"Probably."

"It's like – you got a new jacket, but you won't wear it in case it gets spoiled. You may as well not have it in the first place."

"I know. I'm stupid."

"No, you're not."

"Although it's not like a new jacket, is it. It's not *there*, all ready made. We've got to make it."

"Yeah, but—"

"When we were just friends it was OK, it just kind of happened, we got on great, but now this is – this is *pressure*. And I'm scared I won't do it right. I won't be good enough."

I try to turn her round to face me, but she won't budge. "Look, Bonny," I say, "you're making this all complicated. We've just got to trust what we feel and – you know. *Go* for it."

"I know. I know we have. I'm just so scared it won't work out."

"But that's a risk you've got to take. You can't know how it's going to turn out – us being together – neither of us can."

"I know."

"What we've got between us – it's changed already, and it'll change more. We've just got to let it." I push my face into her neck, into her sweet-smelling hair. "It's going to turn out great, Bon. Have a little faith. I really, really like you."

The rest of the evening is ace. We sit down, arms round each other on the blanket with Pitbull curled itchily against our legs, and we talk lazily, relaxed and joking like the old days. Only there's the new energy there too, the wanting each other, that's charging everything up; but we don't do a lot with it that night, just a bit more kissing. It's good just to know it's there, it's waiting for us.

At about midnight Bonny says she's going to drive home, then come back and get me early for our day out. It feels fine. Slowly, steadily, the weirdness is fading, and we're turning into a couple.

Chapter 10

I'm woken up the next day by loud hammering on the flat door. I stagger blearily over to open it, and Nick erupts into the room, taking me with him. "*Boy* are you in trouble, Richy boy!" he gloats.

"What?" I rub at my eyes. "Nick, I *told* you I wasn't working today –"

"Nothing to do with work, darling. Barb wants your goolies on a skewer."

The penny drops. "Oh, God, the barbecue. Freddie's magic show."

"You got it. And it was a *tremendous* success. He got every trick ace-perfect, just about. Trouble is, no one was watching the magician. All eyes were fixed on the magician's assistant. And – more crucially – the magician's assistant's *mother*. Polly saw her son mince out in gold stilettos and a tiara, and just about *passed out* with shock. She was wringing her hands, giving out these little agonized moans . . . her old man looked like he'd been pole-axed. He didn't *move*. But Hugo wasn't put off by the reactions of his parents, bless 'im. He's a trouper – he just upped his act. Twirling round in his tutu, camp hand flourishes whenever Freddie pulled off a trick, blowing lipsticky kisses to the audience . . . Scarlett had drilled him *brilliantly*. . ."

"Oh, *shit*, Nick. How did it end up?"

"It was *hilarious*. I just about pissed myself laughing. And Barb, who is nicer than me, headed over to comfort Hugo's mum, but she wasn't quick enough."

"What d'you mean?"

"Tigger got there first. Took hold of Polly's hand and started telling her about a very dear friend of hers who was learning to come to terms with the fact that her son was gay."

"You are *joking*."

"Nope. *As mothers we must love our children whoever they are, however much we want them to be different. It's a lesson I've had to learn.* Polly burst into tears. Barb put her arm round her, assured her Hugo's just a brilliant actor. Tigger told Barb she's *not helping by denying the truth*. Barb told Tigger to fuck off. More or less. And then *Scarlett* enters the arena."

"Scarlett?"

"It's not often she sticks up for her little brother, but when she does it's like Armageddon. She *exploded.* Icily. Said how much effort had gone into the show, how hard Freddie had practised. And no one was really looking at him because they were distracted by *superficialities.* It was tremendous. I applauded. I was the only one, oddly. Then she swept upstairs, taking Freddie and Hugo and the two dogs with her. Minutes later, we heard her and the dogs howling. You know how she does sometimes."

"Yeah. That must've been the final crowning touch."

"It was. Especially when we heard Freddie and Hugo join in. Tigger announces that Scarlett's a psychotic brat, a bad influence on the boys and so on. Then Barb *really* goes for her."

"I bet!"

"Tigger leaves, all tragic and misunderstood. I get more drinks all round. Everyone pitches in to support Polly who ends up laughing as everyone tells her how fantastic her kid is. Barb persuades the kids to come down, rerun the show. Big applause, then I get Freddie and Hugo in a good game of footie to prove to Hugo's parents how macho he is underneath."

"Fabulous. Almost sorry I missed it. So why does Barb want my goolies on a skewer?"

"She doesn't. I just said that to wake you up, matey. Although she did think you and Bonny might've warned us."

I manage to get rid of Nick by offering him coffee ("Are you kidding? That instant muck? I'm off downstairs, darling.") and then I get ready for my day out with Bonny. Around ten o'clock, the time we agreed on, I head downstairs to wait outside for her. I'm feeling weirdly nervous but I won't really admit it to myself. I sit on the front step and occupy myself by adding a bit more graffiti to one of the stone lions by the entrance.

At ten past ten, Bonny chugs into the car park and winds her window down. "Hooligan!" she shouts.

"Crap, I'm improving it. It needed a chain on its monocle." I pull open her driver's door, smack a huge kiss on her. "Get in, then," she says.

"Actually, Bon, I thought we'd take the bus."

"What? Why?"

"'Cos I want to go out to The Unicorn. It's this brilliant pub – you can get to it across the fields. It does fantastic lunches. And it'll kind of spoil it if I'm drinking beer and you're having an orange juice, won't it."

"God – the other night you were lecturing me on getting so pissed!"

"There's a difference between getting over the driving limit and getting completely legless, Bon."

"You sound like my dad. OK, let's take the bus."

She parks the car and locks it up, and we swing along to the bus stop. I don't tell her the real reason I want to take the bus, that I want to feel level with her, equal. I'm not even sure I can totally admit that to myself.

It's a good decision though. When the country bus comes we scramble up to the top deck, sit right at the front, and we chat and act like kids, holding hands and swaying about as the bus turns corners. "So was Liz pissed off?" I ask. "When you blew her out for today?"

"Well – a bit – we haven't seen each other for ages. We were going to go shopping, catch up on each other's news, then I was going to meet her new boyfriend. And. . ."

"And?"

"And I told her about you. She's dying to see you again."

"Again?"

"She came to that party you had – remember? At the flat? When you and Portia shut yourself away in my room and –"

"Yeah, yeah. Sorry."

"Liz can't remember much about you – just the flat."

"Flattering."

"She kept going on about how amazing it was. So I hope it's OK – I said it'd probably be OK if the two of them came round tonight? Her and her new man? It is, isn't it?"

And I can't help it, I'm invaded by resentment. I had vague, hopeful, sexy plans for tonight, when we got back all tired and happy after a great day out, and now. . . "Sure," I say sourly. "Except I thought we were going to have today on our own, like we talked about. . ."

Despite the fact I'm moaning, Bonny glows with pleasure. "Oh, Rich, we *will* be on our own. They'll only be there for a couple of hours, then I'll kick them out. It's just – Liz was so disappointed I couldn't make it, I felt awful –"

With her explanation, my resentment evaporates. I sling my arm round her shoulders and say, "You know your problem, Bon? You're too nice."

The bus leaves the outskirts of town, starts to chunter down narrow country roads. And the rest of the day is the kind of day that makes you wish it could always be like this. I tell her about what happened at the barbecue after we left, and she laughs, and then we're off, talking. We talk loads, real, joined-up talking, mostly about our past, and how we left home, what we want, what we feel. As we talk we walk across the fields, following wonky old pathway signs, me trying to remember where the pub is. The sun comes out, low and mellow, the air gets warm, and Bonny takes off her thin sweatshirt, ties it round her waist. She's got gorgeous arms, toned but not too muscly, brown as anything. It suits her, walking like this, shorts and flat shoes on. She looks lovely. The leaves are turning gold and red in the woods, a few fall on us as we pass by.

"I'm hungry," she says. "And I bet we're lost, aren't we?"

"Nope," I reply, half truthfully. "See those houses, on the horizon? That's the village where the pub is. Just over there."

There's some brambles hanging over our path, heavy with late blackberries. "You see?" I say. "Nature provides." I pick some and feed them to her, and she feeds me back, and we're standing close and I know she wants to start kissing like I do, but I wipe the purple from her mouth and say, "Come on. It's after one-thirty. They'll stop serving lunch soon."

As soon as we get on to the narrow road beyond the field and I see the squat little Post Office, I know I've found the pub, and I feel cocky with relief. "Just round that next bend, Bon. The best pub you've ever been to."

We head through the doors of The Unicorn, and I'm praying our good luck lasts and we're on time. The landlord tells us severely that the lamb chops and mash are all finished, but we can have ham on the bone, beef and ale pie, a ploughman's . . . we both settle for the pie, and beer, and as we're scanning the room for seats two old codgers seated between the inglenook and a window creak to their feet. I'm over there before the two suits at the bar next to us can move, and soon Bon's sitting opposite me across the ancient oak table.

We get through our first beers pretty quickly; the alcohol hits our food-hungry bloodstreams, jazzes up our moods, and we're all happy and hungry, waiting for the food to come. She's *looking* at me. No one's ever looked at me the way she's looking at me now. Like they're completely crazy about me, melting with it. It's a lot to take, but I manage it. "Still scared?" I ask, grinning.

"Terrified," she says.

"Good. That makes two of us."

"Don't talk bollocks. You're not scared. You've had *loads* of girlfriends."

"I haven't. I've had the Porsche, who doesn't exactly count as a girlfriend, more like a brief encounter with a barracuda, and a few grisly one-night stands, and one serious relationship."

"Well, that's one more than me. Who was she?"

I tell her all about Emma, how functional and flat it got, how I finished it. Bonny's face clouds over. "What?" I say.

"I was just thinking – poor Emma. You were a bit harsh."

"No I wasn't. I was stupid to let it drag on as long as it did. And before you start getting any wrong ideas, she never meant as much to me as you do right now."

"But you were –"

"Sleeping together. So?" Then I can't handle the emotion any more, I stand up to go to the bar and get more beer, and by the time I've got back to our table our food's arrived and soon we've been swallowed up by the fabulous smell and taste of it.

When we've cleared our plates I suggest staying on, having another beer, but Bonny says she won't be able to walk straight if she has any more. She says she'll have a lemonade if I want another beer, but in the end we go. And outside the pub, the light's changed, the sun low on the horizon glowing like a great Halloween pumpkin that's out too early. "You know – I could get into light," I announce.

"What?"

"Painting it. Not bloody sunsets over the sea and stuff – I could do it different."

"Do it sad," she says.

"What?"

"The way the year's dying. It's still all so beautiful, but it won't be for long."

There's not a lot I can say to that, but I take her hand to show her I'm glad she said it, and we start to walk again across the fields. We're silent as we walk now, all talked out. I can't think of anything to chat about, I'm too full of what I feel for her. I'm horny, but it's more than that. I keep looking at her sideways, at her gorgeous, soft-strong profile, the way her cheek dimples up when she smiles, the way her hair falls on her neck. "You want to sit down for a bit?" I say. "Have a rest?"

She doesn't answer right away – she knows I'm not talking about resting. "OK," she says.

Chapter 11

We turn off the path through the fields, wander over to a little copse of trees on a raised bit of ground. "It'll be good to be in the shade for a bit," I say. "The sun's hot, isn't it?"

"Yeah," she agrees, a touch awkwardly. Going into the trees has got nothing to do with wanting shade. I wonder if she's as turned on as I am, so turned on I can't walk right. We sit down on the outskirts of the little copse and we're lost in high, dry grasses. "This day has been *fabulous*," murmurs Bonny.

"It's not over yet," I murmur back.

Then I put my arm round her shoulders, and she turns towards me, says, "I never had you down as a keen walker, Rich."

"Keen? I'm obsessive. Backpack, boots, the lot."

We're just making chat before we kiss, it doesn't matter what we say.

"Yeah? Youth hostelling?"

"You bet. *I love to go a-wandering . . . along the mountain track. . .*"

While she's laughing, I kiss her. It feels so good to kiss her at last, all the close feeling that's been building all day put into that kiss. We kind of hutch down, still kissing, till we're lying on the ground. We're hidden by the tall grass now, grasshoppers whirring up as we stretch out together. I stroke her arms, her neck, move on to her chest, move on to her breasts, the first time I've touched them. I can feel her stiffen, like she might stop me, and I'm waiting, but she doesn't stop me, she puts her arm round my neck, pulls me on to her.

I say her name, kiss her again. I push my hand underneath her little summer top, trace into her cleavage, under the lacy edge of her bra. Then I work my fingers round her back, and she's arching up like she's wanting to make it easier for me, and I wrestle with the two hooks of her bra, and at last it falls loose.

She's amazing. She feels so good. When I start to slide her top up, though, she stops me, she wants to stay covered. That's fine. I'm really trying to read what she wants. We kiss, stronger and stronger, and I move my hands lower, down her stomach, but she shifts away so I stop. It's fine, it's good, it's more than enough.

The sun's so low now it's almost setting. "We

ought to get back, Rich," she mutters. "I told Liz to come round any time after eight."

I check my watch. "We've got hours!"

"Yeah, but —"

"Bonny, we're fine — just relax!"

She doesn't though — we kiss again, but it's not so good. Maybe she thinks I was trying to bully her — maybe I *was* trying to bully her. "OK," I say at last. "Let's hit the trail again." And we stand up, and I'm aching and stiff like my groin has aged before the rest of me, but Bonny's smiling, she swings along chattering and happy, almost like she's glad she's got it over with, got through it OK. I can't ask her about it, about how she feels — I want to but I can't, I can't think of a way of talking about it without sounding dead crass and crude. We hold hands and scramble along, back on to the main path, and I remember back to when we were flatmates and she had a real go at me about what she thought was my casual attitude to sex. She said then that her first time had been just about the only time, that it had been a disaster. I'm dying to ask her about this, talk about it, but she's chatting about her holiday in Spain and how she fell in love with the splat-footed geckoes that lived near the light fittings, eating all the bugs, so I can't.

She was right about needing to head back. By the time we've got a bit lost finding the right rural bus stop, and waited ages for the bus, and ridden back to the flat via a burst water main and a road-diversion, it's nearly half past seven. We're both famished, and I'm trying not to feel bad-tempered about the imminent arrival of Liz and her new man. I peer in the fridge and the bread bin and suggest making toasted sandwiches with the rind of cheese and the bit of stale bread Andy's thoughtfully left for me, but Bonny goes all coy and mutters that she'd *sort of* said Liz and her boyfriend could eat with us.

"Yeah?" I go, ungracefully. "And what are they going to *sort of* eat? Half a toasted sandwich?"

"Well – I've got a bag of stuff in the car. You know. For a meal."

"Bloody hell – you got this planned, didn't you?" I can't help it, I feel hurt. I'm thinking: *After all we'd said about wanting to be on our own.*

She shrugs, won't look at me. "It's just – I wanted to make it up to Liz. For letting her down today."

There's a pause. Then I say, "Why didn't you bring the bag up with you?"

"I forgot," she snaps.

I know this isn't true, I know she was embarrassed about it, but if I pursue it I'll sound niggly as hell, won't I. And I know I've got to give in but I don't feel like giving in, or at least not yet. "Won't it've gone off?" I demand. "In the heat?"

"It's only peppers and courgettes and stuff. No meat."

"Groovy."

"Well – Liz has gone veggie. Her new man – he's really into it, apparently."

"Oh, God – he's not one of these tree-huggers, is he?"

"No, Rich. Look – if you're going be like this about it, let's just forget it OK? I only told Liz I might cook something. I'll just leave the bag down there. It's not a big deal."

There's another pause, then I enquire, grumpily, "What were you going to make?"

"Stir-fry. And noodles. With cashew nuts."

She still won't look at me. What I want to say is – cook it, but just for us. But she'd probably refuse. And even if she agreed it would hardly lead to a joyous meal, would it? And anyway we'd have to wait till Liz and her stupid veggie tree-hugger left. And I'm *starving*.

"Oh, all right then," I mutter, "go on."

"Not if you don't want to."

"It's fine."

"Look, if you're not keen—"

"Bonny, I said it's *fine*! Shall I get the bag out the car for you?"

Fifteen minutes later, she's frying garlic and chopping up peppers and I'm doing some low-level sulking with a bottle of beer in my hand out by the windows. I know she'd like me to join in, all enthused and domestic, but I'm buggered if I'm going to.

"Ri-ich," she calls out, a bit wheedling.

"What?" I wander into the kitchen.

"Look," she goes, "I'm sorry about this. It's just – Liz is one of my best friends, I wanted you to meet her."

I shrug, scoop up a handful of cashew nuts and cram them into my mouth.

"And I thought if I made a meal things would go easier, OK?"

"OK. I've said it's OK." I feel a bit better, now she's said that. I move in on the nuts again.

"*Hey* – don't have any more of those! There won't be enough for the stir-fry."

"Sorry, babe," I say, through a mouthful, and head back to the window.

Not long after this the front-door buzzer goes and Bonny springs over to the intercom shrieking *Liz!* and Liz crackles back in alien-intercom talk. Bonny presses the front-door release button and turns to me, smiling and trying not to look too enthusiastic all at the same time.

"What's her boyfriend's name?" I ask, begrudgingly.

"Kell."

"*Kell?* What kind of a stupid name is that?"

"Oh, *shut up*." She opens the flat door, and we stand and wait for the lift to clank up to the top. "Rich – be nice," she mutters.

"I *will*," I say. *Kell*, though. Pretentious git.

The lift opens, and Liz speeds out towards us, followed by this black-haired box of a guy. Boxy face, boxy body. Powerful looking, but shorter than me. Good.

Bonny and Liz exchange girly hello kisses and hugs while Kell and I square up to each other across the threshold. I'm all "Yeah, this is *my flat*," and he's got a ready-made sneer on his face, determined not to be impressed by anything he sees.

"Come in!" cries Bonny.

"Oh, isn't this room *fabulous*," Liz gushes, speeding over to the huge arched windows. "I mean – when it was full of people at that party, you couldn't really see quite how brilliant it was. Oh, look at the *view* from here, it's *stunning*, so open and *high*—"

"Liz, you're jabbering," Kell snaps.

"Sorry," she says.

Sorry? He insults her and she's *sorry*? "It's just – it's beautiful," she mutters, looking at him all contrite. "Don't you think it's beautiful?"

"It's a nice enough space," he says, in a voice that implies *space* is pretty low down on his list of Life Priorities.

There's an awkward pause. Then Kell turns and stares at Liz, hard, and she looks away, down at the ground. What the hell's going on here? Bonny clears her throat, asks, "Want a beer?"

"Sure," says Kell.

"I'll get them," I say, and stomp off to the kitchen. *Nice* of Kell to bring some with him, I think. He's clearly tight as well as ugly and an idiot. I knock the caps off four beers, stomp back into the main room, and pointedly give one to Liz, then to Bonny, before I hand one to him.

Liz has got her eyes fixed on Kell. She watches him take his first swig of beer, then she takes one too. Weird.

"I've made dinner," says Bonny, all eager. "Veggie."

"Oh, Bonny, you are great!" exclaims Liz.

"It's ready. I mean – if you want to eat now."

"Kell?" says Liz, all kind of respectful.

"I'm not that hungry," he shrugs. "But if it's ready – sure, why not."

Rude, unenthusiastic bastard, I think, feeling all protective towards Bonny and the effort she's put into her meal, even if I didn't want her to cook it in the first place. "It smells fantastic, Bon," I say. "You want to eat here or on the balcony?"

"It'll be a bit difficult to carry it down," she says, looking at me gratefully.

"Right. I'll get some pillows, we can eat in front of the windows," I say. I hope she's noticing how much nicer I am than Kell. Liz asks what the balcony is and Bonny explains and says we can take a look later and Kell looks pointedly bored by the whole conversation. He's finished his beer already. I'm not about to offer him another one, the bastard.

Soon we're all sat on the floor like Indians, eating Bonny's tasty meal. "This is *great*, Bon," I say. "You are one hell of an ace cook." And I stare hostilely at Kell, who doesn't look up, just keeps filling his boxy mug.

"Where did you two meet?" asks Bonny, brightly, trying to get the chat going.

Liz glances over at Kell, who ignores her. "At a bus stop," she says.

"Original," I say. Kell glares at me.

"We just got talking. And we let bus after bus go, and then we discovered we were getting the same bus anyway."

"*Aw*," says Bonny, dimpling up. "And it went from there, did it?"

"Yes. We went out together that night, and well, we've seen each other just about every day since. . ." She trails off, glances over at Kell again. He's having this effect on the conversation, killing it, like a bloody great granite block.

"That's lovely," says Bonny.

Pause.

"Bonny and I met up again by chance," I announce.

"Did you?" says Liz.

"I was down by the town hall, and there she was, sitting on the wall, swinging her legs all brown and sexy. . ." Both the girls laugh. This is more like it, I think. "We got chatting. I told her what an idiot I'd been, letting her move out like that."

"Oh, Bon, how lovely," squeals Liz. "She used to go on about wanting to bump into you, Rich."

Bonny says, "Liz, *shut up!*" and I crow, "Yeah? Well why didn't she come round, then?" and Liz laughs, says, "Maybe she wanted *you* to come to *her*," and in all this I think, but can't swear, that Kell makes a flicking movement with his hand towards Liz. Who stops laughing, goes quiet, and just looks at him, like he'd just have to say the word and she'd lay down her life for him.

Then Kell puts down his fork and speaks. "So. How d'you fund this place then?" His voice is flat, like he couldn't really give a shit, he's just making conversation.

"It's rent-free," I say, equally off-hand.

"It belongs to friends of ours," Bonny breaks in. "It's the most amazing bit of luck . . . it's above his office, you see, his ad agency. . ."

"*Ad* agency?" sneers Kell, in the sort of voice you reserve for *heap of maggots* or *dysfunctional sewage works.*

"Yeah. . ." falters Bonny. "It's brilliant, 'cos Rich works for him loads, he does storyboards and. . ."

Kell fixes me with a stony stare. He's got weird eyes, kind of cold grey and unblinking. "You work for an ad man, do you?"

"Yeah. It's great pay."

"And you don't care that you're making money by screwing people's minds?"

"*What?*"

"You don't mind being part of the whole sick machine?"

"Sorry, mate, I don't follow."

"Adverts work by making people feel inadequate, empty – brainwashing them into believing that *buying stuff* is the only way to fill the void."

"Oh, *please*. Don't give me that crap. This is the real world, mate. Adverts – they're part of life."

"They *poison* life. They're slavery – a twisted distortion. They've got no truth."

Bloody hell, I think, who *is* this guy? John the Baptist?

"Well, I'm *so sorry* if the way I earn a few bucks offends you," I snarl. "What d'you suggest I do instead? Arms dealing? Rent boy?"

Kell looks at me like I'm sticking to the underside of his shoe. "Don't overreact. I'm just suggesting there are better ways of earning money."

"Well, it might be more moral to help out in an old folks' home for twenty pence an hour, but it won't pay the bills. This is the real world – you need real money. You try doing without it."

"Oh – the *real world* again? You're pretty sure that this pigs' race you're caught up in is the real world, aren't you?" Kell smirks, all superior. "And as for living without much money – I have done."

At my side I'm aware Bonny's twitching, breathing fast, wanting me to stop this fight, but I can't. The red mist's in front of my eyes. "So have I, mate," I spit. "It's called sponging off your friends, and I don't like it. How much d'you think the food you just shoved down your throat cost, eh? Or the beer?"

Damn. I sound petty as hell. And Bonny's *glaring* at me.

Kell smiles, nastily. "I was invited here. But food can be grown. Beer isn't necessary."

"Won't offer you another then, mate," I rap out, before I can stop myself.

"*Rich!*" erupts Bonny. "Kell – have another beer!"

But Kell doesn't even look at her. He puts his plate on the floor, says, "I think we'd better go now," stands up, and holds out one arm to Liz. Who scrambles silently to her feet, scurries over to his side, and inserts herself obediently under his arm.

"What about the balcony?" falters Bonny. "You said you'd like to see it, Liz. . ."

"Some other time," says Kell.

And they leave.

Chapter 12

"*Jesus – H – Christ*," I explode, as the door slams behind Kell and Liz, "you didn't tell me I was going to have to eat dinner with some kind of psychotic *hippy*. Where the *hell* was he coming from?"

"You didn't have to be so *aggressive* to him!" Bonny explodes back. "Just 'cos he had a go at ad agencies!"

"Bonny – he was a patronizing arsehole!"

"He's got strong views, that's all. Liz said he's a real idealist. He was into Sufism, then Buddhism—"

"And now full-of-*shit*ism. . ."

"Oh, *shut up*. I think it was good, the way he was talking. I agree with him about adverts."

"Oh, Bonny, *come on*."

"I do. All these images everywhere of impossibly beautiful girls with impossibly thin bodies—"

"Yeah, but you know they're fake! You've got to be really sad to let that kind of thing get to you!"

"Well, *fine*, I must be really sad then, me and about 99.9 per cent of all other girls. . ."

"Oh, for *God's* sake –"

"You don't realize, you don't know how it affects us!"

"And Kell does, I suppose?"

"He seemed to know how—"

"Oh, well, *sorry*!" I erupt. "Sorry for not being a touchy-feely all-round-great-guy like Kell!"

"Oh, Rich, stop being such a *dickhead*." Bonny stamps back across the room, starts picking up the plates and cutlery. "Liz is my *best friend*," she adds, bitterly. "You might've made more of an effort."

"I *was* making an effort!" I howl. "Not that I got a chance to, with her. She hardly said a word to me, she spent the whole time gazing at that git like he was God or something—"

"She's just in *love*. She told me. And how he's the only guy she's ever felt really loved *by*."

"He was ticking her off, ordering her about—"

"She said he really cares about her. She's so secure with him. And he's . . . *helping* her."

"Helping her what?"

"*I don't know!* I had about two seconds on the phone with her before she came over tonight! If you hadn't been so bloody antagonistic, maybe I could've talked to her a bit and found out!"

"Oh, great, so it's all *my* fault, is it?" I explode.

"I didn't say that—"

"My fault your friends are complete *losers* who can't take a bit of discussion? I couldn't bloody wait for them to go!" I stomp back into the kitchen for another beer.

A couple of seconds later, Bonny appears at the doorway with the plates. "D'you want me to go too?" she demands.

When she says that I feel like I could kick the fridge in. Shit, *shit*, how can a day that went so brilliantly end up so badly? What happened, how did I lose it, how did I lose control of everything? I want to ask her to stay, but what I do is shrug and say, "If you wanna go, go."

She pushes past me, dumps the plates in the sink. "If you're going to keep on acting like this – fine, I will."

"Go on then."

She starts to walk out of the kitchen. At the very last moment I shoot my arm out and bar her way. "For *God's sake*, Bonny, of course I don't want you to *go*! I'm just pissed off with you – asking those two retards for a meal, when I wanted you all to myself!"

I'm expecting her to be really mad at me now, calling her best mate a retard and everything, but what she does is droop her head and kind of butt it into my chest. I put my arms round her immediately, say, "Bonny, I'm *sorry*."

"Me too," she whispers back.

"Yeah, but I'm *sorrier*. Honest I am. I was out of order then."

"Yeah, well – I shouldn't've asked them over."

"Yeah, you should. After you cancelled Liz and everything."

"But we'd had such a brilliant day, and . . . it spoilt it."

"No, it didn't."

"I shouldn't've cooked for them."

"Yeah you should." I hug her tighter. "It tasted great, Bon. Is there any left?"

She laughs at that, and the tension between us starts to ebb away. She pulls down a clean plate and scrapes what's left in the cooking pan on to it. "I did try with them," I say, as we wander out of the kitchen. "He just got my back right up and I lost it. What a sanctimonious prat."

"Rich – I've kind of *grasped* what you feel about him. You don't have to go into it all again."

"Sorry." We sit down on the floor again and I start forking in my second helping of stir-fry. "Did you like him, though?"

"No. Dunno. He was *different*, he had his own views, and I kind of admired that, but. . ." She watches me for a moment, then says, "Liz isn't usually a retard."

"I know, I know. I shouldn't've said that."

"No, I mean – I've never seen her like that before. She must be really gone on him."

"No accounting for taste, babe."

"She, like, *deferred* to him the whole time. Like he was between us the whole time. Not that either of us could get a word in towards the end, with you two on at each other."

"Well – no more cosy foursomes, Bon, eh."

"Don't *worry*! Your friends next time."

"OK – there's a party on tomorrow night. Someone Chris knows, from college. He's got a free house."

She looks a bit scared when I mention the party, but she doesn't back down, just nods, says, "Fine." And actually I wasn't going to mention the party, I didn't really want to go. I'm not sure what made me mention it – rising to the challenge? Revenge? Anyway, it's too late now.

After I've polished off my food, we go down to the balcony and curl up together on the rug. I start kissing her, but when I slip my hands under her top like I did in the fields she says, "Rich – d'you want a massage?" She takes off my shirt, makes me lie on my front, and works on me. She's good, she's got all the moves, and she's strong too, pressing hard on my muscles. She's so good, and I'm so knackered with all the fresh air that's been blasting through my lungs, and the row and everything, that I fall asleep. I'm half aware of her kissing me and saying, "See you tomorrow," then I wake up alone just before dawn, cold and stiff. I stagger up the fire escape ladder and fall into bed.

Chapter 13

It's Saturday the next day. I phone Bonny's mobile around noon and pull her leg about running out on me when I was asleep. I want her to come over but she says she's got a big-deal family birthday she has to go to, so we arrange that she'll come over at eight for Chris's mate's party.

At ten past eight she parks her car in the mill car park, beeps for me to come down. She looks amazing. She's got this stunning top on that's incredibly sexy but not a bit tarty, probably because it cost loads. And she's done something to her eyes that makes them look huge. "Bonny, you look the business," I say. "You really do." The party isn't far away, so we agree to take the bus, maybe a cab back. She seems pretty on edge. Perhaps she's nervous at meeting up with my mates again now she's my girlfriend.

As we lurch along on the bus we don't say a lot. My mind's full of whether she'll stay the night with me. I suppose she will, as she's left the car behind. I want her to, so much. Not to go the whole way, I know it's too soon for her, but just to go . . . well. A bit further. And to fall asleep together afterwards. I really, really want to ask her, but I don't, I can't make myself. Scared she'll make an excuse, I guess.

When we get to the party, Bonny copes fine with all the teasing from Chris and Ollie, and would-be-lover wounded looks from Ryan. She also copes with Natalie loudly making friends with her and making a big, big deal about how much my brain and taste has improved since Portia. In fact, she's on great form. I find myself just standing back, listening to her, watching her, thinking how fantastic she is. Unlike the party. Not even Bonny can disguise the fact that that's monumental crap.

"God, Chris," I mutter, after about an hour of total non-action. "No wonder your mate was so laid-back about you asking a load of people along to this. He only knows two other people apart from you."

"Nat and me are sloping off pretty soon," Chris mutters back. "To the pub. Coming?"

But when I put this to Bonny, she isn't keen. "Would they mind if we didn't?" she says. "They're great but – I dunno. I just don't feel like it."

"Anti-social cow."

"*Look —*"

"*Joking.* It's fine. Come back to the flat for a bit?"

She hardly says anything on the bus on the way home. Neither do I. She seems dead tense. Riding up in the lift, she hardly looks at me. I open the front door and she stalks over to the windows and just stands there, looking out at the purple night. I walk over, put my arms round her waist, but she feels rigid, rejecting. "Sorry about the shitty party," I say.

She shrugs. "S'OK. It was nice to see Chris and everyone again."

"Yeah?"

"I really like Nat."

"She likes you."

There's a pause, while I think in panic — Christ, what is it? Has she suddenly gone off me, or what? Then I say, "Want some wine? I thought it was about time I bought a bottle."

"I'd love some," she says. I go into the kitchen, de-cork the bottle, find the only two wine glasses the flat possesses, wash them, dry them, and fill them to the brim. She still hasn't moved when I get back. I walk over and hand her the glass without the chip on the rim and say *cheers*, and she takes a big gulp.

And mumbles, "I wanna sleep with you."

I'm not sure I've heard her right at first. "You what?" I say.

"Oh, *God*! You heard me. I want to. I s'pose you want to. Don't you?"

"Bonny, you know I do, but—"

"It's stupid waiting. Just 'cos you're supposed to wait for two months or something after you start going out together. We *know* each other, and – and the other night, you were going on about taking a risk, letting things move on and . . . and I . . . I don't want to wait."

I fix my eyes on the black windows, try to ignore the inevitable groin–clench I got when she said she wanted to sleep with me. The windows are reflecting nothing, not even our faces. "That wasn't what I meant," I say. "When I talked about taking a risk and stuff, I didn't mean –"

"I know. I know. I just –"

I put my arm round her waist, press my mouth onto her skin, right behind her ear. "Can't you just relax a bit? About all . . . *this*?"

"No," she whispers. She's still rigid against my arm – she'll start crying in a minute if I don't do something.

"Bonny, have some more wine. Come on." She takes a mouthful and I steer her over to sit on the cushions on the floor. Then I open up the windows, so the warm night rushes in on us. "Look at that sky," I murmur, settling down beside her. "Amazing or what?"

"It's beautiful."

"And we're OK, aren't we?"

She sniffs. "Yeah. Except I'm ruining everything. Like I always do."

"Bonny, for Christ's sake. Don't talk like that. You're not ruining anything."

She doesn't answer me; she still won't look at me. "You're tense, though," I say. "You've been tense ever since we left the party. What's up?"

There's a kind of crackly silence, and I'm wondering if I dare bring up the whole subject of sex, just to talk about it, just to ask her how she feels, 'cos I'm sure that's the problem, when she gulps down another load of wine and mutters, "I had a phonecall before I came out tonight."

"Who from?" I say, although something in me already knows who from.

"Mum."

"Oh, great."

"Yeah. She was drunk. She's started knocking back vodka again. She stopped for a while but . . . she's back on it again. She wanted me to go and see her. Tonight. I refused, said I was going out, and she . . . she totally lost it."

"What'd she do?"

"Oh, the usual. Whining, accusations. . . She went on about how *badly* she was treated at Nick and Barb's barbecue, like it was all my fault, and she'd found out about me going to this birthday party today – Ellie's niece – she was jealous as hell. She started laying into me, screaming down the phone at me, blaming me for running out on her, *abandoning* her, blaming *me* for her drinking again. . ."

"Why didn't you put the phone down?"

"I couldn't. I wanted to, but I couldn't. I just sat there, holding the receiver away from my ear but I could still hear it all – one minute she's begging me, the next she's screaming foul things at me. . ."

"Oh, shit, Bonny. No wonder you're –"

"What? What am I?"

"Unhappy."

Bonny drains her glass. "Don't go getting plastered," I say.

"Pour me a bit more. Rich, I *need* it!"

I pour her half a glass, and she says, "Mum's waiting for me to phone her back. That's the only way I got off the phone, by promising to phone her tonight, when I got home."

"Well, you're not home. You're not breaking any promises. Has she got your mobile number?"

She shakes her head violently, gasps, "Are you kidding?" Then she sighs, huddles her hands round her wine glass. I have this sense of her sliding down, slipping back into some pit her mum's dug for her, and I don't know how to grab her, how to save her.

"I'll have to phone her back," she croaks. "Before it gets too late. I promised."

Then I have a brainwave. "Give your dad a phone instead," I say. "Offload on to him."

"What can he do?"

"He can phone the old cow up, tell her to lay off you!"

"He hates to have anything to do with her."

"Well that's just too bad, isn't it? She's his ex-wife – she's *his daughter's* mother! If he can't step in, who can?"

"But Rich – you don't understand – he had a complete break from her, he *hates* talking to her—"

"And you *like* it? Look – you're going to be all on edge till you phone. Or someone phones. Get him to!" I hug her to me, warm to my theme. "You go on about how protective he is – get him to show it! You need protection from *her* a hell of a lot more than you do from me."

She laughs a bit at that, and I risk saying, "No wonder you want to have it off with me, Bon. Sure way to take your mind off all this."

There's a frigid pause, and I think I've blown it, and then Bonny laughs again. It's a lovely, gurgling sound, like a stream unfreezing. "Oh, *Rich*. You're fantastic."

"Am I right, though?"

"A bit."

"So are you going to phone him?"

"Yes." She's cuddling up to me, happy for me to take over.

"And when you're on to him, tell him you're staying here. In your old room. I mean – you can't drive now you've had all this wine, can you?" And I empty the last of the bottle into her glass. She seems to need it.

"And am I going to be in my old room?" she says.

"No. Unless you fancy shagging Andy."

"Not him, I don't," she says.

"Glad to hear it. But – look, Bon. I don't think we should – you know – sleep together. Not tonight. You're too upset. You're all screwed up over your mum." She looks up at me, all kind of grateful and surprised, and I think, *Blimey*, if Oll and my mates could hear me now, turning down sex, they'd be more than surprised, they'd be stunned.

"There's no rush, is there," I go on. "After all."

"No," she agrees. "I just –"

"What?"

"It's just kind of – hanging over us, isn't it."

"Is it?"

"Yeah, you know – when, if. I just want to *jump in.*"

"Blimey, Bon. What sex manuals have you been reading?"

"Oh, shut up. You know what I mean. I just feel an idiot, that's all."

"And you thought sex would solve that? Never worked for me."

She laughs, butts me gently with her head. "You *know* what I mean. It might stop me being so neurotic. About you and me being together."

There's a pause, then I say, "Bonny – sleeping together – it won't guarantee we work out."

110

"I know that," she whispers. "Nothing's a guarantee."

We sit there in silence and I hold her to me, then I say, "Come on. Give your old man a bell."

Bonny doesn't answer for a moment. Then she presses her face into my shoulder, says, "Pass me my bag, Rich. I'll phone him now."

Chapter 14

I wander into my room while Bonny bells her dad, 'cos I don't want to eavesdrop. I'm wondering whether I should tow my bed out in front of the windows again, like I did that first night Bonny stayed, but I decide not to. I don't want Andy stumbling past us again in the middle of the night.

Ten, fifteen minutes later, Bonny calls out to me. She's on a high. "I told him what'd happened," she says, "all the stuff Mum was saying, and he *exploded*. He went off about how she had no right to *spew her twisted neuroses* all over me – I think that's what he called it – so then it was pretty easy to get his arm up his back and get him to agree to phone her and tell her to leave me alone. I think he was going to phone her right away – I hope he does – while he's still mad at her. He said –" Bonny breaks off, makes a noise that could be a giggle or a sob – "he said she should have serious treatment, that she's like someone walking round with a disgusting open sore, not getting treatment for the state her mind's in. . ."

"God," I mutter, not wanting to hear this. For a creepy moment Andy's words come back into my head, those words about Bonny being damaged by her past, but I shove them away. "Is he going to call you back?"

"Not tonight. I said I was staying here again, 'cos I'd had too much to drink, and he didn't even question it."

"Good. Anyone'd need a drink after their mum went sick at them like that."

"Yeah. Actually, Rich, I could seriously do with another. Got any more?"

It goes through my head to tell her to watch it or she'll end up an alkie like her mum, but I veto this as insensitive. "Andy's got some beer, I think. In the fridge. Want me to go out for more wine?"

"No. Forget it. Make me some tea, eh?"

She slumps against the kitchen counter as I put the kettle on to boil. "So your dad wasn't twitched about you staying here again, then?" I ask.

"Not really."

"Even though you'd told him we might be getting together, and how much you fancied me. . ."

"Oh, shut up. He thinks my old room's still empty. He thinks it's all just like before."

There's a pause, as we both reflect on how different it is to before, then I say, "You look knackered."

"Thanks!"

"I don't mean you look *bad*. I just mean you have this . . . this *air of tiredness* about you."

"Yeah? If you hadn't just told me you weren't going to sleep with me, I'd think you were trying to get me into bed. . ."

"Ha, ha. Look – I was being *noble* when I said that, all right? I'd love to get you into bed."

She goes a bit red, mutters, "Well, you're right, I am knackered. Mum's scenes – they're exhausting. I can block them out for a while, but they always come back to you."

"I bet," I say, uneasily, and hand her her tea. "Maybe you should get some sleep."

"Yeah," she says.

It's weird, going to bed together when you've decided all you're going to do is sleep. Bonny fishes a bright yellow sponge-bag out of her shoulder bag and heads off to the bathroom and I think about pulling her leg about coming all prepared, like she was planning to spend the night with me, but I decide that would be a bit crass, because she did plan it, didn't she. After she's come out of the bathroom I go in and clean my teeth and strip off, but I keep my T-shirt and boxers on. When I get into my room she's under the duvet already. She looks gorgeous, tanned skin against the

114

creamy pillow, blonde hair spread out. My boxers are only just about containing me. "I'm not sure I can do this, Bon," I say. "I think I'd better sleep out here."

"Turn the light out," she says. "Turn it out and get in beside me."

I do what she says, lie down beside her so we're almost touching but not quite. She's kept her top on too. Her hand slides down, takes hold of mine. It's sweet, but it's kind of a barrier too. Well, that's fine, isn't it? Fine for tonight. We lie there on our backs and look up at the purple-black lozenge of the skylight. "Three stars," she whispers.

"It's cloudy. Sometimes you can see more."

"Rich – I'm sorry about tonight. I'm sorry I was so weird."

"Bonny – it's fine. Anyone'd be weird with a mother like yours. Oh, shit, I don't mean – " Luckily, she's laughing. "You know what I mean," I say, squeezing her hand. "It's tough. You do great."

"You think?"

"Yeah. I'm just glad you weren't having second thoughts about me. You know – when we first got back here and you wouldn't say anything."

"No way."

We lie there, side by side, and I'm so turned on I daren't move. And yet it's easy to talk, too, the easiest yet, side by side in the dark with the skylight glimmering above us. "You know," I murmur, "back at the start of the week, when we met up again?"

"Yeah?"

"You seemed so sure of yourself, all sophisticated, with your *car* and everything."

"*Did* I?"

"Yeah, you did. I was dead intimidated. You made me feel like a right yob."

"I intimidated *you*? Brilliant!"

"You blew it pretty soon, though. The sophisticated act, I mean."

"Shut up. I *am* sophisticated."

"OK, you are. Just not when you get drunk."

"Oh, shut *up*. I know I had too much but – I *needed* it. Meeting up with you again – it was a real shock. . ."

"You were stunned by how good-looking I am, weren't you? You'd forgotten."

"Yeah, Rich, ha ha."

Her knee's touching my thigh. I'm all seized up with wanting her. "Why didn't you try and contact me?" she says.

"What?"

"This summer – if you wanted to see me, you could've got hold of me. . ."

"I tried. Barb wouldn't give me your new number."

"You are *kidding*! You asked for my number?" We've turned towards each other on the pillow now, talking into each other's mouths.

"Yeah. She said you were seeing someone else and I ought to leave you alone. 'Cos you were just getting over me."

"Blimey. She acts more like my mother than my mother does."

There's a pause; I listen to her breathing. Fast, faster than normal. "What was he like?" I ask. "The guy you were seeing?"

"Loads of money, twenty-two. Suave, up himself. A total pain in the arse, actually."

"Good." And then I can't help it, I smooch a little kiss down on to her face, just beside her nose.

She smooches me back.

And then we're kissing, really kissing. I feel mad with how great it is. We both kind of rear up and I wrap my arms round her, she pulls me in close and I cover her and all the time we're kissing. She slides down in the bed beneath me, her top's riding up, she's got nothing on underneath. I can't believe how beautiful she is, I'm stroking her, touching her, and I'm waiting for her to call a stop, but she doesn't. Her legs are winding round mine and her top's all rucked up round her neck and she tugs it off, lobs it off the bed on to the floor.

Maybe *I* should call a stop. We said we wouldn't – won't that seem like rejection, though? She's holding me so close. I let my hand slide down her stomach, slowly so she can tell me to stop, but she doesn't. We're not kissing now. She tucks her hands down just inside the elastic of my boxers, like she's not exactly sure what to do. Then she croaks, "Rich. *Rich.* It's OK."

I don't answer. I want to make this very, very good. I'm very gently peeling her pants down, kissing her again. I'm going very slow, very careful. We don't have to go the whole way, do we? We can just get used to each other, touch each other. . .

It's like she doesn't want to be slow, though. She wriggles away, scrapes her pants off with her foot, kicks them away. "Please, Rich. Just – *please*. Have you got – have you got something?"

"Bonny – are you sure?"

"Yes. *Yes*."

I reach over the bed, into the bottom of my wardrobe, find a condom. Half of my head's telling me to stop, ask her what's wrong, ask her why she's rushing it like this, but the other half's pounding away, just wanting to get inside her, and that half's stronger.

So we do it. She's very tight, too tight. I think I must be hurting her but she's holding on to me, she won't let me go. I stop moving; I look down at her, and kiss her. "Hey," I say. "You all right?"

She's got her eyes screwed shut, she won't answer, like there's a law against speaking during sex. I still don't move. I kiss her again, but this time I nudge at her mouth and kiss her really deep, and then I think – *I'm making love to Bonny* – and it kind of fills me up and I just keep kissing her, really slow, really deep, really warm, and then – at last – she kisses me back. "You all right?" I whisper again.

"Yes," she breathes. She's relaxed, she's warm, too, it's better. I start moving again, moving into her. I don't try to stop myself coming though, I let myself come; I know she won't.

After it's over she's kind of shaking. I stroke her hair, and I tell her she's great, and we don't talk much, just hold each other. Then she goes off to sleep, face squashed against my shoulder.

I watch her for a bit, sleeping. I know she didn't enjoy it, not the way she should, not the way I know she could. And it's not the best sex I've ever had, no way. But it's with *her*. And I know it's just the start.

Chapter 15

When I wake up I'm all on my own in the bed. My first thought is that she's run out on me. That she's flipped, and done a runner. Then I hear clattering from the kitchen. "Bon?" I call.

"Just making some tea," she calls back, in a loud whisper, like she's trying to avoid waking Andy up.

A few minutes later she appears at the door, with a tray and two mugs, and even some toast she's made, all laid out on a plate. She dumps the tray down on the bed, sits cross-legged on the end.

"How are you, beautiful?" I say.

"OK," she says. She's put her top and pants back on, brushed her hair. She looks great.

"Listen – I'm sorry – you know. I said we shouldn't make love and then –"

Her eyes get wide, stricken. "You're sorry we made love?"

"No! No – that's not what I meant. I meant – we weren't going to, were we, and then –"

"Are you sorry we did?"

"*No*." This is hard work, especially when you're not really awake yet. "No – it was great, Bonny. It's just – oh, come here, won't you? Get back into bed."

"Have your tea," she says, and hands me a mug.

I take a sip, say, "Can I tell you something?"

"What?"

"You have got the most fantastic breasts in the whole entire universe."

"Shut up," she says, going red, looking delighted.

"And I bet aliens have *great* breasts. I bet they have four pairs each."

"*Rich!*"

"Sorry. Come on, get back into bed with me."

She shakes her head. "I ought to get back. Daddy'll be waiting to see me, he'll be –" She suddenly breaks off. All the colour drains from her face. She claps a hand over her mouth and wails, "Oh, *no-oo. . .*"

"*Shit*, Bonny, what's up?"

"*Lunch!*" she howls, in sheer panic. "You're supposed to be coming to *lunch!*"

Panic hits me too. Eating lunch with big, powerful, protective Daddy just hours after I've laid his daughter for the first time is not exactly top of my relaxing-things-to-do list. There's a stricken silence, during which we gape at each other like beached cod. Then I rally. "It's OK, Bonny. We've got hours, haven't we?" I check my watch. "It's only just eleven. What time we supposed to be there?"

"One, Ellie said. Oh, shit. That's only two hours. . ."

"That's long enough to get a shower, wipe the afterglow off our faces. . ."

But Bonny's anything but afterglowing. In fact she looks like she's about to throw up. "It's not the *time*. It's just going to be so awful. Oh – *God*! I can't go through with it. I feel so . . . so *strange*."

Strange. *Strange?* Strange shouldn't be how she feels. Brilliant, yes. Amazing, *yes*. Not *strange*.

"You'll be fine, Bon," I say, trying not to sound too pissed off. "Get a glass of Daddy's posh plonk down you, you'll feel great, then the only thing you have to worry about is holding yourself back from crawling across the table towards me. . ."

She looks over at me wildly, like I've gone completely mad. " 'Cos I'll be looking so gorgeous," I explain. "'Cos you're so turned on."

She stares at me blankly for another second or so, then, thank *God*, she laughs. "Oh, *Rich*. Shut up. Look. I have to go. I have to shower, get myself together."

Now it's my turn to turn white. "Go? Why have you got to go? Can't we pitch up together?"

"Oh – *I don't think so.* I'm just supposed to have

dossed in my old room, aren't I. If we turn up together we'll look like a real couple, and that'll get Daddy's back right up."

I want to say *well, tough* but I don't. "I don't know his address," I whine.

She scrabbles in her leather shoulder bag that she'd dumped down by the bed, finds paper and pen, scribbles frantically. "Here," she says, "it's not far. The 248 bus is best. Or you can walk it. Or d'you want me to come and collect you?"

"No," I say, a bit sulkily. "I'll get there."

And two hours later, all showered and fresh-shirted, I am there. In front of a big mock-Georgian front door with paint so new and bright you can just about smell it still. Bonny had warned me her new home was on a pretentious, executive-type new estate, warned me to be prepared. Even so it's hard to stop my lip curling as I lope up the steps.

I wish I could get it out of my head that I've got a sign stapled to my forehead saying *I've just shagged your daughter.* I wish I could convince myself that Daddy isn't going to know. I spent about fifteen minutes in the shower, and I've OD'd on aftershave. Just in case he can *smell* her on me.

I extend my trembling digit, press the mock-Georgian electric bell, and wait.

Ellie opens the door. I assume it's Ellie. She's about thirty, with an OK face, a mass of black curly hair, one toddler balanced on her hip and its clone clinging to her leg. "Hi!" she says, all revved-up girly enthusiasm. "You're Rich!"

"Er – yes," I say. I wonder about shaking her hand but it's fully occupied trying to stop the hip-balanced toddler launch itself into space.

"Come in!" she says. "Great to see you. Melvin's making the lunch – Bonny's helping."

So Daddy's called Melvin. Hilarious. And I might've known he'd be cooking lunch. Second family, got to be all hands on and evolved man this time.

"Come through!" she carols, and limps slowly ahead of me.

Daddy – I can't call him Melvin, I can't – and Bonny spin round as one from the flash open-range cooker. Daddy's all hearty geniality, Bonny looks like a young deer caught in a trucker's headlights with nowhere to run. I'm overcome with wanting to go over to her, wrap her up in my arms, bury my face in her hair and inhale her . . . if I had a laser gun I'd zap Daddy and Ellie and the twins, I'd evaporate them. . .

"RICHARD!" Daddy booms. "Glad you could join us. Now – settle a dispute between my daughter and myself. We're having lamb. I said I was sure you were a mint sauce man, preferably fresh. She thinks you'll like that terrible sickly redcurrant jelly she and Ellie like."

My immediate response is *couldn't give a stuff*, but as that doesn't seem appropriate I plump for siding with Daddy, the men against the girls. "Oh, mint sauce, every time," I say. "The more vinegary the better."

"You see?" booms Daddy, all triumphant, like I've passed some kind of test. He takes a step towards me and for one dodgy moment I think he's going to sling an arm round my shoulders. "I knew Richard was a man of taste. Now – drink?"

Great. Test Number Two. I either ask for beer and risk sounding like an alcoholic yob, or a soft drink and risk sounding like a complete nancy. "I'm having a beer," says Bonny, rescuing me. I smile at her and our eyes collide, just for a second, but even this feels risky, too exposed.

"Yeah, great, beer," I go, and she knocks the top off a bottle of Rolling Rock and hands it to me, then she takes a swig from her own bottle before I can get uptight about whether Daddy expects me to use a glass or not.

"Right!" pronounces Daddy. "Now Richard's here, I'll put the green vegetables on. Bonny darling – did you lay the table? Richard – how's your potato mashing technique?"

Oh, bloody hell – Test Number Three. This is exhausting. He hands me a gleaming implement that looks like it might belong to a large-animal vet, then propels me towards a vast vat of spuds.

"Not too heavy handed," he warns. "Light and fluffy. Then you can *fold* in the caramelized onions."

Fold them in? What, like in a blanket? And *caramel* onions? Yuck.

I start nervously mashing. Suddenly, with no warning, Daddy tips about a gallon of olive oil into the vat, timed perfectly so that it hits the masher and sloshes over my hand. "Careful!" he barks. Then he shovels in a ton of fried onions, hands me a spatula, and tells me to *fold*. Then he directs me to glob the lot into a classy-looking dish he bangs down beside me. I realize he's not actually doing anything, just overseeing me. "Back in the oven!" he booms. I'm about to pick up the red-hot dish and burn all the skin off my hands (probably what Daddy was hoping for, the bastard) when Bonny thrusts an oven glove at me. I ram the *olive oil mash* as Daddy pretentiously calls it back in the oven and then I take a long pull of beer.

Jesus. I'm shattered.

"Three minutes!" Daddy bellows. This is the cue for Ellie and Bonny to wheel two hideous high-tech high-chairs out from the corner of the room and hoist an infant into each, Ellie saying stuff like *oooh, num-nums, is oo hungry, baby?*

A bit more scurrying, and we're all sitting round the groaning table and Daddy's poised at the end in front of a huge leg of lamb, slowly and deliberately sharpening an unnecessarily large knife on a steel.

He knows. I know he knows. He knows what I was

doing last night. He must do, he's staring at me non-stop. He's psychic, or he bugged Bonny's bra or something. You could do that. You could get a tiny microphone down alongside the wire of her bra, no problem.

"This meat is perfect," he says, slicing it bloodily off the bone. "Not too overdone. Lamb should be *rare*. Ellie – *plates*, darling."

Ellie jumps to it. No amount of wearing a pinny and doing the cooking can disguise the fact that Daddy's a good old-fashioned paterfamilias. He's the type who's used to having his orders obeyed on the double, the type to beat the shit out of any yob who laid an amorous hand on his little girl. And I've as good as got *I screwed your daughter* stapled to my forehead.

Calm down, I tell myself. He's not going to finish slicing the lamb and start on you. But I still feel sick. I look down at the huge plate of food slammed in front of me and wonder how the hell I'm going to gag my way through it.

As we're eating, Daddy makes conversation. He grills me about sport and takes my preference for football over rugby as a clear sign of degeneracy or homosexuality or both. Bonny tells him how good I am at art but he bats this aside as further proof of my weak character. He asks me my opinion of the wine we're drinking and leaves a long silence after my stuttered "Good. Yeah, er, great." Then he moves on to the flat: how long I've been there, who else stays there, machine-gunning questions at me and all the time watching me like a hawk in case I slip up and confess it's a full-time shagpad and his daughter and I like doing it on the kitchen counters.

The twins save me, though. Normally I've got no time for mucky little kids but in this instance I'm quite keen on them. Once they've smeared food all over their heads they get bored and keep up a stream of demands and chatter that deflects Daddy from concentrating all his terrible attention just on me.

Second helpings. Then a French tart from a *marvellous* patisserie Ellie discovered locally. Chew it up, gag it down. And all the time Bonny's sitting there, beautiful and frozen and so far away from me she could be behind a brick wall.

"What are your plans for later?" Daddy suddenly barks. My mind goes blank. Does he mean later today? Or later in life?

"We haven't any plans," says Bonny.

"Those were the days, eh Ellie?" Daddy sighs. "No plans, no pressure."

No pressure – is he *kidding*?

Finally, lunch is over. And Ellie's insisting she doesn't want any help clearing up and Daddy's balancing a twin on each arm carrying them upstairs to have a nap and Bonny and I escape into the over-styled garden at the back. "*Sorry*," she gasps.

I'm not even going to pretend there's nothing to apologize for. I collapse down on to a poncy wrought-iron bench and go, "*Grooooough*."

"Was it that bad?"

"Worse."

"*Sorry*."

"He hates me."

"No – that's just him. And – you know."

"Yep. I'm a threat."

"He was far worse to that other guy."

I drop my head lower. "Don't wanna hear about it."

"You're sick of me, aren't you."

"*What?*"

"You want to go back to just being friends."

"Bonny – what are you *on* about?"

"I'm not worth it. I'm not worth the hassle."

I look up at her, at her anxious, open, lovely face, and say, "You know what I want? I want to go back to the flat now, and take off every bit of what you're wearing, and—"

"Shut UP!" she hisses, but she looks pleased.

"Can we go now?"

"Well – pretty soon. Or –"

"Or what?"

"I'd really like a walk. You know? I'd like some air."

"More than you want to go to bed with me again?" I rap out, and instantly regret it. Bonny's eyes are shining, like she could cry any minute. "Hey, come on," I say. "What's wrong?"

"It's just. . . Oh, God. It's been a hell of a weekend. Mum flipping, and this awful lunch . . . and . . . and you know. . ."

"Yeah," I say. "Come on. Let's get out of here."

Chapter 16

There's a sticky moment of potential horror when our exit from the front door coincides with Daddy bouncing down the stairs all successful-dad ("Out like lights, the pair of 'em.") and booming, "A walk? Great idea! Ellie – fancy a walk?"

Ellie wearily calls out from the kitchen that they can't leave the twins on their own, and Daddy replies that they won't wake for a good hour, they're flat out, and Ellie responds that it's actually *illegal* to leave them on their own and while Daddy's harumphing about the horrors of the nanny state Bonny and I slip out the front door and leg it along the road.

One of the good things about the executive housing estate is that it's right on the edge of a wood. There's these dinky little man-made footpaths into it, and signs saying stuff like "The Bluebell Walk" and "Woodpecker Way". Really naff, but useful too. I get hold of Bonny's hand and we swing along. "Thank God that's over with," I say. "D'you reckon I passed the test?"

"I think you did great. I nearly died when he made you mash those spuds."

"Tell me what he says about me, won't you."

"Oh, he won't say anything. Ellie thinks you're *hunky*, though. She mouthed it at me. Or was it funky?"

"Hunky. *Must*'ve been."

She laughs, says, "What are your parents like? You hardly ever talk about them."

"They're OK. They'd like you."

"I'd like to meet them."

I get this sudden picture of our grotty little kitchen-diner at home, washing hanging down from the ceiling-rack, formica peeling off the counters, and I think – I can't take Bonny back to my old place. Not yet.

"Yeah, no rush," I say. We walk out into a clearing with a bench, huge sun coming through the trees warming it.

I pull her over towards it and she laughs, says, "Oh, Rich. You lazy sod. We've hardly *started*."

Sitting on the bench has nothing to do with being tired and she knows this, but I play along with her. "I'm too full of lunch to move. I am, honest. Come on, just for a minute."

We sit down, and I put my arm round her but before I can move in for a kiss she says, "I phoned Liz yesterday. I meant to tell you. Only Mum calling kind of put it out of my head."

"Yeah? What she say? She apologize for her boyfriend being such an aggressive wanker?"

"*No*. And neither did I."

"Glad to hear it."

"I did say I was sorry the meal didn't exactly go smoothly. You know."

"Yeah." I'm stroking her neck now, the bit I love just below her ear, but she doesn't seem to be enjoying it. Or even noticing.

"I wanted to arrange to meet up with her soon – just us on our own," she goes on. "But she was really *weird*."

"What d'you mean – weird?"

"I dunno. Maybe she's offended with me or something. It just didn't sound like her. She wouldn't get into chatting – she didn't laugh *once*. I felt like I was pushing a big stone uphill, just trying to keep the conversation going."

"Didn't you ask her what was up?"

"Yeah – sort of. I said – *are you OK?* And she said – *I've never been better*. But in this kind of dead voice, like actually she'd never been worse."

"Weird."

"Yeah."

"I bet *Kell* was listening," I say, darkly. "I bet he

was sitting right next to her. That's why she sounded so inhibited."

"Well, if she was inhibited, why didn't she kick him out? Or move to another room?"

"Maybe you interrupted them screwing." *Damn.* Shouldn't've mentioned sex again.

Bonny shifts on the seat, says, "Maybe. Not from the sound of her voice, though."

"So when are you seeing her again?"

"This is it, I'm not. She wouldn't fix a date. Not even vaguely."

"Well, that's nice."

"It's just not *like* her. If she's pissed off with me, she tells me. We've known each other for *years*. She's just about my oldest friend."

"Maybe she was just having a really bad day. Maybe she had a hangover."

"You think?"

"Yeah. She'll call you back." And then I do move in for a kiss, and Bonny kisses me back, but when I slide my hand down on to her breast she freezes, seizes up.

"Someone could *walk by*," she hisses.

"Well, if they do, we can stop," I say, but she pulls away from me, and she's trying to laugh like it's all lighthearted, but I know it's not; and I know something's wrong, but I can't ask her, everything's too raw and new, I can't say a word.

Chapter 17

There's a kind of fakeness between us after that, both of us pretending things are fine. We get up from the bench, we stroll hand in hand along the woodland path, we talk about this and that, everything but what we ought to be talking about, which is what happened last night, what she feels about it. She asks me if I want to come back for a cup of tea and I say, *I think I've had enough torture, thanks*, and she laughs and I say, *I'll just come back to say thanks for lunch and then I'll scarper*. I suggest she scarpers with me but she starts saying how knackered she feels after everything that happened over the weekend, how she wants to get an early night.

I look at my watch; it's only four-thirty. She's planning to get her jim-jams on at four-thirty? Then just as I'm feeling dead rejected and upset she throws her arms round me and says "Rich – *thanks* for being so great this weekend. Thanks for helping me about Mum and everything. I just – I need a bit of time, you know?"

Saying goodbye and thanks to Daddy isn't too unpleasant, I suspect mainly 'cos he's deliriously happy to see the back of me. Bonny offers me a lift home and I refuse. I can't kiss her goodbye properly 'cos Daddy could be watching out of a window somewhere. So I just peck her on the cheek on the front path, and promise to phone.

Then I set out for another walk, a proper fast walk, back into town. Walking always helps me sort out my head when it's mushed up. What feels like ten miles later, though, my head's as mushed up as ever. I need advice on this relationship. I need someone to chew it over with. Who? Not my old man, no way. He and I stopped talking about anything meaningful as soon as I hit puberty. Not my mates, not about having sex with Bonny. Not –

Barb, that's who. She was desperate to know how things were with Bonny, wasn't she? I'll get a mature, open-minded woman's perspective on this – if Nick's there I'll get a dual perspective. And as fate would have it, I'm only ten minutes' stroll from their house right now.

As I walk up their wide drive I can see them

through one of the front-room windows, curled up side by side on a sofa watching TV. I feel a bit mean knocking on their door, but I still do it.

Nick's all mock-disgust as he opens the door to me. "What the hell do you want? I get enough of you all week!"

"Nick!" yells Barb from the sofa. "Don't be so sodding rude. Come in, Rich. You want something to eat?"

"I've just had lunch with Daddy," I groan.

"Great! How's it going with Bonny?"

Barb knows I want to talk. She's psychic, I swear she is. She sends Nick (grumbling loudly) out to make tea and then they both listen to me while I give them the rundown on everything that's happened with Bonny so far. I don't tell them we've slept together or anything, but I do say how it's not exactly going smoothly. How it gets good, we get close, then something happens – like when Liz and her toxic boyfriend Kell came round – to make it go bad. And how uptight Bonny seems an awful lot of the time.

Barb doesn't seem that sympathetic though – it's like she doesn't really recognize what the problem is. She lectures me about all the hard times Bonny's had to go through (like I wasn't fully aware of them *myself*) and winds up with "Just take it slow, Rich. Be patient. She's going to take a bit of time to trust you."

"*Why?*" I demand.

"It's not personal. She'd take time to trust anyone.

She's dead scared of getting hurt. And also – well, she's always been pretty keen on you."

"Well, in that case – why does she keep freezing me off?"

"Oh, come *on*. The more you like someone, the more scared you are. Try and see it from her side."

"I *do*. We've talked about it. Oh – *God*. Why does it all have to be so *complicated*."

"Rich, stop acting like a typical *male*. You let someone in your life – I mean really in your life – and it *gets* complicated. You've got to face that."

"People mean problems," intones Nick from his slumped position on the sofa. "You're not the only car on the road any more. You get slowed down, barged aside, smashed into, wrecked."

"Blimey, what roads do you drive?" I ask, sulkily.

"It's an analogy, stupid. I'm just saying – it's hard. Have another biscuit."

I select a choccy digestive and start to munch, and the lurchers zone in on me. "There's always too much *else* going on," I moan. "Her mum – her dad – friends. . . I wish I could get her on her own. I wish we could go to a desert island for a week."

"Well, you can't," says Barb. "You're going to have to deal with this in the real world."

I toss both dogs a bit of biscuit to try and get rid of them but they lean towards me and chew, ecstatically, foul breath hitting me in duplicate. "Shit," I complain. "It smells like some sea mollusc died in their gobs."

"No, it doesn't," snaps Barb. She's really not being that nice to me. "Nick – are you going to take them out?"

"Oh, OK," grumbles Nick. "Wanna come, Rich?"

As we're bowling along towards Bannerbury Park in Nick's old Lotus Elite, the dogs crammed in the back breathing decomposing mollusc down my neck, he says, "You don't want to worry too much about Barb's lecture. She's dead protective of Bonny."

"Anyone'd think I was treating her bad, the way Barb was going on."

"Yeah, well, Barb'll always take the girl's side. She's female. It goes with the territory."

"But I'm being really *nice* to Bonny. I mean – I'm crazy about her. I act crazy about her."

"I'm sure you do, mate. But in Barb's book, no man will ever treat a woman good enough. Trust me. I've suffered with that all my life."

We drive on in silence, then Nick starts to laugh, and I join in. "We'll never get it right," he says. "We're poor, hard-done-by blokes. Maybe we should just give up right now." He pulls into the old tree-shaded car park, and we get out and start striding across the grass, the dogs wheeling happily around us.

"I didn't tell Barb everything," I say.

"No?"

"Thing is – Bonny's gone all weird. You know – about sex."

"*Yeah?*" crows Nick, face lit up with curiosity.

"Yeah. *No!* Not like you mean. Not like – handcuffs and stuff. What I mean is – we did it. You know. She wanted to – she really did. Then she went all distant. I don't know what's going on, Nick, honest to God."

"Maybe you were crap."

"Oh, *fuck* off –"

"Sorry. Couldn't resist. Look – why don't you just ask her?"

"What – just come out with it? Like – what's wrong?"

"Yeah, Rich, just come out with it."

"But she's acting like there's nothing wrong –"

"Women do that. But if you see past their act, they love you for it. Trust me."

"She won't want to *talk* about it –"

"I think you'll find she doesn't mind. I think you'll find girls are OK about talking about that kind of stuff. It's guys who find it impossible."

We follow the dogs into a little copse of trees. "You've just got to get up the balls to be direct, mate," says Nick. "It's a question of picking a good time, and then just going for it. And relationships – they're like a game of snakes and ladders, aren't they. Up the ladder, fine, then blam, before you know it, down a snake. Only when you think about it – Freud an' all – the snake bit ought to be the good bit, the snake –" Nick breaks off. A horrible ear-splitting squealing, like a small hysterical pig being knifed, assaults our ears. "Oh, *shit*," he gasps. "They're killing something. Come on!" And he legs it towards the horrible sound, me following.

We crash round the trees and come face to face with a spindly, agitated woman holding a tiny pooch up in the air, shrieking "Get ORFF! Get ORFF!" The lurchers are closing in like wolves. One starts pogo-sticking up and down, trying to snatch the tiny pooch in its slavering jaws. The other crouches menacingly on the ground, ready to launch forward and help tear the tiny pooch apart.

"*Willow!*" roars Nick. "*WILF!*"

The lurchers clock Nick and look cowed. "Are these your DAWGS?" screeches the woman. "Call them ORFF!"

"HERE!" thunders Nick. "Wilf – Willow – COME!"

The lurchers head stiffly and unwillingly over to Nick, as though they're suffering from chronic arthritis, and he attaches their leads to their collars. Then he looks towards the woman and says, "Look, I'm really sorry about—" but his words are obliterated by a torrent of cut-glass complaints.

"Your horrible dawgs nearly killed my Tosca! I've never seen her so scared in my whoal *life*! I had to pick her up or they'd have torn her *apart*! I'm going to report this! What's your name? I said, what's your name? You can't let horrible murderous dawgs like those off the lead. . ." She screeches on, so posh it's damn near impossible to follow what she's saying. Nick hands me the murderous mutts' leads, and oils over towards her.

"Look, I'm *really* sorry," he murmurs pleadingly. "You're right – it is a problem, letting them off. They're rescue dogs, you see."

The woman's eyes soften. If Nick has Rescued Some Dogs, he must be a Nice Man.

"To be frank with you," Nick smooths on, "they had a really rough start in life. They'd been abandoned – tied up and left."

"Oh, *no*," croaks the woman. "Heow can people treat animals like that?"

"They were half starving when they were found."

"Oh, how *sad*!"

"I know. And the Animal Welfare people were pretty sure they were used for –" he lowers his voice – "*hare coursing*."

"Oh, my goodness," bleats the woman, who's practically sobbing on to Nick's shoulder by now, "how fraightful!"

"So they've kind of got it in them, to chase things, I'm afraid. I shouldn't let them off, but –" here his voice cracks a bit, like the emotion's getting to him too – "I just can't bear to see them – you know – *not free*. I mean – they may as well be dead as tied up all the time."

"Oh, I *agree*! Look – my little Tosca's fine. Please – forget all abowt it."

"Well – I don't know." Nick's really into his stride now. "I can't risk letting that happen again."

"Oh, but you must! I'd feel dreadful if they were denied their freedom because of what happened today!"

Nick looks consideringly over his shoulder at Wilf and Willow, who've slipped into a vacant doze, unaware that their whole doggy future is apparently hanging in the balance. "We'll see," he says, solemnly. "Maybe they can have just one more chance."

Once the woman's tottered off, Tosca clutched to her emotion-packed bosom, I turn on Nick. "*Great* performance, man! You practically had her in tears by the end of it!"

"Not bad, hey? I'm particularly proud of the way I had *her* persuading *me* to let them off the lead again."

"I never knew they were rescue dogs."

"They weren't."

"*Wha-at?*"

"Made the whole thing up. Those two had the cushiest start in life you can imagine."

"But that poor woman – you had her completely taken in!"

"Yep. I've got the knack of making crap sound convincing. That's how come I've got so far in the ad business. You should take lessons, Richy boy."

"What about all that stuff about being used for hare coursing? Was that all porkies too?"

"They go squirrel-coursing. Same kinda thing. Stop looking at me like that, kid! She shouldn't keep a dog that looks like a rat if she doesn't want a *real* dog to mistake it for one."

"Bloody hell, Nick."

"Oh, bollocks. People who name their dogs after operas deserve what they get."

"After *operas* —?"

"God, you really are an illiterate yob, aren't you. Now speed up. I want to get back."

Chapter 18

Back at the Hanratty residence, the kids and Barb are involved in some kind of theatrical event in the back room, and they don't even notice us come in. Scarlett's made Freddie up as a Victorian villain, and he's spouting melodramatic lines, and Barb's nearly killing herself laughing.

"Look at her," says Nick fondly. "That's one of the reasons I married her, 'cos she does that. People talk about getting doubled up with laughter – she actually does it. It is *so* incredible sexy, I can't tell you."

"Sexy?" I echo, doubtfully.

"Oh, to a callow youth like you sexiness is all high heels and bum-twitching skirts. To a man of mature and sophisticated tastes, sexiness is a whole lot more subtle, darling."

I look over at Barb. I can't see anything either sexy or subtle in the way she's clutching her guts, or the loud snorts coming out of her nose.

"It's all to do with the way she lets herself go," he says, then he winks at me, really irritating and superior, and goes over and puts his arms round Barb. "Don't give yourself a hernia, doll."

Pretty soon after that I leave. I'm going to get an early night, then I'm going to talk to Bonny. I'm going to get up the balls to be direct, just like Nick said.

Next morning I get down early to graft at Abacus Design, then I phone Bonny's mobile around eleven. "Feeling better?" I ask.

"What?" she says edgily. "I wasn't feeling bad."

"You said you were tired. After the weekend."

"Oh. Right. Yes. Yes, I'm fine, thanks."

Not a brilliant start. "Fancy doing something tonight?" I say.

"Sure," she goes. "What d'you want to do?"

"Oh, I dunno. We could have another barbie here. On the balcony."

She leaves a pause just long enough for me to be convinced she doesn't want to be on her own with me, then she says, "Sure. Great. When shall I come?"

"I'm finishing here around six—"

"Seven-ish, yeah? Shall I get the food this time?"

"This time? You made that meal when your friends came round. . ."

"Yeah, well that hardly counted, did it. In fact – I should probably cook you two meals to make up."

"Just get me some meat," I say. "None of that veggie crap."

I spend the rest of the day physically grafting over storyboards and mentally rehearsing what I'm going to say to Bonny. I weigh up whether I should launch into my chat as soon as she gets here or wait until we're all cosy on the balcony with the food cooking. In the end I decide a bit limply to see how things go, and head back to the flat to shower. I'm still pulling on my shirt when Bonny bursts into the flat.

She's forty minutes early and she's *really* upset. She doesn't even give my superbly-honed chest so much as a glance. "Liz is going!" she wails. "She's just – *going*!"

"What d'you mean?"

"She says she's *leaving*. Home, school, everything! I've just had the weirdest phone call from her. It was horrible – she sounded sort of *hysterical*, you know, frenzied, like she was high on something, all kind of *weird* and shrill. . ."

"Bloody hell, Bon. Where's she say she's going?"

"*Scotland!* To live in some kind of commune place up there –"

"*Commune?* What kind of commune?"

"She wouldn't say. She wouldn't answer *any* of my questions – she said she didn't have long to talk –"

"Melodramatic or what?"

"It was horrible, Rich. I couldn't get through to her at *all*."

Her face is all scrunched up and worried and gorgeous. I head for her to give her a hug, but she turns away. "Kell's behind this, isn't he," I say, darkly. "He's the weirdo commune sort."

"Yes – she's going with him. It's all dead sudden. He got some kind of *summons*. She was going on about how thrilled he was, he's had a connection with this commune group for ages, and he was waiting for the call."

"The *call*. Bloody 'ell."

"I know. They made this major exception to let her go along too, even though she wasn't *connected*, because he'd told them they were so devotedly in love – it was ghastly, listening to her burbling on."

"So what's this group *do*?"

"She wouldn't tell me. She said the group doesn't want the outside world to touch it, they make anyone going there promise not to give out details."

"Dodgy."

"I know. She said they'd been trying out some of the group's *directives* – that's what she called it – something about men and women, but she said I'd take it the wrong way if she told me about it. . ."

"I bet it had something to do with the way he was ordering her about."

"Maybe. Or maybe that's just Kell. I don't think *she* knows much about this group, to be honest. She's just so blown away by Kell wanting her with him, she's not thinking further than that. I tried to talk to her, said it sounded dodgy, said she should check it out more. She wouldn't talk about it though. Just said Kell had warned her 'outsiders' would be like that about it."

"Outsiders. Groovy. So you've got no idea of the address?"

"No. I haven't even got a name. Oh – and something else really worried me. She was phoning me in secret, that's why she was so rushed. Kell had *forbidden* her – she used *that* word! – he'd *forbidden* her to contact anyone. He just wanted her to leave a note for her mum saying, *I'm fine, I'm safe, don't try and trace me*."

"Don't the alarm bells go off for her? That he's a total psycho?"

"Apparently not. She said something about betraying him by phoning me, but she couldn't bear to think of her mum worrying about her. I'm supposed to stop her mum searching for her."

"This gets worse."

"She's sworn me to secrecy, about the commune, in case her mum gets all these ideas about it being a mad cult—"

"Which it clearly *is*! Jesus, Bonny – what you gonna do?"

"What can I do?"

"When's she going to leave?"

"That's it. She's already left. I don't know where she was phoning me from, but she said she'd left. And her mum will get back from work and read her note —" Bonny checks her watch — "round about now."

Chapter 19

"I'm going to have to go round," Bonny's saying, "aren't I."

"Yeah," I agree, unenthusiastically, recognizing that my plans for a frank talk about sex and life and stuff have been shoved *well* back on the back-burner. "How well d'you know her mum?"

"Oh, pretty well. Carol's on her own, like my mum, and they struck up a friendship when we were little—"

"I thought your mum didn't have friends."

"It wasn't a real friendship. It was just, you know, taking it in turns to take us to ballet and stuff. . ."

"Aw, Bonny – can you do ballet?"

She smiles faintly, but she's clearly as tense as a steel spring. "I'll try not to be long," she says. "I just need to make sure Carol's OK. . ."

"Will you tell her about the cult?"

"Rich – we don't know it's a cult."

"No, but we've got a pretty good idea if that freak Kell's caught up in it."

"I'm just going to tell her it's a commune, it's a group of Kell's friends, tell her it's just a phase, and Liz has to get this out of her system, then she'll come home—"

"If she can," I put in, darkly.

"What d'you mean?"

"If it's a real cult, they'll brainwash her. Keep her prisoner if she tries to leave. Starve her if she won't pray fifty times a day."

"Oh, for *Christ's* sake, Rich!"

"You want me to come with you?"

"I don't *think* so, thanks! You're not exactly going to cheer her up going on like that, are you."

And Bonny leaves, with just one dry kiss planted on my forehead.

The rest of that night, I make two trips down in the lift and all the way along the road to the phonebox, cursing the fact that I can't afford a mobile. Both times I dial it, Bonny's mobile is switched off. I leave one message saying, "How'd it go, babe? Come round and see me. Doesn't matter how late." The second time I hang up before her message is over.

She doesn't come round.

* * *

The next morning Andy and I collide, yawning and nasty, in the kitchen. "Bonny not here?" he asks.

"Nah," I say, blearily.

"Thought she might be moving back in, mate."

"Not yet."

"Oh. Well, look – I thought I'd move out soon. Shift back home. Don't want to cramp your style."

"There's no rush."

"Well – thought I'd get it sorted before the start of term. I'm a lot nearer college at home."

"And you miss Mummy's cooking and washing service, you mincer."

"Yeah, well," he mumbles, goofily. "It takes a lot of time, all that domestic crap."

Just for a moment, I get this rush of self-pity, for me the lone struggling orphan fending for himself. I know I could move back home again if I wanted to, but the cost would be too high. Not in money – other things. Way too high.

"You pathetic bastard, Wilkinson," I say, shoulder-barging him from the sink so I can fill the kettle. "Giving up freedom for roast chicken and clean socks."

"Yeah, but I'm pretty free at home, mate," whines Andy. "I got a phone in my room. And you know how relaxed my mum is – I can have girls to stay over."

"Yeah, but that's only theoretical. Like your whole sex life is theoretical."

"Get stuffed, Steele. You think you're such a stud, don't you."

"I don't think it, mate, I have proof," I say – then I decide to go easy on him. After all, I don't want to shame him into staying on, do I? I want more space – this place – for me and Bonny. "Look – you spotted Bonny isn't here," I say. "It's not exactly got to the five-shags-a-night stakes yet."

"She OK?" asks Andy. "I mean like – you know – *OK*?"

"If you're asking me if she's flipped out and gone mental yet, no, she hasn't. And she won't either. She's great. But she is a bit – I dunno. Not relaxed."

"Well – it'll go one way or the other," he says, completely pointlessly, and staggers out of the kitchen, picking up my mug of tea on the way.

I try Bonny's mobile constantly all that day from my desk in Abacus, but I don't get hold of her until the evening, just as I'm about to go upstairs. "Why you been switched off?" I demand.

"Sorry," she says. "There's no reception in Kingsmead Shopping Centre. I was there with Ellie, trying to get the twins some winter clothes. . ."

"Fun, eh?"

"It was horrific. They're hyperactive little bastards, all over the place all the time. And Ellie wants them to dress the same but they never want the same things. . ."

"I thought twins were supposed to share a brain?"

"*What?*"

"I thought it like – divided in the womb or something?"

Bonny laughs. "Oh – you're thinking of identical twins – they're not. They *fight. God.* And Sammy went psychotic, threw a real wobbly in Mothercare, they nearly banned us, I mean for *life.* . ."

"Yeah, OK, Bon. When can I see you?"

"Tonight? I'll come and cook, like I promised. I've still got the food."

"Brilliant! Hey – how'd it go with Liz's mum?"

"*Uuuurgh.* I'll tell you tonight."

Bonny turns up around eight. It's a dry, warm night; we scramble down to the balcony, fire up the barbecue and do the steaks. And then she talks. She tells me all about her visit to Carol, how she only got away at about one in the morning and only then by the skin of her teeth. . .

"Carol went on a *total* guilt trip. Things have been pretty bad between her and Liz for a while now, she said. They'd been rowing loads – mainly about Kell. Carol didn't like him – didn't like the way he seemed to be taking over Liz's life, the way he pushed her around. But she didn't think things were so bad that Liz would just leave without even talking to her face to face. I was caught between wanting to tell her it wasn't her fault, and not wanting to *scare* her by giving her the reason why it's not her fault, which is that her daughter's under the influence of a control-freak psycho. . ."

And on and on, all about how Bonny managed to walk the long wobbly tightrope between truth and reassurance. How Bonny got round it by saying Liz was just out of her mind with love, quite sweet really. How Carol got stuck into the vino and got into reminiscing about when Liz was a kid, how she got the photo albums out. How Bonny and she talked about the way you have to let your kids go if you really love them, that a stint in a commune might make Liz appreciate ordinary life once again. . .

Now I like to think I'm the kind of thoughtful, generous bloke who's usually quite a good listener, but even my limits are being reached when it hits eleven o'clock and Bonny's still mulling over the whole Liz drama. And then – when I put my arm round her, hoping we can get into a clinch – she gets all chatty about the twins again. How nightmarish they are, how she'd like to whack them hard when Ellie isn't looking, how she's ultimately very sorry for Ellie because – surprise, surprise – Daddy's always criticizing the way Ellie copes with them. And how she's promised to go shopping again tomorrow because they only got coats today and they need shoes as well.

"Oh, *what*?" I grouse. "I thought *we* could do something!"

"What?"

"What's it matter *what*? Just be together. Be *here*. I mean – haven't we been through this before, Bon? Letting other people get in the way the whole time?"

Bonny shifts away from me, all uneasy. "I thought you'd be working. At Abacus."

"I've done *loads* of work in the last week or so. There's nothing urgent on, now. I could take a day or two off, easy."

"Come shoe shopping with us?" she teases, then, when she clocks my face, "Oh, Rich, *sorry*. I can't get out of it. I *promised* her. She was nearly in tears on the way home yesterday."

"Bonny – I've said it before. You're too nice. To everyone but me that is."

"I *am* nice to you!"

"Prove it." Corny, but it works. She flings her arms round my neck, and we start kissing, and then I'm sliding my hand up under her top, wrestling with her bra hooks, and it's too fast, but I don't care, I feel desperate to get us physical again, at the back of my mind I'm afraid we'll end up just friends again, like we were when we were flatmates.

It's not good though. She doesn't stop me but that's about it. It's like she's letting me do this 'cos we've slept together, like it's what we do now. I can't explain it, but it's not good.

Pretty soon we make our way upstairs. I'm thinking: if she stays, we can go slow, we can open up

157

together in the deep dark. But Bonny says the shoe-shopping trip kicks off at nine, 'cos the twins get up before seven. And she leaves to get a full night's sleep at home.

For the next week or so, everything's pretty much the same. Working, meeting Bonny when she can fit me in, lots of chat about Liz and Family Life still (I hear all about the huge row Daddy and Ellie have at six-thirty in the morning just before he catches a flight to Vienna) but no chat about why our sex life has stayed a one-event wonder. Somehow, it's never the right time to bring it up. Probably because I'm sulking big time. I reckon too much is coming from me – asking her to be with me, asking her not to hide from me. Wanting her more and more, in this weird kind of vacuum we're in. I reckon it's her turn to make a move in my direction. September arrives, filling me with depression. That night (Friday) I'm too sulky to go with her to some crap eighteenth birthday she says she has to go to, despite hardly ever seeing the birthday-girl in question any more, and then it's Saturday.

And on Saturday, everything changes all at once.

Chapter 20

I'd forgotten about Chris's plans to make his five-a-side team attend a torturous start-of-the-season footy festival the first Saturday in September but I'm pretty bloody rudely reminded of it the next day when he goosesteps into my bedroom at the crack of dawn and tries to haul me out of bed. "Come on, you lazy *bastard*," he yells. "We gotta be there by ten-thirty."

"Oh, *what*?" I groan, burrowing further under my duvet. "How did you get in?"

"Andy let me in. *He's* all up and ready. *He's* all set to play. Not like you, you lazy scum."

"I thought you were *joking* about this five-a-side festival. I mean we've hardly played all summer, have we. We're not fit."

"Speak for yourself, Steele. I'm fit. Been going to

the gym, haven't I. Now come on, *shift* it. Olly's outside, with his brother and his van. I got it all organized. All *you* got to do is get up."

I decide I hate Chris when he's in one of his keen, self-righteous moods. "We'll get slaughtered," I moan. "Knocked out first off. We haven't trained."

"Look – that doesn't matter. It's just meant to be *fun*."

"*Fun?* This isn't my idea of fun, mate. Being dragged out of bed by some insane fascist sadist is not *fun*."

"Oh, for *God's* sake –" Chris interrupts himself by yanking my duvet, hard, off the bed. As I'm hanging on to it, hard, I end up off the bed too. "Now shift it!" he roars, and stomps out of the room calling back, "Like your boxers, mate. Palm trees. Nice."

Fifteen minutes later, I'm crammed next to Andy in the back of Ollie's brother's van, bumping along to the Athletics Grounds. I had time to stick my head round the door of Abacus and explain why I wouldn't be in that day, but no time for breakfast. "I'm *starving*," I moan. "And I can't function without tea, first thing."

"Yeah, well it's not first thing, is it mate. It's late. Now stop whingeing, you can get breakfast at the café there."

But when we get there there's no time for breakfast, of course. Chris checks the schedule as soon as we

160

arrive and we find out we're on Pitch C in four min-utes' time. Chris frog marches us along to Pitch C, trying to fire us up with his pre-match chat. "Andy – use Ollie, use his speed. Ollie – you gotta find space before you strike. Don't waste it. Ryan – keep the ball moving or you'll lose it. Rich – *for Christ's sake, wake up.*"

The whistle goes, the game's on. And I can't quite believe it, but at half-time we're a goal up, due to a flash of brilliance from Oll. And due to some hard graft from Chris and Andy, two minutes from the end we're two goals up and at full-time we've won. Chris turns to us, incandescent with triumph. "Two more knock-out rounds to go – best of three and we're in the quarter-final!"

Oh, *goody.* "I need *food,*" I wail.

"No time mate, we're on Pitch D now."

"If I don't get food I'll pass *out.*"

"Yeah, well, no one would exactly notice, mate, the way you were playing. Except you'd be horizontal instead of standing up."

Although we play even better the next game, we lose it, but only just. And then there's a longish break and Chris harangues us while Ollie's brother, the saviour, brings over bacon rolls and hot sweet tea. Natalie, Chris's girlfriend, turns up to watch Game Three, on her lunch hour from her Saturday job. She's as fierce on the touchline as Chris is on the pitch and between them, they goad and bully us to a narrow victory.

Best of three. We're through to the quarter-finals.

"You see?" Chris crows. "Don't you doubt your captain again, you bastards. If we can do this when we're all slack and unfit, we'll be bloody *dynamite* when we've trained. . ."

The next team we meet is definitely a notch up from the other three. But we're on a roll. Even I'm inspired – I score from the sweetest pass from Andy. And we beat them, three goals to two.

On to the semi-finals. Natalie goes back to work, kissing all five of us first for luck, snogging Chris so hard on the touchline that one of the refs blows his whistle on her. I'm feeling shattered but Chris is now a man possessed. "Look, men," he says, coming on all World War Two, "I'll level with you. I thought we'd get knocked out first off. These guys we're up against – they're good. But if we can go this far, we can go the whole way. We can go to the finals, and we can win. How much d'you want it? *How much d'you want it?*"

I stop myself saying "not as much as a hot bath", and jog on to Pitch B. When I clock the opposition, though, I know it's over. They're big, mean, deter-mined bastards, and you can tell *they* haven't let their training slip over the summer. They've even got a proper team kit.

We put up a valiant fight, but they get a goal past

us straight off. Then Ollie has another flash of genius, and puts one past them. We fight, and fight. We defend like madmen. But in the last three minutes, they score again. Twice.

Chris is very philosophical as we head for the changing room. "We were in the top four," he says. "That's brilliant. And those bastards are going to win, easy, so really we're probably second. And that's with no training. Soon as college starts – we get back to it. Regular. Like – Tuesday and Thursday. No excuses, no let-outs. . ." We let him chunter on as we shower and change, then head for some food. And as I walk in the café I stop dead. There, standing behind the cafeteria counter, serving up chips, is the last person in the whole wide world I'd expected to see serving up chips.

The Porsche.

Chapter 21

Ryan's nudging me furiously. "In't that your ex?" he hisses. "In't that Portia?"

"Yes," I snap. "Stop poking me."

"Bloody hell, she's gorgeous," breathes Andy, before he can stop himself.

Despite my finer intentions, I do feel kind of proud. "Yeah," I say. "She is." She's standing there, unbelievable body covered but not obscured by a naff pink apron, sexy cat-face turned to the girl serving alongside her. She's gorgeous, all right, and *I* went out with her.

I *slept* with her. Three times.

"She dumped you, right?" chokes Andy.

"No," says Ollie, "He dumped her."

"*What?*" squawks Andy. He doesn't know whether to be impressed or appalled. "What on earth for?"

"Don't go just by what you see, man," says Oll, all man-of-the-world and superior. "Rich done the right thing."

Portia's yabbering in this phony, head-wobbling-on-neck way to the starstruck girl next to her, who I don't recognize and who is clearly almost passing out with the honour of being the Porsche's confidante. Five small footballers — average age about twelve — are queuing silently and in awe on the other side of the counter. Portia and starstruck girl ignore them.

"Come on," says Chris. "We gonna get some chips, or not?"

Ollie saunters over to the counter, and we follow. Portia clocks him and spins away from starstruck girl mid-sentence. "Oll-*eeee*!" she squeals. "*Guys!* What you doing here?"

"Modelling swimwear," grunts Chris.

"Oh, *Chris*! Don't be such a joker — you were in the tournament, weren't you? How did you *do*?"

"Second," lies Chris, although he probably believes it by now.

"That's *brilliant*! God — guys — well done!" She turns to me, gives me a lingering, longing look. "Hi, Rich. Long time no—"

"Anything," I say. "No." I'm experiencing routine groin-clench but I'm safe in the knowledge I don't want her back.

"This is *so* embarrassing," she squeals. "I mean — the one day I do this *shit*, you guys turn up!"

"Don't you work here, then?" asks Ryan, who's visibly drooling on account of being within grabbing distance of her.

"No, I *don't*! God! I *couldn't* – I'd go *mad*. Mo does –" she indicates starstruck girl, now looking mortally offended – "and they were shortstaffed today, and offering double time and Mo put me up for it."

"Are you gonna serve these kids?" grunts Ollie. "Only I'm starved."

Portia sneers down at the five small footballers, who look back, transfixed with wonder and admiration. "Mo, serve that lot," she snaps, and turns back to us.

"O-*kay*," she goes. "Wadda you want?"

She makes a complete pig's ear of dishing up our hot dogs and chips, mainly 'cos she's done something bizarre to her nails. They're hugely long, and shining wetly. She's holding the serving tongs all awkwardly because of them. She's fake, she's ridiculous. She's fabulous. "Nice to see you again, Rich," she purrs.

"Yeah," I go, all smooth. "You too." Then I nudge Ryan – who's stock-still clutching the plate she handed him, gawping at her – and hiss, "Shift it, prat."

We make our way over to an empty table, and Andy says, "Blimey, I never realized you were the one who ended it, Rich. I just assumed—"

"Yeah, well, you assumed wrong," I retort, smugly.

"But what she *do* to make you dump her?" wails Ryan.

"God, Ry – a girl'd have to hack your dick off before *you* dumped her," snaps Chris, and while we're laughing I say, "Yeah. You need to develop some discrimination, mate. Portia looks fantastic, but I realized pretty soon she was an idiot."

"And that's good," approves Ollie, "'cos a lot of guys woulda let the way she looks affect their brains and hung on a lot longer."

"Yeah, and a lot of guys woulda given anything just to go out with her *once*," bleats Ryan.

We shake our heads over Ryan's sadness, while Andy smirks lecherously into his Coke. "She look as good without her clobber as she does in it?" he asks.

I can't resist it, can I? I'm basking in the envy all round me. "Better," I grin. "Once – she came round, asked me to draw her. And started taking her clothes off right there and then. She looked amazing. I mean, I hadn't actually got to really look at her before – not from a distance, like. And she's all – *How d'you want me, Rich?*"

"*Jesus*," sobs Ryan.

"Those were the pictures up in the Art Department, right?" demands Andy.

"Yeah."

"God, I remember. It was *all over* the college –"

"They were hot," grunts Chris. "Everyone

queuing up to see them, guys going green with envy – Matt was on about photocopying them. . ."

"You shoulda done a whole load," says Oll. "Sold 'em."

"Have a heart, mate," I smirk. "You saw them. You imagine having the real thing there in front of you. *Wo-oow.* I reckon it was pretty good to manage *three* before I jumped her."

And everyone's all huh-huh-huh masculine laughter at this, and then Ryan suddenly coughs. "Er – Rich?"

"What?"

"I think Bonny just walked out."

"*What?* Where was she?"

"Right behind you, mate."

"How long *for*? Why didn't you *tell* me?"

"Well, you were so into how great Portia looked without her kit on, I couldn't get a word in edgeways. . ."

I spring to my feet. "You *bastard*, Ry. You fucking *wait*."

Then I leg it desperately out of the cafeteria.

Chapter 22

Car. She'd have to have her car to get here. *Car park, car park.* I race over there, top gear, just in time to see a blonde-haired girl who could be Bonny disappearing speedily round the corner ahead of me. I force my shattered five-a-side legs to accelerate a bit more, and make it round the corner just as her little blue Polo's pulling out of its parking place and making for the exit gates.

I fling myself in front of it, arms windmilling like a bad cop film. Behind the windscreen, Bonny's face looks like an ice-age mask. She swerves round me; I jump in front of the car again. This time she stops. She's staring ahead, face still frozen. I grab the driver's door, wrench it open. "Bonny!" I gasp. "Come on. Park this thing. I know what you heard, but we were just having a laugh –"

She won't look at me. "I have to go," she says.

"But – come on. You'd come here to see me, hadn't you? And then you overheard all that shit about Portia. . ."

Her mouth twitches. "Look – it doesn't matter. Can you shut the door."

"*Bonny!* Talk to me, *please!*"

"I'm late. I shouldn't have come in the first place."

"But you did, and then you heard stuff you shouldn't –"

"It doesn't matter. Rich – let go of the door."

"No! God, Bonny – this is such an overreaction!"

"I'm not overreacting – I've got to *go!*"

"Oh, come on – not like this! You heard me being a wanker, and you think it's important, and you're all upset and—"

"Look – it doesn't matter."

"Fucking *hell!*" I explode. "If you say *it doesn't matter* once more I'm going to kick this door in!"

It's like a touchpaper to dynamite. She turns on me spitting like a lynx with its tail on fire. "Don't *you* swear at *me*! *Jesus!* You get back with her if you want! That's what you want, isn't it?"

"*No.* You mean Portia?"

"No, the Little fucking *Mer*maid! *Yes,* Portia! 'Cos she's so gorgeous and wonderful and you loved drawing her – nearly as much as you loved *shagging* her – so just bloody well go back to her, then your mates won't think you're mad for dumping her any more, *will* they?"

I'm gobsmacked and delighted by her ferocity. "Bonny – park the *car*!" I yell. "We gotta talk!"

"No, we *fucking* haven't," she snarls, and lunges past me to grab the door handle and slam it shut, but as she's leaning out I dive in and snatch her keys out of the ignition.

"*Give those back!*" she screeches. "You bastard, give me my *keys* –"

I leg it round the front of the car, get in the passenger seat. She turns on me like she's going to smash me in the face, but instead she twists back and smashes both fists down on the steering wheel. Then she collapses down after them and starts crying.

My heart's thumping, stunned by her passion, guilty as shit for what I've done to her. A car draws up behind us and honks, loudly and impatiently, 'cos we're blocking the exit road. I put both my arms round her, press my face in her hair. "Bonny, c'mon," I murmur. "Move the car, over there." The car behind us honks again, even louder. I flick a V over my shoulder, then I put the key in the ignition, turn it. She starts to move the car and I help her steer, still with my arms round her, over to the far side of the car park.

We park, not straight, under a huge old sycamore tree, the other side of a derelict shed. It's almost private. "C'mon, Bonny," I croon. "It doesn't matter, it didn't mean anything. . ."

"*I'm sorry,*" she gasps, face still on the steering wheel.

"*You're* sorry?"

"For – for going sick at you like that. . ."

"Oh, come on – I preferred you bawling at me to that frosty act you were pulling at first!"

She looks up at that, eyes all wet, mutters, "I lost control."

"Well, what's wrong with that? I do it all the time." There's a potent silence, and from it I learn that her weird upbringing has given her some hang-up about losing control, and she's deeply amazed and glad I don't seem to mind. "Shows how much you care, Bon," I add. "Bit of a turn-on, actually."

She half sniffs, half laughs, looks down at the steering wheel again. I think of saying a bit more, then I think: Now is not the time to start unravelling all that, now is the time to put things right about Portia.

"What you heard," I venture, "what you heard in the café back then, it was just crap, it was showing off, it was—"

"You were saying how fantastic it was to draw her naked," she says, in a monotone.

"Look – yeah, OK, I did say that. But it was like – just to my mates."

"So what? You said it."

"Yeah, but Bonny – everyone talks to their mates different to normal."

172

"Yeah, they do," she says, looking up at me again. "They're more honest with their mates."

"Not always. This was a wind-up, showing off. I didn't mean it. Well – not in the way it came over."

She's staring at me like she's got lie detectors in her eyes. "Look," I squirm, "blokes just – *do* that. Boast and stuff. Like they look at page three, and porny mags if there's any about, it's like dogs, they just *do* it. I admit it, I was an arsehole, what I was saying, it was just too tempting, that's all, making out I was this big stud. . ."

There's a silence. Wind shakes the sycamore above us, and a few yellow leaves sense summer's over and spiral down on to the windscreen. "I wouldn't blame you if you wanted her back," she says, in the mono-tone again. "She's gorgeous. And I bet she's great in bed."

"Not particularly, she isn't."

"Better than me. She has to be."

More stuff we have to unravel, more stuff to put right, but not right now. "You and I have hardly started," I murmur.

"Look – I think you should go back to her. You still like her, you *want* her – the way you said *wo-oow*. . ."

"The way I said *what*?"

"*Wo-oow*. You want her."

"I *don't*! Look – I'm here in the car with you, aren't I? Not up at the food counter chatting her up? You heard me behave like an idiot, like a *prat*, but it's you I want, I promise you, and I don't know what else to say to convince you, Bonny. Just – I'm sorry you heard it, but it didn't mean anything, it was just guys wanking on. OK?"

Another silence, a few more drifting leaves. Then I say, "How did you find out I was here, anyway?"

"Were you trying to keep it quiet?"

"*No.* God, you're suspicious. I got dragged here with no warning by Chris, for the five-a-side tournament. I had no idea Portia was going to be here serving up burgers and chips, and it wouldn't've made any difference either way if I had." I tighten my arm round her. "Look, Bonny – I'm not gonna lie, it was pretty good when that happened with Portia, when I drew her. But it was phoney too – all the time I was doing it I was thinking how I was gonna *tell* people about it. Sad or what? And it's over with Portia and. . ." I stroke her hair, decide to risk it. "I'd sooner it never happened at all if you're hurt about it."

I'm not sure I've put it right, but Bonny visibly softens, relaxes back against my arm. "What made you come down here anyway?" I ask.

"I had to see you – I've got something to tell you. I turned up at the flat – got no answer. So I went down to Nick's office – he was just leaving. He told me where you were."

"What have you got to tell me?"

"I've got to go away. Like – *now*. Today."

I get this thud of panic. "What? Why – *where*?"

She heaves in a huge sigh, says, "God, I feel shattered. I need some coffee."

"Just tell me about it and I promise I'll get you some."

"What – from Portia?"

"No – we'll go somewhere. Bonny – *tell me*."

"I will," she says. "But I need some coffee first." And she starts up the car, reverses all efficiently, and heads out of the Athletics Grounds without another word.

Chapter 23

Five minutes later she's parked in front of a sprawling transport café, and we're queuing at the counter for coffee. "*Monster*," I hiss. "I'm suffering here. Why can't you just *tell* me?"

"Put up with it," she says. "I put up with thinking you wanted Portia back."

"Just tell me if you're going away for good."

"No," she says.

"No, you won't tell me, or no, you're not going for good?"

"Rich, you *baby*! Can't you wait just for two seconds?"

"Nope," I say, looking soulful.

"No, it's not for good."

"*Good*." We pay, and head for an empty table. As soon as we've sat down she pulls a postcard out of her bag and hands it to me.

"It's from Liz," she says.

It's a picture of some bide-a-wee-while cottages nestling at the foot of a purple Scottish hill. I flip it over, read:

Dear Bonny,
We're here, and everything is wonderful! Please don't worry about me, this is exactly what I want. I'm beginning to discover who I really am, I'm so happy. I feel it's so right for me, to be here with Kell.
I-love-you-and-you-love-me,
Liz.

"Bonny, call me thick, but what the hell has this got to do with you going away?"

"Look at the way she's signed off."

"Yeah, weird, soppy—"

"It's a sign. It's a cry for help."

"*What?*"

She takes the postcard back from me, studies it. "We were dead close when we were little, I told you. The end of primary school, we went through this real best friend phase. We hated being apart. When we got dragged off by our mothers to visit people or go on holiday – we wrote to each other, sent cards. We'd always sign off like that and what it meant was – *This whole card is lies and I'd sooner be with you than what I'm doing now.*"

"I don't understand."

"Rich — it was a *game*. You know — kids having secrets. Our mothers would think how sweet we were to send postcards and they'd post them for us and what we'd do, we'd make a game out of writing the exact opposite of what was true. 'Mummy and I are having great fun' meant it was shit, 'The food is fabby' meant it was shit, 'I've met a really interesting new friend' meant whoever it was was a real creep—"

"OK, Bonny, I get the picture, but come on, a little kids' game? Maybe she's forgotten the rules or something?"

Bonny shakes her head. "She wouldn't forget. We joke about it — you know, get nostalgic about it. She kept all my postcards."

"And you don't think this is just nostalgia? Or having a bit of a laugh?"

"No, I don't. Especially after the way she was acting, the way she's been with Kell, those awful hysterical phonecalls. . ." Bonny takes in a big breath, smoothes one corner of the card. "When I read it, I felt this great shock, this *jolt* go through me, and I knew something was wrong with her, really really wrong. You look at it. 'I'm so happy' means she's miserable — 'it's so right for me to be here with Kell' means it's so *wrong*. . . And 'Please don't worry about me' means *Help me*."

"Yeah, OK. I just think it's a bit melodramatic, that's all. I mean — if she wants help, why doesn't she just write a letter, phone you up. . ."

"Maybe she *can't*! Maybe she had to do a card, just like we had to as kids – it was the only way to communicate. I can't get that last time she phoned out of my head, when she said Kell had *forbidden* her to phone. . . Look, when I read it, it was like she was shouting for help. I can't just ignore that, can I? I mean – yeah, it could be a joke, or a mistake, and I'll get up there and she'll explain and I'll feel like beating her brains out. But suppose it *isn't*? Suppose she's locked up somewhere in that weird commune place? I've gone over and over it this morning and I just can't *afford* to ignore it. I can't."

"No," I say, finally. "OK, you can't. So what you gonna do?"

Bonny takes in another shaky sigh. "The card says 'Pittlowrie'. I'm going to drive up there and see if I can find her. I'm gonna leave today."

"OK," I say. "I'll come with you."

Chapter 24

There's a long, long silence across the coffee cups, so intense I think the china might shatter. "D'you mean that?" Bonny croaks at last.

"Yeah. I want to come with you."

"I . . . I don't believe you. . ."

"*Fine.* I'm lying again. I don't want to come with you at all, what I really want to do is go back and snog Portia senseless over a big tray of sweaty chips." She starts to laugh, the sort of laughing that's near crying. I look at her, all shaky and brave and loyal to her friend, and I want to tell her, but don't, how great she is to do this, how much I want her, want to *be* with her.

"Don't you want me to come?" I demand.

"I'd *love* you to come, Rich, it just never crossed my mind you would – I mean, you can't just drop everything –"

"You are."

"Yeah, but she's my friend —"

"And you're my girlfriend, whatever you think."

She reaches across the table, searches out my hand. "I thought you'd just say I was mad —"

"Maybe you are, but I can see you gotta go."

"What about things here? Your work for Nick, the flat —"

"I'm well up on work for Nick. Andy can take care of the flat. He's not moving out yet."

"He can feed Pitbull," she says. She's smiling at me now, all hopeful.

"So," I say, and I suddenly feel dead excited, "an adventure, eh? When we setting off?"

"I've got my stuff in the boot. I'm all set to go, I just had to see you first—"

"Drive by the flat, let me pick up some clothes, leave a note for Nick and Andy, and we'll be off then."

"You sure? You sure it's OK?"

"Sure I'm sure. Hey — what've you said to your dad?"

"Well — not the truth, he'd have a fit if he knew that — he'd never let me go on my own."

"Yeah, well — I agree with him."

Bonny dimples up at that — her man getting protective and all. She looks gorgeous. I'm starting to feel really horny at the thought of heading off into the unknown with her, just the two of us on the road . . .

maybe it's exactly what we need to get close, and I won't ever have to get into that embarrassing sex discussion I've had planned since way back, 'cos it'll all just solve itself. . . "I invented this sudden invite," she's going, "to a cottage without a phone up in Pittlowrie. I told him I was going *with* Liz. I told him I wanted to get away for a bit to think things over, and he was pleased 'cos he thinks I'm getting in too deep with you. . ."

"Great," I groan. "Hey – what if he contacts Liz's mum, to check?"

"Carol's in on it. She's been phoning me just about every day since Liz left, wanting to know if I've heard anything – she phoned this morning, right after I got the postcard. I told her about it, but not the – you know –"

"Hidden meaning."

"No. If I told her that she'd freak completely. She'd be straight on to the police."

"Bon – you sure you shouldn't go to the police?"

"And say what? Tell them I've got *doubts*?"

I get a flash-vision of a typical Mr Plod perusing the postcard, trying to get his dinosaur brain round their childhood game. "No – maybe not," I say.

"I told Carol Liz was fine, but now I knew she was in Pittlowrie I fancied going up to see her, and checking the commune out. Carol was delighted, of course. Wanted to come with me, said I shouldn't go on my own. I told her Liz would be embarrassed if her mum turned up and anyway, I was going with you."

"So you had thought of it!"

"I didn't say I hadn't *thought* of it – I just didn't think you'd come. She's given me a load of cash."

"Useful."

"Yeah. And she says I can phone her, any time, and she'll put more into my bank account."

"She feels guilty."

"A bit. Grateful, mostly."

"Well, it won't cost much more for me to come, will it," I say, leaning across the table towards her. "Same car, same bed. . ."

She goes ever so slightly stiff on me, and laughs. "True. Just food."

"I got some cash, Bonny."

"I don't want you to pay for anything. I'm just so glad you're coming."

"So am I. And not just to be with you – I'd hate to think of you driving round on your own. Anything could happen."

"Don't be daft," Bonny replies, but she's kind of glowing, too.

"You want another coffee?" I ask.

She smiles. "Nope. Let's get off." And she stands up and heads for the car park again.

I'm an efficient type, so it doesn't take me long to stuff a few things in a bag and leave mysterious, dramatic notes for Nick and Andy. Then I'm down in the lift, and in the front seat of the Polo beside Bonny. "I thought we could drive till dinnertime, then find somewhere to stay," she says, turning on to the road. "I've looked at the map, and we can do well over half of it by tonight. . ."

"I wish I could share the driving," I say, ruefully. "I feel like a right useless wuzz."

She reaches down beside her, pulls out a map, pitches it on to my lap. "You can tell me where to go," she says.

We drive through to the outskirts of town and hit the main road, talking non-stop. First we analyse Liz's mental state and Kell's nastiness, then we discuss how we're going to track down the commune once we get to Pittlowrie. "Just bowl into the local, ask if they're heard anything about a loony religious cult," I say. "Bet they'll know all about it. That kind of stuff always makes for good gossip."

"Yeah," agrees Bonny. "It's how we handle it once we've found the right place that worries me. I mean – do we try and make contact with Liz in secret, or what?"

"You've read too many *Famous Five* books, Bon. We just breeze up to the front door, say we've come to take Liz home."

"Yeah, but Kell might get nasty."

"I can handle that box-faced berk!"

"Come on, we want to avoid a fight if we can."

184

"Do we?"

"Rich – *yes*! I think we should try and see Liz in private first. Then we can find out what she *really* wants to do, without that git influencing her, and take it from there. . ."

"Well, I'm just saying, if it comes to it – I can take Kell. Easy."

"My hero," she says, all taking-the-piss, but I bet she's impressed underneath.

After an hour or so on the road, we hit the motorway. I'm pretty damned impressed by the way she handles it, if you want the truth. True, she tends to stick to the slow lane, and she stares fixedly ahead like she's playing a very fast video game, but she's cool. I don't tell her this, of course. I don't want to distract her.

We turn off, and after half an hour, with me mapreading more or less flawlessly, Bonny says she's parched, and we stop for tea in a no-nonsense little town in South Yorkshire. Bonny glugs hers down like a tin-throat, then orders another with scones to go with it. "I feel better now we're actually on the way," she says. "Now we're actually doing it. I was so on edge before."

"I'd never've guessed."

"Oh, shut up. I know I went over the top."

"*Over the top?* You were like a self-launched missile. Powered by insane jealousy."

"*Don't* flatter yourself, Rich. I just couldn't believe your taste had taken such a back-slide, that's all. . ."

"You nearly ran me over."

"Yeah, well – I'll drive straighter next time."

She's looking across the table at me, mock angry and a bit turned on. I grip one of her legs between mine, say, "Don't be mean, Bon. I'm all yours on this trip. You can do what you want with me."

Our waitress – who has a face like a tank and a bosom to go with it – collects my tea cup and plate, snorting loudly with disgust. "Anything more for you two?" she demands.

"No, thank you," I say, flashing her a smarmy smile. She snorts again and writes out the bill, which Bonny picks up and pays. The waitress gives one last reverberating snort – to show her disgust for this softy southern gigolo who lets his girl pay the bill – and stomps off.

We stand up to leave. I put my arm round Bonny as we get outside, try to turn her towards me for a kiss, but she's all stiff and unyielding. "Aw, loosen up, Bon," I say. "I don't mean to be insensitive to Liz or anything, but there's no reason we can't enjoy ourselves too, is there?"

"No," she says, ducking her forehead down on to my chest. "No."

"Come on, then. Let's do another few hours before we stop for the night."

Chapter 25

It's getting dark by the time we finally stop on the outskirts of a large, anonymous-looking town. We drive past a couple of posh-looking small hotels, and find a B&B with "Vacancies" in the window. Bonny parks outside and we spend about ten minutes winding each other up, saying how we'll have to pretend to be married, how they'll get the vice police on to us if they suspect, all that stuff. Then when we finally get up the courage to go inside, the woman in charge is so utterly bored and indifferent I mutter, "Bonny, for all she cares you could be a sheep in suspenders." This sets Bonny off with a fit of nervous giggles, which starts me laughing too, and the bored woman switches to hostile as she shows us up to the room

Which isn't bad, considering how cheap it is. Nice big window, nice big bed. Shabby, but clean. I'm all for pulling Bonny on to the bed there and then but she insists that we go out for dinner first because she's famished.

We eat at a cosy, smoky little burger and steak place. We flirt and joke and she seems very intent and I feel sure everything's going to be great once we get back to the B&B and shut the door on the world.

But it isn't. Instead of pouncing on me lustfully, she heads for the bathroom. I wait patiently; she takes hours. After that I feel obliged to trek all the way down the corridor myself to clean my teeth. And then we get into bed together, still half dressed – and she freezes up. I try everything I know to relax her: kisses, cuddles, caresses; she freezes up more.

It's awful, crushing, and I don't understand. It's not like it's our first time, after all. And OK, she was tense our first time, but this should be better, shouldn't it? So I ask her what's wrong, and what she says is: "I can't."

"What d'you mean?"

"I'm sorry, I just can't, OK?"

"You mean you don't want to."

"Look – don't get all offended. I'm tense, I'm all on edge about Liz, about finding her—"

"Oh, come on, Bon – leave that for tomorrow. Why don't you just relax and—"

"For *God's sake*, Rich!" she erupts. "Would you stop trying to *bully* me?"

It's like a smack in the face. "I'm not! Look,

Bonny – I just don't get it. Earlier today you flip because you think I'm after Portia again. Now you're freezing me off. What's going on? If you've gone off me, just say it, will you?"

But she doesn't say a word. She just slithers off the bed, grabs her silky kimono and stomps out of the door. And I'm left staring all hurt at the ceiling of the grotty little B&B wondering what the hell went wrong.

Well, she can't go far in her kimono, can she? Maybe she'll just sit in the bathroom for a bit.

Probably not a good idea to go after her.

I'm pretty upset, but I know one thing – this time, when she comes back, we're going to talk about it. I lie there staring up at the ceiling, telling myself I'm man enough to take whatever she tells me: she hates me, she's found someone else, she's a lesbian, whatever.

And then I do something awful.

I fall asleep.

Chapter 26

When I wake the next day Bonny's fully dressed, putting things in her bag. I slept like a log and I have no idea if she got back in bed beside me or if she sat up all night glaring at me from the wicker-work chair by the window. "Shit!" I groan, hoping for sympathy. "I must've been more tired than I thought – that football tournament really knackered me. . ."

No answer. I try again. "Have you had breakfast, Bon? Wasn't a Full English included in the price?"

"If you want breakfast," she says, all expression-less, "you've got fifteen minutes before they stop serving."

I get out of bed, sharpish. Already, I'm starving. "What time did you come back to the room?" I ask. Again no answer. So I give up, head along to the chilly bathroom, take a fast, tepid shower, and go back to the room.

Bonny's not there. My first thought is she's driven off without me, but I won't let myself panic. I hurry down to the ground floor, find the dining room. There she is, at a table by the window, staring out. I join her. I'm not sure what I'm feeling right now, to be honest. Relief that she's there, certainly. But I'm starting to feel pissed off and angry, too.

"I ordered a fried breakfast for you," she says, coldly. "And tea. The woman was threatening to shut up shop."

"Thanks. Aren't you having one?"

"No," she says, "just toast."

I get the feeling she thinks I'm pretty damn insensitive to be tucking into fried eggs and sausages. "We got to talk about last night, Bon," I say.

"Not here," she says.

"Why not? No one can hear us."

"They might. I wanted to talk when I got back to the room. You were asleep."

Before I can answer, the bored woman from last night slams a great greasy plateload down in front of me. Bonny turns away as I eat it.

We check out and get on the road again in complete silence. After ten minutes, I've had enough. "Look – this is crazy. I'm not carrying on like this."

"You want to go back home?"

"No. But I will if you won't talk to me."

She drives on, mute. I stare at her profile – her bottom lip's going on a wobbler. I don't feel that sorry for her, though. "You're not making sense," I say. "You don't add up. Hot one minute, cold the next. You gotta tell me what's going on."

Another long silence. "Look – some girls just don't like sex," I say. "I know that. If you're—"

I break off because she's slammed on the indicator, she's exiting the road we're on at speed. Now we're bucketing along a small country road, trees either side. A grass verge appears; she pulls over on to it. "OK, you asked," she kind of explodes, turning off the engine. "Look – d'you remember me telling you my first time was awful?"

"Sort of. You didn't go into details."

"No. That's 'cos the *details* are – horrible."

"Oh."

"Yes. It was a horrible, ghastly experience. It was *shit*. It's made me –"

There's a pause. "What?" I prompt.

"You know. Uptight. *Useless.*"

"Bonny, you're *not* –" I put my hand over hers on the steering wheel, but she throws it off.

"Why don't you tell me about it?" I say, gently. "About what happened?" Another pause. Her hands are sliding up and down the steering wheel. I want to get hold of them, hold them, stop that angry sliding, but I daren't.

"OK," she croaks, finally. "Although I don't know what good it'll do. This guy – everyone was after him. He was in the sixth form of this boys' school we did plays with, and had debates with and stuff. He was really good-looking – really full of himself. I got off with him at an end-of-term party—"

"When?" I ask. I know I shouldn't interrupt but I have to know, I have to know she hadn't met me then.

"Last summer. Over a year ago now. *God.* You'd think I'd be over it, I ought to be over it –"

"Why should you? Go on, Bon, tell me."

She takes in a breath, says, "It was like a competition, me and my mates all going after him. I couldn't believe my luck when I 'won'. I acted like an idiot – I drank too much – I was dancing with him, showing off . . . he must've thought I was on a plate. He kept getting drinks for me – then he hauled me upstairs – and then it was just – let's get down to business, let's do it."

"Didn't you push him off?" I demand. "Didn't you tell him to go fuck himself?"

Bonny's subsided in her seat. "At first I thought it was maybe OK," she croaks. "See – I'd been – like – *fantasizing* about him the night before. Thinking – wouldn't it be great if he was my first. Stuff like that. And by the time I realized what a pig he was –"

"It was too late."

"Yeah. It was *horrible.* I hated it, I hated every minute of it. He didn't look me in the face, didn't say anything . . . I *hated* myself for going along with it, for not having the guts to tell him to get lost."

I'm overcome with wanting to find this vile opportunistic little shit and smash his skull in. "What a *bastard*. He must've known the state you were in. Was he drunk too?"

"Not as much as me. Afterwards I was sick."

She starts crying then, and I put my arm round her, hold her to me. I can't stand to think of anyone treating her like that – like she's a piece of meat. My heart's thumping with anger, with what I feel for her. She fishes a paper hanky out of her pocket, wipes her eyes, sniffs, "I'm OK now."

"Did you tell anyone?" I ask. "I mean – afterwards?"

"No. My mates were all jokey and jealous, you know, that I'd got off with him, and I played along with it, 'cos I was too upset to . . . I dunno, face it I s'pose. . . I told Mum, the next night. I had to, 'cos I burst into tears over dinner. I told her what made it worse was really liking this guy and she said . . . *she* said. . ."

"What?" I ask, gritting my teeth against the answer.

"She said it was easy to get carried away, and everyone's first time was awful, and why didn't I phone him, maybe we could start going out."

"Oh, Bonny. That's appalling, even for Tigger."

"She was desperate for me to find a boyfriend. . ."

I squeeze her shoulders, hold her to me. "So you never told anyone?"

"Only Liz, after about a week. She was great. Let me get it all out. And now you. God, I can't believe I've told you all that."

"Well, I'm glad you have. Tell me where he lives, Bonny. Tell me his address and I'll go round and beat the *shit* out of him."

"Thank you," she sniffs, smiling. "Oh, God, Rich, I wish –"

"What?"

"I wish I'd waited for you."

"It won't matter. You'll get over it. You will. You know when we –"

"What?"

"Our first time. Was that as bad?"

"*No!*" she wails. "Oh, God, Rich – no! You were gorgeous – I wanted to – I just – I froze up, I panicked – I ruined it, I spoilt it. . ."

"No, you didn't. You *didn't*. I just wanted you to enjoy it as much as me, that's all." She rubs her face against my shoulder, silently. "So, Bonny – what's scaring you the most – is it the thought of freezing up again? Like – you know – panicking?"

She nods.

"Not that you find the thought of doing it with me too disgusting to contemplate?"

She shakes her head so hard I put my hand up on the back of it, to stop her cricking her neck.

"We're going to be all right, Bon," I say. "We are."
And I'm suddenly grinning with happiness, and even
the grey Scottish drizzle against the windscreen looks
pretty good.

Chapter 27

"You know what I really wish, though?" I say, as (after quite a bit of kissing and cuddling) we turn back on to the main road again. "I wish you'd explained this right at the start."

"Oh, sure," says Bonny. "*Yes, Rich, I'd love to go out with you but I have a severe sexual hang-up.* You'd've thought that was a real bonus, wouldn't you."

"I *swear* it wouldn't've made any difference. You've had a dodgy start, that's all."

"And you're the fresh start."

"You said it. I'm the guy to put it all right again."

"Bighead."

"I'll be your sex therapist. *God*, that is such a horny idea. . ."

"The thing is, I thought it would sort itself out," says Bonny, smiling. " 'Cos I fancy you so much."

"Aaaaah. Say that again."

"You heard! I felt so good, you know when we kissed and stuff, and I thought if we kind of did it soon, I'd get over that first time –"

"You tried to go too fast, that's all. I knew it was too fast, that time we . . . I said so, didn't I?"

"Yeah, you did. But then you –"

"Yeah, I know, OK. I'm only human."

"It was my fault, Rich."

"You know what you did, don't you? You put me in the same position as that guy."

"What – on top?"

"Don't be crude, Bon. I'm talking psychology here. You kind of – you were waiting for me to do it to you."

"Now who's being crude?" she gasps.

I can't believe we're talking like this, so openly. Talk about moving a stage closer, making it more real – I'm almost shaking with it. I bet she is too. She shouldn't be driving, probably. She's slowed right down.

"What I mean is," I say, "you left it to me to take over. . ."

"Yeah, but you're the experienced one. That serious girlfriend you had, and . . . and everything. . ."

"I know what you're saying, Bon, but it didn't work, did it?"

"No," she croaks, "you're right, it was too much like him –"

"And I'm not," I say. "I'm not like him at all."

We drive on a bit in silence, then a Greasy Spoon looms out of the drizzle. "I could really do with a break," Bonny says. "From driving."

Over our hot, sweet drinks, we talk some more. It's harder now, 'cos we're face to face, not side by side. We kind of go over what we've already said, both doing a lot of looking down at the table, then I mutter, "You know what we should do?"

"What?" she mutters back.

"Take it slowly. What you've been doing is – it's like someone who's had a scary time swimming trying to get over it by jumping straight in the deep end." Bonny nods, doesn't say anything. And I'm suddenly inspired. "You know Andy's mum's a therapist? A while back, he was going on about how one of her things is telling couples with sex problems to agree not to do it for a while – they can do everything else but the full thing." I break off, 'cos at the time Oll and I had fallen about laughing. Now, I can maybe see the point. "It takes all the pressure off, and they end up gagging for it, Andy says. We should do that. We should ban sex."

"*What?*"

"Not for ever. Just for – I dunno, a week or so. Two weeks, maybe. We just agree we won't do it. Till *you* want to."

Bonny's silent again. "Reckon it'll work?" I say.

"You think I'm worth it?" she croaks.

"Bonny, what a question. Yes, of course you are." She looks at me, and I meet her eyes. There's a little piece of my brain going, *Watch it, mate, watch it – she's been screwed up by this, maybe you're letting yourself in for a heap of trouble.* But I push it down. "Come on," I say. "Let's go."

Outside the café, I put my arms round her. "You're schizophrenic, you are. Of course you're worth it."

"Why d'you call me schizophrenic?" she says, into my shoulder. It's easier to talk now we're touching.

"'Cos a good half of you *knows* how great you are. Funny, and intelligent, and great. But the other half thinks you're crap."

"As far as sex goes, I am crap."

"No way. You're dead horny. You just want to relax about it."

"I'm scared."

"I know."

"Not just that – I'm scared of being useless at it. You know – boring. Mum used to say how most women were boring in bed, how bored men got—"

"God. That is *crap.* Bored with sex? *Crap.*"

"– and how critical they were, if you didn't look completely sensational without your clothes on."

"But Bonny – you do. *Completely.* You're beautiful, whatever your insane mother says."

"To her, dieting and getting laid are just about the same thing."

"Shit, I hate your mother. I wish I could take a *can opener* to your head, and open it up, and pull out the bit that's all screwed up by your mum."

Bonny laughs, says, "So do I," and we start to walk towards the car.

It's not till we're back on the road again and Bonny spots the sign for Pittlowrie that I remember about Liz and why we're actually up here in Scotland at all. Sorting out our relationship had really taken over. I tell Bonny this and she laughs and agrees. "But I really need to find something out soon," she adds. "I absolutely promised to phone Carol tonight."

"She could get you, couldn't she? On your mobile?"

"I know. But she made a big thing about not wanting to interrupt anything."

We drive into Pittlowrie around lunchtime, just as the sun makes it out from behind the grey clouds. Pittlowrie isn't too long a drive from the Midlands where we live, but it's different right down to its soul. The small, dour houses, the low stone walls, the hills like dead dinosaurs on the horizon. . .

"Wishing you'd brought a sketch pad?" Bonny asks, telepathically.

I look at her profile, at the dimples which appear when she knows I'm staring at her, and say, "You're great, you are."

"Why?"

"You just are."

We tour about for a bit, checking it out, and stop outside a busy pub which looks like it's the sort to be full of locals who'll gossip to strangers. Inside, the landlady's dead friendly as she takes our order for beer and steak pies, so I risk asking her if she knows of any communes in the area.

"Communes?" she frowns. "You mean where folk all share a house, raise the kiddies together, that kind of thing?"

"Well – not necessarily. More weird, a bit religious maybe –" I shy away from using the word *cult*.

Her face clears. "Oh, you mean The Larches. That's a kind of commune. Well, you know – community living."

I throw Bonny a triumphant glance, and she asks, "What's it like? Is it friendly?"

"I'm sure it'll welcome you with open arms, lass."

"*We* don't wanna join up!" I blurt out, but Bonny nudges me, so I hastily add, "Can you tell us where it is?"

And half an hour later, we're leaving the pub, with full stomachs and a little sketched map showing us where The Larches is.

Chapter 28

"You think we should just knock?" I ask, eyeing the vast, sludge-green door of The Larches a bit nervously. A thin rain has started drizzling again.

"I don't know," breathes Bonny. "I mean – if it's as cut off from the outside world as Liz was making out. . ."

Just then, the decision's made for us. A man wearing an orange padded waistcoat and looking a bit like a benign troll comes round the corner of the huge house. He's got a spade in one hand and a flowerpot in the other, and he holds them both out towards us. "Greetings! Welcome to The Larches!" he pipes.

"Hi!" I respond. "We're after a friend of ours. Liz –"

"McGowan," supplies Bonny.

"Yes. Liz McGowan. We've come to see her."

"Have you? Yes, perhaps you have."

Bonny and I slide our eyes sideways at each other. "Is she here?" asks Bonny.

"D'you know, if I were to remember the names of all the children who come to us, I'd have no room in my head for anything else! Let me put these in the potting shed –" he waves the spade and flowerpot again – "and we'll go to the kitchen and get dry and see Wonderful Mrs Travis."

As soon as he disappears into the shed, Bonny hisses at me and I hiss back.

"He's barking!"

"You said it, babe."

"How come he doesn't know if Liz is here or not?"

"Maybe he murders everyone soon as they get here –"

"Yeah, and mulches them down for potting compost –"

"Or boils them up for soup – no, meat pie fillings –"

I shut up as the jolly troll reappears, and motions to us to follow him round the side of the house. As we walk, he says, "You know, you don't need to be visiting anyone to come here."

"Well that's . . . great," I go. "But we *are* visiting someone. It's the reason we're here—"

"Perhaps, perhaps," he says, irritatingly, and opens a heavy, half-glassed door.

"Mrs Travis!" he cries. "More young wanderers, in

need of sustenance. If you could provide for their bodily needs – perhaps a cup of tea? A couple of ginger biscuits? And then I'll attend to their –" He grins, breaks off, and exits the kitchen. Bonny and I exchange glances again.

Wonderful Mrs Travis – bony, fifty-ish, no make-up – sighs, puts down a huge saucepan and picks up an equally large kettle. "We don't want to put you to any trouble," says Bonny. "We're just after Liz McGowan."

"Don't recall the name," asks Mrs Travis, tiredly, filling the kettle. "Have you got a photograph?"

"Well – no," says Bonny, beginning to sound anxious, "but – I thought people all got to know each other? I mean – if it's a commune?"

"Commune – *hah*!" explodes Mrs Travis. "In a commune – people share the *work*." She bangs the kettle down on the stove. "Can you describe her to me?"

"Hang on," says Bonny eagerly, "I *have* got a photo!" She jerks her bag up front, starts rummaging, and soon she's pulled out a diary and a dog-eared photo from the back of it. "It's pretty out of date, but that's her," she says, thrusting it at Mrs T, who takes it and holds it way back from her eyes to examine it.

"When would she have arrived here?" she asks.

"About two weeks ago?" says Bonny. "And she was with her boyfriend, who's—"

"Dark, square-faced. Plug-ugly," I supply.

But Mrs T has already handed the photo back to Bonny and is busy lighting the stove. "No, she's not here," she says. "She's a bit like someone I remember from Easter-time, that's all."

Bonny looks absolutely stricken at this news. "Calm down, Bon," I say. "I'm not sure this is the right place."

"Oh, it's the place all right," grumbles Mrs T. "It's where they all come."

"But you said it's not a commune –"

"No. More of a refuge. A rescue station. Some people take in stray cats or dogs, the Reverend –" she jerks her head at the door the troll left by – "takes in kids in trouble."

"What – they just come here?"

"The Reverend thinks everyone comes here by God's Will. Even if they're sent direct by Social Services, who love him, of course. He's got private money. And big church connections. Word gets around. Kids pitch up here – or get dumped off by their parents."

"And what do they *do* here?" I demand. I'm still not convinced they don't end up as meat-pie fillings.

She laughs, mirthlessly. "Not a lot. They *experience the silence*, according to the Reverend. They *listen*. To God's voice in the silence, he says. No telly here, no modern music. What the Reverend won't face is half of them are shutting out God's voice with those blasted Walkman things they smuggle in." Bonny and

I laugh awkwardly. "It's not all they smuggle in either – the Reverend still thinks it's scented candles he can smell. They get lots of therapy sessions, and they're meant to help in the vegetable plot, and here with me . . . well, I won't have 'em any more, not in my kitchen. More trouble than they're worth. Breaking things, stealing food. . ." She breaks off, picks up a large brown teapot. "I shouldn't complain. He pays my wages and he does really good work with the damaged ones. As I say, the Social Services love him."

I turn to Bonny, who's looking a bit devastated. "This isn't the place, Bon. This isn't any kind of cult."

"I know," says Bonny. She turns to Mrs T. "Thank you for making tea – but we should get off. If my friend's not here."

Mrs T is looking hard at me. "Did you say cult?"

"Well – yeah," I go. "I mean – from what we can make out, you get a summons to go there, it shuts out outsiders. . ."

"It sounds so weird," breaks in Bonny. "That's why we're scared for my friend."

Mrs Travis's whole face is suddenly energized, like a terrier spotting a rat. "I know where you want! A few years back, this group of Americans took over the old mansion, foot of the Lairy Hills! No one calls it a cult, no one likes to, but there's been talk. . ."

"Where is it?" asks Bonny.

"You got a map?"

"It's in the car," Bonny says, pulling her keys from her bag.

"I'll get it, Bon," I say, and she looks at me all grateful and tosses me the keys.

When I get back, map in hand, Mrs T and Bonny are seated across from each other at the enormous kitchen table, drinking tea. *I hope the old girl hasn't been scaring Bonny too much*, I think, and I sit down to claim the mug that's been poured for me. "Nothing was proved," Mrs T is saying, "and after a while, it all got forgotten. . ."

"Proved?" I repeat.

She turns to me. "There was a to-do with the police a year or so back. Now, let's see that map. I must get on – I've got soup to make for supper." She smoothes out the map on the table, points out the place. "You won't park nearby," she says. "Too rough. Park in the lay-by there, like the ramblers do, and walk the rest."

As she's folding up the map, the jolly Reverend comes back in through the door, beaming. "What a contented scene!" he pipes.

"They're just going," she snaps.

"Ah – *you* can persuade them to stay, Mrs Travis. You know, young people – there could be A Reason why you're here. One you don't understand. There's A Pattern in things, a pattern we don't always under-stand. You've been led here. . ."

"And now we're being led away," I say, a tad rudely. Mrs T grins. As we leave, she calls out, "Be careful."

I turn back. "Why d'you say that?"

"A year or so ago, we had a lad fetch up here from that place. Took us ages to get him right."

I put my arm round Bonny and steer her through the back door before she can hear any more.

Chapter 29

"So was she scaring the shit out of you?" I ask, as we pull out on to the road again.

"A bit. Well – she didn't say anything definite, really. 'I hear things, and I don't like what I hear.' That kind of stuff."

"What was that about the police?"

"Oh – a couple came over from the States, chasing their daughter. They insisted she'd gone to this place – and it denied all knowledge. No one could find her."

"Nasty."

"Yeah. Guess what the place is called."

"What?"

"The Fellowship of Beloveds."

"Oh, pass the *bucket*."

"I know. Puke. Are we on the right road, Rich?"

I've got the map spread out on my lap. "Yeah," I say. "Think so."

After two wrong turnings, which Bonny blames on my directions and I blame on her driving, we think we've found the lay-by and park. It's about seven o'clock now, light but with an edge to the sky. "Mrs Travis said to head that way," I say, pointing ahead into thick trees.

"OK," says Bonny, a bit nervously. "Let's go."

We lock the car up and walk. Autumn's further on up here; yellow and red leaves drift past us in the gloom. It's chilly, too, and damp and dank from the rain. After we've tramped along for a while, Bonny asks, "Can you see anything?"

"Not yet."

"I'm sure we should be there by now. Mrs Travis said there were huge iron gates to the place, and a broken down wall. . ."

"How broken down is broken down?" We're passing piles of stones, crumbling segments of wall half covered by brambles and ivy.

"This could be it," says Bonny, doubtfully.

"Not gonna keep many people out, though, is it," I say. "*Or* in. If that's what this cult-thing is into – *JESUS!*"

Two huge teeth-filled snarling dog-mouths are lunging at us. They belong to two enormous Alsatians, surging top-speed round the wall. My terrified brain takes in the fact that they're on chains, takes in the fact that the chains are attached to a man, and I manage – *just* – not to piss myself in sheer terror.

"Well, I do apologize," the man says, in unmistakeable Yank. He's lanky, blond-haired, early twenties maybe. "Did not mean to frighten you. *Quiet*, guys! *Down!*"

The dogs growl their way to almost-silence, and stand there glaring at us, chains clinking.

"OK, Bon?" I whimper, flinging out my arm to cover her shoulders.

"Yeah," she breathes. "Bloody hell, though."

"You want to be more careful, mate," I say, turning back to the Yank angrily, "getting those brutes to tow you around like that. Supposing we'd had weak hearts?"

"Well, with respect, sir," he responds, voice all on a level like a robot, "you are, strictly speaking, trespassing. The boundaries are unclear, which is why I patrol with the dogs, but this is private property."

I decide to cut to the chase. "Are you from the Fellowship of Beloveds?"

Just for a second, he looks hunted. "How do you know that name?"

"Someone from the town told us. Are you?"

"I am indeed. Do you have business with us?"

"We think a friend of ours is here," I say. "Liz McGowan."

The guy says nothing. "Is she here?" demands Bonny. "We want to see her."

"If you come to the main gates," the guy says, "tomorrow between the hours of ten and twelve midday, and approach the front door, Rupert may see you."

"Rupert?"

"Our leader."

"We haven't come to see your *leader*. We've come to see our friend."

"I am afraid you must clear it with him first. Ten o'clock to twelve, tomorrow."

"We're here now, mate. We'd like to see this friend tonight."

"I am afraid that is impossible. Audience is only possible between those hours."

"*Audience?*" I sneer. "Who is this Rupert guy – the pope?"

"I am not in a position to argue with you," he says. "Those are the hours. No exceptions." And he tightens the chains on the dogs, who growl throatily.

"Where are the main gates?" quavers Bonny.

"Back the way you came, ma'am. From where you have parked the car, walk in the opposite direction."

We all stand and look at each other in silence, apart from the dogs, who are growling like a storm about to break. Bonny takes me by the arm, tugs. I stand my ground for a moment, glaring at the Yank, then I allow myself to be towed back the way we came.

* * *

"Scary or *what*!" Bonny gasps, as we hurry along between the trees.

"He knows we've got a car," I say, darkly. "He must've been watching us."

"Maybe he just assumed we came by car. . ."

"No, he knew where we were parked and everything. He must've *decided* to jump out at us with those psycho dogs."

"Did he actually say Liz *is* here?"

"Well – not in so many words. But she is, or he'd've denied it, wouldn't he? Come on. Let's go and take a look at the main gates."

"*No*, Rich. I just want to go. I feel freaked enough as it is."

"Stupid mutts. Should've booted them."

"Oh, sure. And left your foot in their teeth."

"Up their arses!"

"Come *on*!"

"OK, OK, calm down, he's not coming after us!" I put my arms round her, and she hugs me back, and then I kiss her, just quickly, but it's a dead turn-on, in the woods with our hearts already pumping and everything. She laughs, then she breathes, "Did you hear that?" and we both start running, laughing as we go.

We reach the car at a trot, and I say to Bonny, "I'm going on. I'm gonna take a look at those gates, see if you can see the house from the lane."

"Oh, *Rich –*"

"You don't have to come! Get in the car and lock the doors."

"Suppose you don't come back?" she wails, and then we look at each other and laugh and I say, "Or s'pose one of the Fellowship turns up and drops my decapitated head on the car bonnet."

"I'm not staying here on my own," she gurgles, "and I don't care how soft that sounds."

"God, Bon – what would you've done if you'd come up here on your own, eh?"

"Oh, all *right*, action hero! Come on, let's go."

After ten minutes, we reach the gates. No mistaking them. Huge, black, elegant and imposing. Brambles are growing through the rails on each side, as though the gates don't get opened very often. "Straight out of *The Addams Family*," whispers Bonny.

"Yeah. They're gonna open on their own any minute –"

"Shut *up*! Rich – let's go."

"I just want to check out what we've got to deal with tomorrow," I say, and walk up to the gates. They're not locked, just bolted. I draw the bolt and slide between them. Bonny lets out this kind of aghast squawk, but follows me, seizing my hand. We walk slowly down the overgrown drive together, round a bend – and there's the house, right in front of us.

"There you go, Bon," I breathe. "Just an ordinary

house. Well, mansion. And there's the door we've got to knock on tomorrow. Fine, see?"

"You still don't think we should try and contact her first?" she whispers.

"Well, we don't want to be caught snooping round the outside of the house, do we? Not now we know they've got killer dogs on the premises."

Just then a light goes on on the top floor of the house, right in the far corner, shining out over the tops of the gloomy trees. Then the light in the room next to it goes on, and then the light in the room next to that, and the next one . . . it's like a chain reaction, like a pile of dominoes slowly falling, all the way along to the other end of the house. It's such a weird way for a line of bedroom windows to behave that Bonny and I get completely spooked. We turn, as one, and race for the gates.

Chapter 30

Back in the warm safe car, driving along and leaving the huge old house behind, we feel braver and better. "What's that about, though?" says Bonny. "D'you reckon they were wired up?"

"Dunno. That guy we met, with the dogs – he acted like he was wired up, too."

"So what shall we do now?" She pulls out on to the main road, back in the mainstream.

"Find somewhere to stay. Somewhere to eat."

"I've got to phone Carol soon. At least I can tell her we're pretty sure we've got the right place, even if we haven't spoken to Liz yet. . ."

Five minutes on we have a bit of luck. A great-looking old country pub looms up, with a swinging sign saying The Green Man, and one underneath saying it's got overnight accommodation and a first-rate restaurant. "Shall we check it out?" asks Bonny, slowing down in front.

"Yeah. Go on – turn in. If we stay here we'll be nice and near for our ten o'clock appointment with 'The Leader'. Jesus. D'you reckon they're all Martians or something?"

The bloke behind the desk is dead grumpy and disapproving when we say we want a room, but he admits he's got some free for tonight. He asks if we want double or twin and Bonny says double, which makes me go very hot inside, especially when she takes hold of my hand under the cover of the desk front.

"Shall we eat here, too?" says Bonny, as we pound up the old oak staircase behind the grumpy pub bloke.

"Well – it's a bit pricey," I reply. "I looked at the menu. And the room costs more than that B&B –"

"Rich, if you knew how much dosh Carol had given me you wouldn't *care*," she says. "Did the menu look good?"

"Extremely."

"Right – we'll eat here then," she says, and we turn into the room.

Which is a whole category up from last night's place. It's even got its own en suite bathroom, the man proudly tells us, pushing open a door on the far wall to show basin and shower beyond. There's an old gateleg table in the big window with tea- and coffee-making stuff on it, curtains with blackberries on, and a very seductive looking bed. . .

I'm not pushing it, though. I'm not pushing anything. We dump our bags, and I say, "I could seriously do with a beer, Bon."

"Me too," she says. "Let's go down. I'll find some quiet and phone Carol, you get the drinks."

Fifteen minutes later I'm sitting on a sofa in a cosy corner of the shabby, comfortable old bar, my beer half drunk, Bonny's white wine on the table in front of me, feeling all right. I'm hungry, looking forward to dinner with my girl, looking forward to the night, too. Just lying next to Bonny, not doing anything she doesn't want to do.

She arrives in front of me, and I put out a hand, pull her down on the sofa beside me. "Everything OK?" I ask.

"I didn't speak to her. Got the answerphone."

"That's weird, isn't it? Shouldn't she be in, gagging for your call?"

"Maybe she's just nipped out for a video. I'll try again later. I phoned Daddy, too."

"Yeah? What did he say?"

"He wanted to know if I was getting you in perspective."

"*Yeah?* And you said?"

She grins at me. "I said, *Right* in perspective, thanks Dad. Now drink up, gorgeous, I'm starving."

Over the chicken risotto special, I say, "I've just realized what's so great about being up here."

"What?" she says.

"All the space."

"What, the hills and stuff?"

"Yeah, they're good. But I mean – the space from people. People we know. No friends winding you up and sticking their oars in."

"No family," she agrees. "No *twins*."

"No scary dads. No Chris and Nat. No Nick and Barb. Just us."

She sighs happily, says, "You going to have ice cream? I am."

We're lying together in the old oak bed. We got into bed just like mates, like the way we were when we first shared the flat together, joking and easy, after we'd cleaned our teeth and stuff. We're sleeping in T-shirts and underpants. Her hair's all cloudy on the pillow.

I want to touch her, I want to kiss her, but I don't, I won't let myself. We just lie there on our sides and look at each other and chat, like kids having a sleep-over. "I suppose you *want* to go and see Rupert tomorrow?" I ask.

"What d'you mean? We've got to."

"We could go the day after tomorrow. . ."

"Ri–ich. . ."

"We could just take tomorrow off, and enjoy ourselves. You know, go up in the hills and stuff. I'd like to see the hills. As soon as we spring Liz, we'll be a threesome, won't we, and on our way home. And I don't want this to be over."

Bonny hutches forward, kisses me. I kiss her back, but reining myself in a bit, and she says, "It won't be over. The way we are now – it won't be over. When we get home – we'll really be together." And she kisses me again, for longer this time, one arm hooked round my neck.

"Don't think I'm not responding, Bonny," I breathe, when she draws back. "I want to respond. I just don't want to – you know – raise bad memories."

She gets a strange look in her eyes when I say that, almost predatory. "You're terrific," she murmurs, and then she kind of launches at me. She wraps herself round me, kisses her way down my neck to my chest, inhaling my skin, her hands gripping my back, stroking it . . . it nearly blows me away. And then we're kissing again, hot as anything, like we want to eat each other up, and I feel so close to her it's choking me, and I know she's feeling the same.

"Maybe you shouldn't've made that sex rule," she breathes.

"Too late," I breathe back.

I won't let myself touch her, not anywhere. I'm

just holding her up against me. A few minutes on I say, "This is killing me."

"Good."

"Sadist."

We kiss again. She's so much sexier now, so much more of a turn on than she was the first night we made it, 'cos she's in on it too, now. I want to tell her this but I don't have the words, and I think she knows it anyway.

She's leading it, it's what she wants. She's like someone walking out, beautiful, from a dark cave, and I've reached her first. I've seen her first.

Chapter 31

The next morning we don't get to the scary gothic gates of the Fellowship of Beloveds' mansion until ten past eleven. We're a whole hour later than we meant to be because we had the best, the deepest sleep together, so deep we slept right through the morning call we'd booked.

I learned something phenomenal about sex that night. I learned it doesn't always have to involve the dick. We slept like babies after endless caresses, and then I made Bonny have breakfast with me because I told her restraining myself the night before had depleted all my energy reserves. She was fine about it, laughing at me as I stuffed my face with bacon and mushrooms. It was light years away from the sour tense breakfast of the day before.

But now, the mood's turned serious. Neither of us

is moving forward to unbolt the huge gates. "*Shit*," she breathes, "I forgot to phone Carol again last night."

"Other things to do, babe."

She smiles. "I know, but –"

"You left a message. She knows we're here. If she's worried, she'll phone you."

Bonny's face relaxes. "You're right."

"When you phone again, you'll have something solid to report. Like – you've got Liz sitting next to you in the car." And I feel a bit depressed when I say that, sorry that our time alone will be over so soon.

"Come on," she goes, and I draw the bolt and we walk down the drive.

We've only just rounded the corner when we come face to face with the rabid snarling dogs again. This time their chains are attached to a different guy, a guy with red hair. "Can I help you?" he demands, in a Scottish accent.

"We have an appointment with Rupert," I say, all smooth.

"I doubt that. Your names?"

"*Look*, buster –"

"Richard Steele and Bonny Davies," Bonny interjects.

"Follow me," he says.

"Let me do the talking, OK?" Bonny hisses, as we set off.

Halfway to the house we walk through eight young

men, divided equally either side of the drive, all on their hands and knees, weeding the edge. They're working in total silence and they barely glance at us as we pass through. One of the dogs cocks his leg over a pile of pulled weeds and pees lavishly. No one comments on this.

When we reach the front door the Scottish guy attaches the dogs' chains to a large hook and disappears inside. "Poor things," murmurs Bonny, looking at the man-eating pooches. "On leads all the time."

She reaches out a hand and I grab it before it disappears into one of their salivating mouths. "Poor nothing, Bon. They probably get loads of exercise tearing trespassers apart. It's those creepy gardeners I feel sorry for."

Before she can reply to this, the Scottish guy reappears and in reverential tones says, "Rupert will see you." We follow him through a phoney baronial hall, all dark oak and pompous pictures. Two drab girls standing at a side table – each intent on polishing a huge brass candlestick – look up serenely as we pass, and then return to their polishing as though it's the only point of their existence. We troop into a large library, shelves up to the ceiling, crammed with musty old books. "Rupert – your visitors," the Scots guy announces, practically bowing as he ushers us in.

Rupert's sitting right at the other end of the library, so we have to approach him like medieval supplicants approaching the king. He's behind one of those pseudy leather-covered desks, and he's *massive*. Not just fat, but tall with it. He makes the big desk look like a child's.

As we draw to a halt in front of him he looks up at us, appraising us. He has longish greying hair swept off his wide forehead, and intense syrupy brown eyes. He's wearing a vast green silky jacket that's half suit, half robe. "*Well!*" he booms, finally. "What brings you here to our house of learning?" He too has an American accent, and a smug, commanding, holier-than-thou voice that gets my back up right from the start.

"We're looking for my friend Liz McGowan," Bonny says. Rupert looks down wordlessly at the paper on his desk; a window to his right is slanting light across it. A little smirk slides across his fat mouth. "Is she here?" Bonny persists.

There's a long silence. "Is she here?" I echo. More silence. "Are you gonna answer me, or what?" I rap out.

Bonny nudges me sharply. Rupert looks up, but at the Scottish guy, not me, and says, "Frazer, will you leave us?" And Frazer creeps out. *Backwards*. All the way.

As soon as the door has shut on Frazer's face, Rupert fixes me with an authoritarian stare, and says, "We will deal better with things if we do it in a spirit of cooperation, not aggression."

"*Aggression?*" I erupt. "No one's aggressive, mate. We just want to see Liz."

"Please," puts in Bonny, hastily. "We're worried about her."

Another I've-got-the-power-here pause from Rupert. Then: "I am a little worried about Elizabeth, too. That is why I am not sure that it is a good thing for you to see her."

Bonny heaves a relieved sigh, reaches out for my hand, and I squeeze hers. Now we know for sure Liz is actually here. "Why would it not be a good thing for her to see us?" she croaks.

Rupert focuses all intently on Bonny. He looks like an opera singer about to launch into a tragic song. "I will tell you, and if you have her best interests at heart you will hear me out. You will strive to understand what I say." He pauses, nodding slowly. "Young lady, we have a very special place here. A place that reveals truth. Sometimes when people join us they find that truth too much to bear. They find the light too blinding. And they are confronted by things about themselves that they find very hard. Their natural – their *mechanical* – reaction is to flee, to avoid having to face those things. Elizabeth is at that critical stage now. She is having a difficult time."

"What d'you mean – difficult time?" Bonny demands. I can see panic in her face, but she's holding it down.

"She is finding our exercises and directives arduous. She is finding it harder than many do to let go of her old ways. But I believe she knows she must stay – knows the battle will be worth it. I believe she has glimpsed the truth, tasted what lies beyond the mechanical level. But if you – friends from the past – appear, she might be tempted back to her old life. I would not wish that for her."

"And I," blurts out Bonny, fiercely, "*would not wish* her to stay if she wants to get out of here."

Rupert's eyelids come down like swollen shutters. "You have not understood me," he intones, with an air of deep disappointment. "If she – as you crudely put it – *wants to get out of here*, she can go, any time. The Fellowship is not a prison."

"Glad to hear it," I say, warmly. "Look, mate, see it from our side. This is Bonny's oldest friend. We just want to make sure she's OK. You can't blame us for that."

Rupert heaves himself back in his chair, sighs mournfully. "No, I cannot blame you for that. But I have explained to you the need for Elizabeth's isolation from the world. It seems you are determined to ruin Elizabeth's chance of finding her life's meaning. Of breaking free."

"Bit of an over-statement, that, don't you think?" I say, as breezily as I can. "If the Fellowship is as good as you say, she's not going to let a quick chat with me and Bon lure her away. Now – we can go round in circles all day if you like. But the fact is, we're not leaving till we've seen her."

"Please – I have asked you before to refrain from threats and aggression. It is anathema to me – poison. I shall call Frazer, have you put beyond the gates."

"And *I* shall go straight to the cops and bring them back here. From what I've heard, it won't be the first time they've been sniffing round this place."

Rupert raises his left hand like he's going to curse us, but looks pointedly at his Rolex instead. "Return at five," he barks. "Elizabeth is in meditation tuition – she cannot be disturbed. At five, you shall see her. If she wishes it. Now I shall call Frazer to see you out. Please leave."

"Thank you," I say, trying not to sound triumphant. Bonny gets me by the arm and we head towards the door, where Frazer is waiting. At the front door, he unhooks the mutts, and shepherds us down the drive. "When you return," he says, "I will be waiting by the gates. I will take you straight to the right room. Do not enter on your own."

In my head, something suddenly clicks about the weird robotic way they talk here. "Hey – why d'you do that?" I demand. "Why d'you talk without running any words together?"

"We avoid the use of connectives," Frazer sneers. "It is an exercise to make us more intentional in our speech."

"Oh, what balls."

"You try it! It is not easy."

"Yes, it is – anyone can speak that way. They just sound like a proper tosser when they do. They sound like they are barking. They sound like they're off some crap sci-fi programme on—"

"You just ran 'they' and 'are' together," gloats Frazer. "You see? It is mechanical."

"Yeah? And how long you been speaking *non-mechanically*, eh?"

"Ever since I got here. For ten months."

"Well, it's *become* mechanical then, for you, hasn't it mate?" I demand, triumphantly. "You try and talk my way, now. Go on. I bet you can't. I bet you a fiver you can't."

"I do not wish to," he says. "Even for a *fiver*." Another sneer.

"That's 'cos you know you'd bog up, and prove me right."

"No. It is because I do not wish to disobey a directive from Rupert."

"Oh, *bloody* hell –" I start, but we've reached the gates, and the dogs are straining and snarling, and Bonny pulls me hastily out.

Chapter 32

We discuss it all over a slow pub lunch. "*God*, I'm glad you came with me," Bonny says. "I'd've been shit scared on my own."

"What – of that bunch of losers?"

"Yeah! They're *sinister*. And *Rupert* – scary or what?"

"Oh, come on, Bon. He's just so far up his own backside he's lost all touch with reality."

"You know – I really thought it was all down to Kell, I thought he'd dragged Liz off and was bullying her into staying, but now I've met the people there –"

"Oh, they're just wankers. With their *directives from Rupert*. What a load of cack."

"What was Liz supposed to be doing –?"

"Meditation tuition, or some such shit."

"That is *so* not Liz," sighs Bonny. "She can't stay still for a moment."

"You know, we should've insisted we saw her there and then. We should've kicked up a bigger fuss."

"What, with those guard dogs outside? You were brilliant, Rich – threatening him with the police."

"So were you, Bon. You might've been scared but you were great, dead firm. I'm proud of you."

And we smile at each other across the table, knees touching beneath.

It feels like for ever, waiting for five o'clock, Bonny all on edge and anxious. We go for a walk; we cuddle up together in a bleak little teashop; and the time drags. There's no point in discussing anything but Liz, and there's nothing else to say about her that we haven't said ten times already. We're there at the Fellowship mansion gates at five on the dot, and so is Frazer with his canine escort. We're shown to the side of the house, this time, into a long, low-ceilinged room with skinny windows. "Rupert won't be long," Frazer says, as he shuts the door on us.

"*Rupert?*" hisses Bonny, indignantly. "We're not here to see *Rupert*."

"Don't worry, Bon. We'll sort him out. We'll see Liz."

The door opens again. Rupert enters like a walking American fridge. And Liz is right behind him.

"Oh, *Liz!*" squeals Bonny. She darts across the

room, throws her arms round her. I can't see if Liz is responding but it doesn't look much like it. And anyway my attention is distracted because behind Liz comes good old box-faced Kell, like he's her other prison guard or something.

He glares at me with loathing. And I glare right back.

"What's up, Liz?" Bonny's pleading. "Aren't you glad to see us?"

"Of course," says Liz, drawing back from Bonny's arms. "But I feel terrible that . . . that you have been put to such trouble, you have come all this way . . . and. . ."

"*Liz*," says Bonny, looking stricken, "this is *me* you're talking to!"

". . .and also it has caused problems for the Fellowship, it has disrupted our studies. I'm really—"

Instantaneously, both Kell and Rupert raise their right hands in the air and bring them down like karate chops. "Sorry," says Liz. "I *am* really ashamed to have been the cause of such trouble to everyone. Rupert tells me you're worried about me—"

Again, Kell and Rupert karate chop. "*Sorry*, you *are* worried about me. But please do not be – I am fine."

"*Jesus – H – Christ!*" I breathe. "You've got her doing it, too. Talking all drawn out and stupid. And what's with the hand chopping?"

Kell looks at Rupert, as if seeking permission to

explain, then says, "The action of the hand symbolizes the shutter of a camera. When we move our hand like that, we are offering a 'photograph' to the speaker of the speaker's speech."

"Bloody *hell*, what kind of *bollocks*—" I start, but Rupert wades in with "I must ask you not to swear. Swearing acts as a conduit for negative energy, and we strive to avoid that here. Although you, my young friend, are sadly so choked by negative energy it permeates every word you utter."

Kell smirks. And I'm just thinking, *I'll show him negative energy, the bastard*, when Bonny, who's been standing there stunned until this moment, croaks out, "Liz – you don't *look* fine!"

"I am," responds Liz. "I do not know why you have come here."

There's a silence, Liz staring all huge-eyed at Bonny. The postcard with its double messages flashes through my mind. "We need to see Liz on her own," says Bonny, voice shrill. "Liz – come out with us now. Come and get a cup of coffee with us, or something."

"Do you wish to go, Elizabeth?" asks Rupert.

"No!" Liz wails. "I must keep free from the Outside World!"

"You're stopping her," gasps Bonny. "You're forcing her to say no. You've scared her somehow."

"Elizabeth – the decision is yours!" booms Rupert. "Just think what you may be losing, though, if you speak with these people – think how you may slip back."

Poor old Liz is visibly shaking where she stands, both hands up to her face. "Just a cup of coffee, Liz!" pleads Bonny.

And then Kell moves towards Liz. He lifts his arm to put it round her shoulders and she flinches. Something in me goes cold when I see her flinch. "I think Elizabeth needs to be quiet for a while," he says. "I think she needs to go to our room."

"Care for the Beloved is paramount," intones Rupert. "Yes – take her to your room."

"*Liz!*" wails Bonny.

"Please go," gasps Liz. "I am fine. *I want to stay.*"

Kell steers her out of the door.

Chapter 33

I turn back to Rupert, and say, "I'm calling the police."

Rupert beams and spreads his fat ham-hands wide, a picture of reasonable innocence. "And you will tell them what? That you turned up here to see your friend, and she did not wish to see you?"

"There's something going on here. You're controlling her."

"Had she wanted to go with you, all she needed to do was step forward."

"Yeah, but how did she know you'd let us go? There's that army of people here, you've got those killer dogs outside. . ."

Rupert chuckles. "Come, come, my young friend, let us not descend into the realms of paranoid fantasy! Elizabeth made a free choice. She did not step forward and leave with you. I am delighted. I thought she would give way; she held firm."

"I need to speak to her," says Bonny, near to tears. "I need to speak to her on her own."

"You heard her decision."

"I don't trust that decision!"

"Then you may ask her again. You must understand – there is no coercion here. Our work is only successful if people agree to it – give themselves up to it with a whole heart. Look – I will make a bargain with you. Stay for our evening meal. It is not Formal Dining tonight, it is Informal. Ask Elizabeth again then. And if she tells you to go – then honour our bargain and go. Otherwise you are hindering her, harming her."

I look at Bonny, raise my eyebrows. She looks back at me and shrugs anxiously. "OK," I say. "It's a deal."

Rupert smirks and holds out one of his ham-hands, but I turn away without shaking it.

We're delivered by Rupert into Frazer's care again, and he tells us it's just over an hour until Informal Dining – whatever *that* is – and we can wait in the hallway or the walled garden. "The garden," says Bonny. "I need some air."

As we enter the garden, the same troop of weeders who were on the front drive earlier are leaving it, eyes downcast. Mercifully, they leave it empty. We find a stone seat in the corner with the low, late sun shining on it, sit down, and hold hands. "I don't know what to think," Bonny says. "I'm just – *stunned*."

"I know. She was weird."

"What's going on, Rich?"

"I dunno. Maybe it's all as Rupert says – she wants to work on herself, but she's finding it bloody hard. And she wrote the postcard when she was really down."

"Yeah, but in that case why play our old game with it? Why not just tell it straight?"

I tighten my grip on her hand. "When Kell went to put his arm round her, did you see the way she flinched?"

"What?"

"She flinched. I reckon he hits her."

"Oh, Rich – you don't know that. Maybe she just jerked back, you know, instinctively –"

"She moved too fast. You only learn to move like that when you know what's coming."

Bonny's looking at me. "You know, do you?"

"When I was about thirteen my dad thought I was getting out of control, and he tried to knock some sense into me."

"Oh, *Rich* –" She puts her arms round me, nestles her face against mine, kissing me. I enjoy this for a few moments, then I say, "It wasn't that bad, Bonny. Honest."

"Yeah, but *hitting* you. . ."

"It was just a few smacks round the ear and stuff.

But I remember – he stopped when I flinched once, when he reached out to put my collar straight or something. Mum said after, it'd made him feel dead ashamed."

"So it should."

"Liz flinched like that 'cos she's used to it."

There's a pause, then Bonny says, "She's got this big bruise on her arm."

"Yeah?"

"I saw it when I was giving her a hug. I mean – she could've done it a hundred different ways, but –"

She trails off, and we both stare across at a couple of fat wood pigeons who've perched on a rowan tree to gorge themselves on the berries. "We've got to get her away," she whispers. "Why didn't she just say yes to us then? *Yes, I'm leaving with you?*"

"I dunno. Maybe she didn't think they'd really let her go. And if she's scared of getting beaten up by Kell. . ."

"I've got to talk to her on her *own*. Without anyone else around. Then I'll know." Bonny suddenly gives a little jump, and pulls out her mobile. "I'd better try Carol again. God knows what I can say to her, though."

But all Bonny gets is the answering-machine. "It's Bonny," she says into it. "We're here and we've seen Liz. She seems . . . OK. Call me if you want to talk. Bye."

As she puts the phone back in her pocket, she's

shaking her head. "Still not at home – that is so weird."

A shadow's unscrolling towards us across the brick pathway. We look up and there's Frazer, mercifully without the rabid pooches. "I am to be your escort for dinner," he announces. "Come with me now."

Chapter 34

On the way over to dinner I ask Frazer how the Fellowship runs things, but his mouth remains zippered, apart from to explain they all have different rotating duties and his – this week – is Security, which is why he's in charge of us two now. From his manner, he'd marginally prefer to be on bog-cleaning duty. He does however explain that we're allowed into Informal Dining because Outsiders are occasionally allowed to take meals with the devotees. Outsiders include would-be novices of the Fellowship or other connected people.

"Such as desperate parents?" I ask, but he doesn't answer.

We're shown into a large hall, leaded windows high up on the end walls, tables laid out in lines like a monastery. All the Beloveds are filing into the room, filling up the tables in some kind of strict rotation, man, woman, man, woman, with one man and one woman at the head of each table. There must be at least sixty of them, and they all have the same phoney-serene, robotic air. They're like some kind of smirking army. I'm dying to stick out a foot and trip one of them up.

"Over here," says Frazer, leading the way.

As we pass, a woman reaches up from her seat, puts her hand on Bonny's arm. "You have lipstick on!" she spits.

"Is that a crime?" I spit back.

"It is falseness. Are you novices?"

"No *way*."

"Cecilia, it is fine," intones Frazer. "They are here because they cannot Achieve Separation from a Friend."

"Ah," says Cecilia.

Beside me, Bonny is stifling a giggling fit, I can tell. But then Frazer indicates where we should sit, and Bonny's giggling dies.

Liz is already sitting there, next to Kell. But this is not a Liz I've seen before. This is a Liz brimming with pleasure and satisfaction and happiness, and beside her, Kell looks completely besotted. "Bonny, Rich – come on – come and sit down!" she cries.

Bonny goes to take the chair next to her, but she says, "No – Rich must be next to me. That way, the male and female energies are balanced." Kell squeezes her hand, and she smiles, adding, "The Fellowship really respects couples. We are all Beloveds, but if you are in a couple, you are Truly Beloved."

I shoot a sympathetic look at Bonny. I know just how lousy I'd feel if one of *my* mates starting coming out with this kind of shit. "Liz," says Bonny in a low voice, "can't we talk in private somewhere?"

"There is no need!" exclaims Liz. "Really, Bonny. I want Kell to hear whatever you have to say to me, there's nothing—"

At her side, Kell karate-chops, and she laughs, seizes his hand, and *kisses* it, saying, "Sorry, there *is* nothing secret between us."

"Elizabeth wishes to stay," Kell intones, smugly. "She has seen the freedom and potential that lie beyond mechanicality. She wishes to work on her-self, as we all do here."

The low chatter in the hall is interrupted by a short, self-important man hitting a stupid little gong three times. Then there's complete silence, and in that silence six people march out from a double door at the end of the hall with laden trays in their arms. They place tureens and baskets of bread on each table, then they depart. The short man bangs his gong again, and the room relaxes, takes up its forks and spoons, starts to dish out the food.

I'm gazing around me at all the weirdos. They look pretty normal, but you can tell they're weirdos underneath. They're acting very intentionally – as if everything they do is a big, big deal. *I-am-drinking-some-water. Wow – here's some carrots for you! Wow – a sprout!* They keep locking eyes, exchanging meaningful silences. Their clothes are straight-laced and boring – no old hippy clothes or anything, nothing tarty or unusual, no make-up on the women. Then I realize something. The women are *serving* the men. Who are all sitting back like smug lords. At our table, Liz serves first Kell, then turns to me. I take the spoon from her, and dob a load of stew on Bonny's plate, just to make a point. Kell sneers, doesn't bother to comment.

"Liz –" begins Bonny, tentatively.

Liz turns to her, all bright-eyed certainty. "Yes?"

"It's just – you seem so different now. From the way you were earlier."

"Oh, Bonny – you do not understand – why should you? It is this *place*. It challenges you – it challenges you to challenge everything you thought was real. So you go through all these changes – and every now and then you get a glimpse of what is really real, a sense of the truth, the *oneness*, underneath it all—"

"Liz, are you *on* something?" I blurt out.

Liz laughs, all tinkly, and starts off again about the really-real and challenging the oneness underneath. Every time she runs a couple of words together Kell's right hand flops impotently up and down. A subtle change is coming over him, like fog rolling in over the sea. He's no longer looking at Liz like he loves her; he's no longer entranced. And suddenly he bangs a hand down over hers and says, "Elizabeth – remember what our leader directs about Unnecessary Chatter."

"But I was not *chattering*—"

Karate chop. "You were. And now you are arguing with your Beloved. Remember the directions on that."

Her face downturns. "Yes – you are right. I am sorry," she says.

Another karate chop.

"But I said—"

Another chop. "Sorry," she whispers.

There's a long, long pause. I glance sideways at Bonny – she's looking completely stunned. The whole room feels like it's choking with careful eating and measured talk.

"*Fucking* hell, Liz," I erupt, loudly. "You sure you don't want to get out of all this?"

Chapter 35

"I believe Elizabeth has been quite clear about that, hasn't she?" demands Kell, box-face thrust towards me and glowing with rage. "She wants to stay!"

"I want to hear it from her," insists Bonny.

"Elizabeth?" barks Kell.

Liz starts, squeaks, "I want to stay."

"Liz, we can get up now, we can get up and just *walk out*, we've got the car outside –"

"No, I really want to stay," she repeats, looking with pleading desperation at Kell. "It's – it *is* amazing, this experience. I cannot just turn my back on it."

Kell sits back smugly. "There! Now – you two should honour the bargain you made with the Leader. Finish your meals, and leave."

Bonny shoots to her feet, scraping her chair back

hard so that all the weirdos crane round and look. She's near to tears. "We'll go now, *thanks*. I just – I don't understand you, Liz! If you *meant* that post-card, you've done a complete about-turn since you wrote it!"

All the colour drains from Liz's face.

"What do you mean – *meant the postcard?*" demands Box-face.

Bonny realizes her mistake and goes red, as though the colour from Liz is flowing into her.

"What do you mean?" Box repeats. "I saw the postcard – it was fine." He rounds on Liz, who shrinks back. "Did you send *another* postcard, Elizabeth?"

"No," she wails. "No – I swear it."

"What's the big deal if she did, mate?" I ask. "It's only a postcard."

"The *big deal*," he snarls at me, like he wants to take a chunk out of my face, "is that *Beloveds* have no secrets from each other. They don't *betray* each other."

I karate-chop him, say, "*Do not*, mate, not don't." Which is possibly not wise. He practically spits in my eye, then rounds on Liz again.

"You have still not explained to me why these two are here, Elizabeth. Why have they come if you did not ask them to come? If you're *lying* to me—"

"Look," says Bonny, "she just sent us that post-card, and. . ." She trails off. She can't think of a way out. "We just thought we'd come and see her," she finishes lamely.

"And now you can go!" Box barks. He gets to his feet, one arm under Liz's, who's jerked to her feet too.

"Liz!" says Bonny pleadingly.

"I'm fine," croaks Liz. "Just please *go*."

I scramble up from the table. "You say the word, Liz, and I'll knock him out."

Box jeers. And Liz wails, "How many times do I have to say it, Rich? *I want to stay!*"

After Frazer and the rabid pooches have escorted us from the Fellowship mansion lands, and said *Goodbye* to us very pointedly and finally, we make our way to the car and sit in it in the gathering dark. Bonny seems too depressed to start the engine up. "There's nothing you can do, Bon," I say, soothingly. "She's made her choice."

"I know. She just seemed . . . so *mad*. You don't think he *had* drugged her or something, do you?"

"Nope."

"He's gonna beat her up, isn't he. About the postcard."

"I don't know. Probably. But she could've come with us then, if she'd wanted."

"I know."

"He didn't have her prisoner. She could've walked out with us."

"I *know*. She's – she's still crazy about him, that's all. The way she was *glowing*, at the start of the meal."

"Maybe Kell's an exceptional lay."

"*Urgh*."

"He'd need to be, with a mug like that. Come on, Bon. Let's go back to the pub. They'll let us stay another night. Let's get a drink."

We make our way back to The Green Man. The guy behind the desk is almost welcoming when we tell him we want to stay another night, informs us it's reduced rates for longer. I steer Bonny into the comfy old bar, see there's an early-autumn fire going, and steer her over to sit alongside it. The place is just crowded enough, just right for talking, but Bonny's completely sunk in gloom, saying nothing. I go up to the bar, order a couple of beers. Of course I feel bad about Liz, but I also feel a trickle of excitement and relief to think that it's just Bonny and me now, up in Scotland, all on our own. . . *Bonny'll come round*, I say to myself. *She'll get over it*. I pick up the beers, go over and sit down beside her. "You know we couldn't've done more," I say, putting my arm round her, "don't you?"

"Hmmm?"

"We did all we could. Short of kidnapping Liz and bundling her into the boot of your car."

"Mmmm."

I'm not entirely convinced Bonny's actually

listening to me, but I ramble on in this vein for a while, dredging up every comforting, we've-done-our-best platitude I can think of, when Bon suddenly twists round, fixes me with a look and says, "We've got to get back in."

"*What?*"

"Look, Rich – I can't just leave her to it, I can't. She's *stupid* about men – she's always getting it wrong. And she's under some spell with him. Maybe he hits her, then makes her feel like a goddess – I don't know. He's messing up her head somehow. I can't just abandon her."

"Look, Bonny, you've *tried* to get her out! What you gonna do – knock her senseless and carry her out?"

"I've got to get to talk to her on my *own*. Without that manipulating *bastard* in earshot. I can make her see sense, I know I can."

"Maybe. But how are you going to *get* to see her now? Don't forget Rupert's poxy bargain. If Liz said – for a *second* time – that she wanted to stay there, you agreed to go away and leave her alone! How you gonna get back in again now?"

A strange look has come over Bonny's face. "By saying we want to join the Fellowship."

"*What?*"

"We go back to Rupert, we tell him we're so impressed by all we've seen—"

"No."

"– that we want to see more, *learn* more, about their work, and—"

"No *way*. *No* way."

"*Ri–ich* – it's only pretending."

"I couldn't do it. I'd choke. I'd spew up."

"Look – I'll do it. You're always saying what a good liar I am."

"Am I?"

"Well, you did once. It kind of hurt me, but I had to learn to lie, living with Mum."

"I know, Bon."

"I'll do the spiel, you just stand there and look mean and moody or whatever you like."

"I don't think I could, Bon. Seriously. That fat bastard Rupert is going to be insufferable if we—"

"Rich – we'd be *conning* him, for Christ's sake! What does it matter what he thinks? Look on it as a challenge – you'll be tricking them, taking them all in. Please, Rich! I can't just drive off and leave Liz. You saw her face when it came out about the post-card. Kell's a monster. He's sick."

"Yeah, but pretending we want to *join up*—"

"It's just a way of getting in again. And if I get some time on my own with her and she *still* tells me to push off, I will, I promise. *Please*, Rich."

There's a silence, while I look in her troubled, pleading, beautiful face. And then I hear myself say, "Oh, sod it. OK."

Chapter 36

After that, Bonny is dead animated. She plonks a great kiss on my cheek, and shoots up to the bar for another two beers. Then she's all into chatting about how she's going to get Rupert to let us into the mansion one more time.

"We get there at ten o'clock on the dot tomorrow, ask to see him again. Then we play on his vanity, Rich. He's so up himself, he'll believe us if we tell him how impressed we were by what we saw. You know – the *harmony* and peace we felt there – this sense that it's what we've been searching for all along. . ."

"Oh, *Jesus*."

"Look – *you* don't have to say that. You just act like I'm hauling you along—"

"That won't be acting, babe."

"I'll be the keen one. They've got a thing about *couples* there, didn't you see? All that stuff about 'Beloveds' – and the way the women served the men? I'll play on that. On us being a couple and everything."

"OK, Bon. If you're set on this, fine."

"You're the greatest, you do know that?"

"Yup. Now finish your beer and let's get up to bed. If I'm going to have to act like one of those crazies I'm gonna need my *sleep*."

When it came to bedtime, I'd already planned to be really sensitive and assume – after a day like she's just had – that she just needs to pass out. But as soon as I slide beneath the sheets beside her she slithers over, face on my shoulder, hand on my chest.

"Thanks for today," she whispers. "Thanks for coming up here with me."

"Bon – I wouldn't've missed this for the world."

"You might not still be saying that tomorrow night."

"What – after Rupert's signed me up as a novice, made me wear a hair shirt and chant?"

She laughs. Her leg comes over on to mine. She's breathing kisses into my neck. I twist round, kiss her back, kiss her deep. The hand on my chest slides lower.

I make myself lie still. I've learned from last night to let her take the lead – not to act like I'm taking over. And then gradually, slowly, I respond a little more. And when my hand's skirting its way down from her shoulder, what she does is, she captures and pushes it on to her breast.

I let out this kind of half groan, half whimper. I don't mean to, but it's fine, because it tells her she's beautiful. She gasps, laughs, presses closer . . . after a while, we're doing everything but the full deed. It's erotic, it's excruciating, it's just about killing me, holding back from where I want to go. And what's really sexy is – I can tell it's kind of killing Bonny, too.

"How long did we agree not to do it for?" she breathes at me, when we surface after another long, lovely kiss.

"Months," I whisper. "*Years.*"

Then I pull her on top of me, crane up to her mouth.

Ten o'clock sharp the next morning – owing to Bonny setting a little travel alarm and bullying me without pity until I get out of bed – we're at the mansion gates. I feel oddly happy about this, like it's a game we're playing. Things have shifted between us. Some kind of barrier has gone and we're behaving like we're in love. It's so sweet, so great, I don't want to spoil it by saying anything about it. It's in everything we do, the way we look at each other, the way we touch. It was even in the way she yelled at me to get up. I find myself wondering how we could possibly feel any closer, even after we've actually made love. I feel so close now I'm shaking inside with it.

"D'you think we should just walk in?" asks Bonny, doubtfully, after we've waited for five minutes or so. "Suppose they see us and set the dogs on us?"

"Well, there's no bell on the gate," I say.

"Maybe if we just hang about here for a bit longer –"

"Or we could shout."

And sure enough, after I've bellowed "*Oi*"! a few times, Frazer rounds the corner at a gallop, towed by the slavering dogs. He reins them in to just within biting distance and the three of them stand there snarling at us.

"You two again! I understood you had made a pact with our Leader not to come back!"

"We had," simpers Bonny, so girlish and twee that I turn to check it's still her. "This is about something different."

"Well – what is it?"

Then Bonny fills her lungs and goes into this amazing act, all about how at Informal Dining last night we were *deeply moved* by the wonderful, harmonious atmosphere surrounding us, and by the new-found bond between Elizabeth and Kell – "how a man and a woman *should* be: together". In fact we were so deeply moved that we'd done nothing but talk about it since, and now we were burnt up with wanting to know more. "It's like something's *drawing* us here. I can't explain it, I just feel it. Somewhere deep inside me, I *know* we need to come back here."

She's so convincing I half believe her myself by the end of it. And Frazer, bless him, is completely convinced. He makes hugely focused eye-contact with her, and says, "The Fellowship has that effect. When one is surrounded by people who are not acting from False Personality but from their true inner selves . . . something true in oneself can respond to it, recognize one's hunger for it." He pauses, smirks meaningfully, and adds, "One becomes a Seeker. One is on the Long Path."

"Do you think the Leader would see us one more time?" Bonny asks, breathlessly.

"Am I to tell him you are Seekers?" asks Frazer.

"Yes," squeaks Bonny, slightly hysterically. "Yes, I think we are. I *know* we are."

Don't laugh, Richie boy. Keep that lip buttoned. Nearly there.

"Very well, Seekers," intones Frazer, "wait there while I seek permission for an audience." And he turns with his dogs on his heels.

There's a long, pregnant silence, then I breathe, "Give-that-girl-an-*Oscar*!"

"*Shhh*, Rich – he'll hear you! Thank God he's gone. My eyes were about to explode, holding his gaze and trying to look all sincere."

"Well done, Bon. You did it. You've got a real skill at telling porkies."

"It's *acting*, Rich. I'm good at acting."

"You're brilliant at it, babe." I put my arms round her. "Well, we've cleared the first hurdle."

"Yeah. It's what happens inside that nuthouse that worries me."

"Yeah. Oh, *Bon* – you've got lippie on!"

"What?" She looks aghast. "Shit, I forgot. What was it that cow of a woman said – lipstick is falseness?"

"Lick it off. Here, let me." We're in a very enjoyable clinch when the hounds come baying into earshot, and we shoot apart just as Frazer is towed round the corner to announce that yes, we will be seen.

Right now.

Chapter 37

As we trek up the long path to the mansion front door, Bonny takes out her mobile to switch it off. "Still no message from Carol," she says, anxiously.

"Weird," I whisper back.

"D'you think something's happened to her?"

"Dunno. We can't do anything about it now, though. Keep your mind on the con ahead, Bon, OK? Then you can phone again afterwards."

Bonny composes her face into that of a Seeker, and we head through the front doors, following Frazer like before. One of the tethered pooches snaps at my legs in a bored kind of way as I pass.

Fat-man Rupert is once again behind his desk as we're ushered into the library. He has such a smug, gloating expression on his bloated face that I damn nearly turn about and walk out again, but Bonny's got my hand gripped like a vice, so I can't.

"Well, well, *well!*" he booms. "You arrive here seeking to take your friend away – you end up Seeking!"

"I know," breathes Bonny, all wide-eyed and saintly. "Kell and Elizabeth seemed to have *found* something together, something Rich and I don't have."

"You are a perceptive girl."

"And this place itself, it just *calls* to me, I can't explain it. I just—"

"There's no need to explain it," says Rupert, waving a fat paw to shut her up. "The Fellowship works that way. It draws people to it. Magnetizes them."

"I don't know what to ask, what to say," Bonny gushes. "I don't know how to seek, how to—"

Rupert waves his mitt again. He clearly prefers the sound of his own voice to anyone else's. "You have made the first step, the all-important first step along the Long Path. Your hearts are empty, starved of the truth. Now it is a matter of keeping those empty hearts open. And your minds, eyes and ears open, too. It is a matter of hearing and listening and keeping faith, holding fast to that which your hearts got the very first sense of last night at Informal Dining."

"Will you let us join?" blurts out Bonny.

He glares at her like she's just farted. "It is not as

simple as that. It is not called the Long Path for nothing. Normally, I correspond with a Seeker for some time before I allow them to come here for Interview. But you are here. Without permission, but here. You have, as you say, been drawn here, irresistibly. And I am not an inflexible man." He spreads his hands, as though inviting us to marvel at how fabulous he is. "I may allow you to participate in some Work Requirements, some Basic Study sessions. . ." Then suddenly, sickeningly, he swings his fat head round to me. "It is you I am concerned about. Your girlfriend's sincerity is evident. She has been touched by this place – called by it. I need to be sure you have too. I need to be sure you are a True Beloved."

Oh, shit. "Oh, yes," I gruff out. "I mean – yes, I have. I am. A – you know. A Beloved."

"You do not understand what you say," he says, smirking patronizingly. "But how can you? The Path is Long." Then he looms towards me across the desk and demands, "Is all well with your relationship?"

Oh, shit shit *shit*. My mind screeches back to last night, back to the spectacle of the women serving the men, and takes a leap in the dark. . . "I'm confused," I burble, as sincerely as I can manage. "It's like – there's no discernible role any more. Between men and women, I mean. Who's in charge and . . . and stuff. It's all so empty. And . . ." I finish lamely, "my girlfriend does the driving and I hate that."

Just as I'm thinking what a prat I am, I realize I've hit

the jackpot. Rupert's melon face is beaming fit to split. "You have felt it, too!" he pronounces. "The imbalance today. Here we believe men must be men, women must be women. Women must *surrender* to their menfolk. Their menfolk must strive to serve and protect them. You may be True Beloveds. You may indeed."

There's a brief, intense pause. I fight the urgent need to burst out laughing in his face. Rupert looks down at the desk for several moments, holding up a podgy forefinger for silence. Then he looks up at us again.

"I have decided." He nods his head silently a few times, as if overcome by the wonder of his own greatness. "You are staying nearby?"

"At a pub," whispers Bonny, reverentially. "The Green Man."

"Continue to stay there. You may attend some of our sessions here. You will work hard. You may attend Informal Dining. And then we shall see."

We both thank him, and Bonny, sounding as awed as she can, asks, "May we attend this afternoon?"

He looks briefly annoyed, then says, "Yes. Two o'clock. At the gates. And before you go – I will give you your first Exercise. You must speak avoiding connectives, as we all do here. It is less mechanical. It makes you more intentional. You are now dismissed."

How we make it down the drive without collapsing in hysteria, God only knows. Bonny manages to maintain a straight face by keeping up a kind of high-pitched humming, all on one note. In case Rupert's watching us from a window somewhere, we hold hands in a reverential way as we mince along, the way we feel True Beloveds would walk. Then once we're safe inside her car we *howl*.

"Surrender to me," I gasp, "Beloved Bon!"

"Serve me, protect me!"

"It is a Long Path! The Way of the Seeker is long and full of shit!"

"Oh . . . *God*! I don't believe what he said back there!"

"What *he* said? You were the scary one. *Jesus – H – Christ*. That creepy voice you did. 'I don't know what to do, what to say,'" I imitate her, squeakily. "'Something's drawing us here, magnetizing us. . .'"

"Shut *up*!" She claps her hand over my mouth, and I suck at it, noisily. "You shut up, Rich. I got us in there, didn't I?"

"You were brilliant. A star."

"Hey – d'you really hate me driving?"

"Yup. It emasculates me. It totally withers my dick."

"No, it doesn't, Rich. Clearly."

"That is not the comment of a Surrendered Beloved. That is the comment of an Oversexed Slut."

She laughs, hugs me, groans, "How're we gonna *do* this? How're we gonna keep it up?"

"We're not, for long. Seriously Bon, I don't wanna

spend *five minutes* longer in that place than I have to. This afternoon, somehow, you've got to locate Liz and find out if she's really lost her marbles. Then we're off. After we've had a bit of fun with Rupert that is. You know – *resigning*. Telling him exactly where he can stick his Long Path."

"How long've we got?" She checks her watch. "It's eleven–fifteen. Two and three-quarter hours to go."

It suddenly goes very quiet in the car. "That's a lot of time to fill," I say softly, stroking her hair.

And she says, "Shall we go back to the pub?"

Chapter 38

The landlord of The Green Man is positively friendly as we roll in again and tell him we'd like to stay another night. It's like he thaws a little every time he sees us. "I'd not got the room cleaned out," he said. "I saw your bags were still in there."

"Fine," I say. "We'll go up now, if that's all right."

"I'll knock a fiver off if you keep those sheets and don't have the room cleaned," he says. "Bit short-staffed this morning."

"Fine," I repeat. "Great." I seize Bonny's hand and turn to the stairs, but he seems to want to chat.

"You having a holiday here then?"

"Sort of," says Bonny. "We're up here to see a friend."

"She at that mansion place?" he asks. "That cult?"

We both stop in our tracks. "Do you know about it, then?" I demand.

"Well – you get to hear things. You know."

"What sort of things?" asks Bonny.

"Just – if you're having much to do with it, take care, that's all." And he smiles at us, says, "Better get on," and disappears through the door behind him.

"I wish people wouldn't keep *doing* that," mutters Bonny, as we pound up the creaky old stairs. "Telling us to take care, I mean."

"Well, it seems to have screwed your mate up pretty tight."

"I still think that's mainly Kell. Well – a combination of the two." She unlocks the bedroom door, and we walk in. It's good getting back to the room exactly the way we left it, more private somehow.

"D'you want a coffee, Bon?" I ask. There's a tray full of tea-making stuff on it on a table in the corner.

She says she does, and I fill the kettle in the bathroom while she pulls back the curtains. The room's glowing. We lie side by side on the bed and drink our coffee and chat some more about what happened this morning. And she says, "Rich – I really do think you're great for coming with me. I know I've said it before but—"

"You want to say it again."

"Yeah," she laughs, and she puts her arms round my neck and kisses me, and I kiss her back, for longer, and then we're away, holding each other close, winding our legs together. . . "Take my clothes off," she whispers.

So I do. Very slowly, and with her permission, I unbutton her shirt and peel off her jeans, and then we kiss again, and I get this thought that it was never this sexy with Portia, it was never this *special*.

"You now," she whispers. She strips me off down to my shorts, and we kiss some more, and I tell her her skin is wonderful, then we shed the rest of our clothes, and she breathes, "Rich, I don't want to wait any longer."

I'm not going to make a crack about breaking the rules, I'm not going to make a crack about anything. I just murmur, "You sure?"

"Yes," she says. "Please, Rich. *Yes*."

Which is kind of what she said the last time we made love, the first and only time we made love, except it couldn't be more different now. Then she was like someone grasping at something, straining for something, now she's warm and relaxed and sure and we're together, we're so close.

I tell her how beautiful she is, each and every bit of her. She tells me I am. And slowly, still talking to each other, it happens. And it's so good, it's wonderful, this time it's the best. OK, I don't last as long as I should do, because it's too much of a turn on and I can't, but it's only the start so it doesn't matter, and already it's the best. Ever.

I tell her so. She's kind of shining. "Thank you,"

she says into my chest. "Thank you. All I seem to do at the moment is *thank you*."

"Bonny, you're great," I sigh. "You're the –" I laugh, searching for a new word – "you're the *totality*."

"So are you."

"We can't both be it."

"Yes, we can. *We* can."

We let the room fall silent, let the happiness flow between us. Then she whispers, "This afternoon, we've got to go back to the mansion and pretend our relationship is empty and we need the Long Path."

"Bloody hell. I can't. It's insane, Bon."

"All that slog they put into being True Beloveds. . ."

"They're missing the point, right?"

"Yes." She laughs. "Let's get some lunch. Let me buy you a beer. I think you're gonna need it."

And we get up and dress and that incredible, close feeling turns into jokiness, but it's OK because we know it's still there underneath, we know we can get it back. Any time.

Over lunch we wind up in fits trying to practise talking without using connectives. "Oh, shit," groans Bonny, "we've gotta take this more seriously."

"I can't. I just want to go back to bed with you."

"Later!"

"Bon – did you come?"

"*Ri–ich!*"

"Sorry. Did you?"

"Sort of. Almost. I don't care, I know I will."

"Yeah," I say happily, "you will," and she goes kind of pink and says, "Rich – we're gonna blow it. This afternoon. We'll be thrown out as frauds."

"Nah – they're all too mad to see past their noses."

"We've got to stop being so . . . *happy.*"

"Nah. They'll just think we're high on being there, when really we're . . . you know."

"What?"

"You *know.*"

She grins at me. "Come on, we'd better go."

We drive back to the mansion at about a quarter to two. The route between the pub and the lane where we park feels pretty familiar by this time. "Hey," I say, "there's another car parked in our place. More Seekers, you reckon? Pull up just behind it. Bon? Bon – *what's wrong?*"

Bonny's swerving almost into the old stone wall, jamming on the brakes. The car stalls, judders to a halt; her face is tight and white. "*Shit,*" she spits. "*Shit.*"

"Bon – what the *hell* is it?"

"*That's* why Carol never phoned me back!" she grits out. "She never got my messages – she wasn't at home! She was driving up here – they've come up here together!"

"*What?* Bonny – what's going on?"

She turns off the ignition and lets her head fall forward on to the steering wheel, just like that, smack. "That's my *mum's* car," she groans.

Chapter 39

I let out a low, comedy whistle. "Tigger. Oh, bloody hell. How come she's got involved?"

"She's friends with Carol. I told you."

"I thought Tigger was too hideous to have friends."

"She is. But they got thrown together picking us up from horse riding and stuff—"

"*Horse* riding? You spoilt cow."

"Shut up."

"My folks couldn't even afford to get me a football. I had to make do with kicking a tin can about—"

"Rich – *shut up*! This is *so appalling* I could die, and all you're doing is taking the piss –"

"Sorry, babe."

"I hate her. Why'd she have to follow me up here?

Just as everything's so good for once, she's gonna bitch everything up, she's gonna—"

"Bonny, *calm down*. This is not about you – it's about Liz. If Carol and Tigger are friends—"

"My mum doesn't have friends!"

"OK, if they know each other –"

"Carol never really listens to anyone, that's how she can put up with Mum."

"OK, so she puts up with her – maybe she told her that you'd come up here, after Liz, and Tigger suggested coming up too –"

"That's it. That's what would've happened. Mum's such an interfering old cow – she can't bear to be left out of anything. And Carol doesn't drive . . . she'd've offered to drive her. *God*. Why can't she stay out of things? Why'd she have to *come* here? Why can't she stay out of my life – why can't she *just die*? *I hate her!*"

"Bonny, I'm gonna have to smack you one in a minute. You're getting hysterical."

"You smack me and I'll smack you right back."

"That's better. Now, calm down."

Her lip trembles, then she laughs. "OK, OK. I'm calm. I just – I felt so *sick* when I saw her car. I can't tell you. She's gonna screw everything up."

I put my hands either side of her face, turn it towards me, rub noses with her. "Bonny – she's not going to screw anything up unless you let her. You've left home. You've left *her*. The only power she's got over you now is what you decide to give her. OK? *OK?*"

Bonny sniffs. "OK."

"Now – it's nearly two o'clock. We have to forget about Tigger. We have to get in there now and hope we don't *see* Tigger, and get Liz *out*. OK?"

She nods. I feel so sorry for her. She looks so crushed by the sight of that car.

"Look – I could throttle your mum," I say, "and I *will* if she tries to mess things up. Don't let her ruin this, Bon. You were ace this morning, you took charge – we're *in* here. *You* did that. Now come on, let's go."

As we walk through the gates we're met yet again by Frazer, but this time the marauding pooches are absent and in their place is a bleak-looking woman in her early twenties with long, straw-coloured plaits. "Welcome, Bonny and Richard," Frazer says. "Follow me." As we head up the path, he says, "To start with, couples are separated. They do separate work so that a space is created in which each Beloved can sense the vibrations of the Fellowship just for him or herself."

Oh, *barf*. Bonny slides her eyes sideways at me, all panicky. I smile back at her, nodding, trying to convey that it'll be all right.

"After a while," drones Frazer, "couples do controlled work together, so that harmony as True

272

Beloveds can be established. Now – to work. Bonny –
come with me into the garden."

I don't like the sound of that. "I thought you were
Security?" I demand.

"I am on gardening, now. *You* are to go to the
kitchens. Helena here is in charge. She will show you
the way."

And with that he stalks off on to a great lawn that
stretches down towards some trees and an oval-
shaped pond. Bonny shoots an anguished look at me,
and follows.

"Would you come this way, please?" Helena bleats.
She has an American accent and she's smirking at
me almost flirtatiously.

I smirk back, follow her, remind myself to talk
Fellowship style, and ask, "Do you know someone
called Elizabeth?"

"I am sorry, but it is forbidden to discuss inmates
with Seekers."

"Oh, great. Helpful."

Her hand chops down. "What's that for?" I
demand, indignantly. "I *did not* use a connective."

"I was photographing sarcasm," she says. "That is
forbidden here. It is not helpful."

She walks on. I resist the urge to turn round and
run in the opposite direction, and follow her.

In the vast kitchen, which has turned its back on the
baronial-heritage style of the rest of the house and gone

for a kind of nasty 1980s modernism, preparations for this evening's Informal Dining are already under way. Eight mixed-sex Beloveds are serenely at work, spaced out along the counters and the long central table. It becomes rapidly apparent that the newest Seeker gets the crappest job. I'm seized on, shoved in front of a towering pile of carrots, and told to peel them.

Next to me at the counter is a creepy-looking guy who's got what can only be described as a bun on the back of his head, half-hidden by his upturned collar. He's busy cutting flower shapes out of radishes.

"Interesting," I remark, nodding at the radishes.

"Food is not just for physical nourishment," he simpers. "I am creating beautiful impressions for the salad hors d'oeuvre."

"Reckon I should carve these carrots into something?" I say. "Swans, maybe? Or ducks?" I'm waiting for him to chop me for sarcasm, but he doesn't. He shakes his head mournfully, says, "You probably do not have the time. Helena wishes you to prepare the broccoli after that."

Oh, great. Use me for slave labour, why don't you. There's a pause, during which I realize with some alarm that he's sidling up very close to me. Hastily, I sidle away. "Are you wondering about my hair?" he murmurs.

"No," I lie, because I *had* just been thinking about what kind of bloke has a bun of hair rammed into the collar of his jacket.

He smiles at me, reaches behind his neck and fiddles for a few seconds. Then his hand reappears with half a dozen or so very long bobby pins. He shakes his head, and this long, snake-like rope of hair slithers down across his shoulders and falls to his waist, separating into oily fronds as it goes.

I concentrate on my carrots, on controlling my lip from sneering with disgust. "I started growing it five years ago," he whispers. "I made a pledge."

"What kind of pledge?" I snap.

"Never to cut my hair. Until my parents asked for my forgiveness."

Oh, bloody hell. He's staring at me, wide-eyed and unblinking, waiting for me to beg him to reveal all. I want to beg him to bugger off, but I say, "Why d'you need to forgive them?"

"Oh, all kinds of things. The term 'child abuse' does not come close, not for their total, *total* unloving failure, the way they tried to break me, smash me up into little pieces that they could make up again into the kind of son *they* wanted. . ."

I feel like I'm at a really bad play, acted worse. "They hit you?" I grunt.

"No. It was all verbal. The destruction was as bad as if they had beaten me senseless, though. They sent me away to school, where again I was *dismantled*, literally, and built into someone I was not."

There's a long, poignant pause. I suppose it's a sad story but I feel like I might start laughing if I don't get away soon, if he doesn't stop staring at me with his nose about two centimetres from mine.

"Rupert's helping me put myself back together again," he says blissfully, turning – *thank God* – back to his radishes. "Rupert can see me, whole, under all the distortions – he is helping me *emerge*."

"That's great, mate," I mutter. "Glad for you."

"My parents *hate* my hair," he suddenly spits. "I grew it just a little, and we had this huge row about it, absurd, just about *hair*, and I suddenly saw in that everything about the way they want to change me, how they hate who I really am. And until they embrace who I really am – I will keep my hair long. Till I die, if need be." He leans on the kitchen counter, overcome with emotion. "It will be my *shroud*."

"*Quentin!*" Helena shrills, from across the kitchen. "What has our Leader directed us about Unnecessary Chatter?"

"Sorry, Helena," gasps bun-head.

"Also, I am sure I heard the new Seeker use a connective which you failed to photograph! He is here to be helped – guided – by us all!"

"Yes, Helena!"

"Now please – both of you – return to your work."

For a second or so, I'm tempted to fall forward on to the pile of carrots, like Bonny fell on to her steering wheel an hour or so ago.

Then I get back to peeling them.

Chapter 40

After what feels like weeks I finish the carrots, and I head over to Helena to report on this fact. "Well done," she gushes. "You are a good boy! You deserve a tea break and one of my special apricot cookies!"

"Er – right," I say. "Can I take some tea out to Bonny?"

Helena's face sours. Shit, she must *fancy* me. "Is it so hard to be away from her?" she bleats.

"I am concerned for her," I say, piously. "I know she will be overwhelmed by the amazing energy that is here." Wow, I'm really getting the hang of the chat here.

"True," says Helena. "But sometimes it is good to let people experience that energy for themselves. To leave them in their own space."

"I know. But I feel I must *protect* her."

Bull's-eye. That's one of the Fellowship buzzwords, and old straw-hair can't argue against it. "Very well," she sniffs. "Take two mugs of tea, and two cookies. Be back here in half an hour, please."

I pick up the enormous blue teapot and pour out two mugs. Then I wait till Helena's turned her back, pocket five cookies, and scarper.

It's not hard to find Bonny. She's down by the lake, with three other girls, dolefully hoeing a patch of ground. Frazer's on the other side of the lake, laboriously scrubbing a nasty statue of two obese cavorting water sprites. When he sees me sidling up to Bonny, he races over and tries to intervene, but I make out coming to fetch Bon for a break is on Helena's strict instructions, and he lets us go.

Soon we're huddled side by side on an old bench behind a bit of screening shrubbery, sipping tea and sharing the special apricot cookies, which are not at all bad. "*Well?*" I demand, mouth full.

Bonny swallows. "I saw Liz, but I couldn't talk to her. Frazer's like the *Gestapo*. She was walking along by the house with another girl, carrying this great pile of towels – I called out to her and Frazer nearly went ape, gave me this fat lecture on how shouting damaged the silence and how *women* shouldn't raise their voices. I nearly decked him."

"What a nerd. So he wouldn't even let you have a quick chat?"

"No. He said I had to put my full energy into the work I was doing, and the time for Limited Socializing—"

"*What?*"

"He called it that! Honestly, Rich, this whole place gets dodgier by the minute. Anyway, he said I could only speak to her tonight at Informal Dining."

"*Shit*. So we're stuck with another grim meal here then."

"Looks like it."

"Did Liz see you?"

"Yes – she stopped, and then the girl she was with said something and she walked on. But at least she knows I'm here – if she wants to speak to me, she'll be trying to get to me too."

"Well, let's make sure you get to talk to her tonight, Bon. I'm not coming back tomorrow if I can help it. I had to peel about a million tonnes of carrots just then."

"Poor baby. Seen anything of my mother?"

"Nope. With any luck they've got her cleaning out the drains."

"She'll be in with Rupert, won't she, cross-questioning him about Liz."

"Maybe she'll try and get off with him."

"Oh, Rich, *please*."

"Well, why not? She tries to pull every other bloke who comes across her path."

Bonny snorts with laughter, puts her arms round

me, and I'm just nudging in for a kiss when a familiar Scottish voice raps out, "Infra-sexual behaviour is not permitted in public spaces."

"*What?*" I snap. I look up to see Frazer heading fast towards us. Bonny squeezes my hand warningly.

"You two Seekers have a very great deal to learn," Frazer barks, pulling up in front of us, jamming his hands on his hips. "If you are to become True Beloveds you must give up your old ways of casual physical interaction. Now both of you – get back to work."

By the time I finally finish my kitchen chores, it's five o'clock. After the carrots I had to trim a great sackload of broccoli and then *redo* the whole lot because Helena said I hadn't done it *intentionally* enough. By this time I am convinced that:

a) Helena is a sadist who gets her thrills by torturing men she fancies.
b) She *seriously* fancies me.
c) I hate broccoli and will never look at it, let alone eat it, again.

I am also convinced that if I don't get out of here soon I'll be barking, just like Quentin who should probably be in a straitjacket.

As I leave the kitchen, Helena puts a restraining hand on my arm. "There is an hour and a half until

Informal Dining," she simpers. "We have prepared the food, so we are not on Serving Duty. I need a brief while to freshen up before dinner, then I could show you the grounds, if you like."

"Thank you, but I have to go and find Bonny," I say gravely.

She sniffs, looks sour. "*Bonny* is not short for any-thing, is it?" she asks.

"No, I don't – do not – think so."

"It is such a silly name. Rupert will probably choose her another one."

I bare my teeth at her, and stalk out of the front door. To be met by Frazer with a stricken-looking Bonny in tow. "Richard!" he barks. "I have come to escort you from the grounds. I have conferred with Rupert who feels that today's experience was enough for you both for one day. You are clearly over-whelmed. If we try to run too early, we end up sprawling on our faces. Rupert says you may come back tomorrow – at ten o'clock."

All the way down the drive, Bonny's gripping my arm, telepathically begging me not to explode and ruin everything. Then when we get through the gates she gasps out, "Look – I'll come back on my own tomorrow."

"Bonny – if you're coming, I'm coming. I'm not letting you go through it on your own."

"Oh, *Rich* – you mean that?"

"Yes. You're bound to see her tomorrow."

"You're a hero. A star. I owe you bigtime. And I'm s*orry*!"

"It's not your fault, Bon! It's that bastard Frazer! I bet he went into Fat-Man Rupert and told him about us having a smooch on the bench –"

She laughs, links her arm through mine and we hurry along the leafy lane towards her car. "What did he call it – *Infra-sexual behaviour?*"

"Yeah. Weird. Hey, Bon – you know that first night we were here, when the lights in the bedrooms went on, one after the other?"

"Yeah – it freaked me."

"I bet Rupert regiments everyone's sex life. I bet that's what it was about. They all have to do it on command."

"Oh, gross, shut up –"

"No seriously, Bon – that was Durex time—"

We both stop dead. "*Why* didn't I park somewhere else?" groans Bonny.

A very familiar figure is speeding towards us, and a hideous, familiar voice is squawking, "There, Carol! I told you it was her car! *Darling!* It's *ME-EEE*!"

Chapter 41

Bonny's frozen at my side. Tigger hurtles towards her, scary, greedy arms outstretched. She's dressed in baggy harem pants and a flimsy purple scarf that billows behind her like toxic steam. She's dressed for the Fellowship – alternative, spiritual, even – but she still looks like a vampire to me. I half expect her to emerge from embracing her daughter with her mouth dripping blood.

"Isn't this *terrible*!" she squeals, letting go of Bonny, face agog with pleasure and excitement. "Such a *drama*!"

"Why are you here, Mum?" asks Bonny, stony-faced.

"Oh – darling! It was *fate*! I phoned Carol, just for a chat – and she burst into tears on me! And then the *whole story* came out, of course. All about Lizzie leaving home without saying a word, without telling Carol where she was going – so hurtful – and all about *you*, darling, coming up here to find her. And *then* she mentioned Lizzie's boyfriend had taken her to a commune. *Well*. Alarm bells went off for me then, I can tell you! *What sort of commune is it?* I asked. *People get up to all kinds of things in a commune. Drugs, orgies, anything. It could be a cult,* I said. *They could be* brainwashing *her*."

"Helpful of you, Mum," says Bonny, dully.

"It's never good to avoid the truth, darling. Well, Carol didn't know anything *about* the commune, of course. Said she was relying on you to find out. She's *desperately* grateful to you, Bonny darling, of course she is, but I *knew* – as a *mother* – she couldn't just sit around at home, leaving it all up to someone else. She had to *act*! Carol said she thought you'd be better at talking to Lizzie, and I said – *Carol, you're her* mother*! Of course she'll talk to you! And besides that, you can't just wait around when your daughter is quite possibly in terrible danger.* I mean – *well*! What mother could? So I'm afraid I was a bit naughty then. I was a real bossyboots, wasn't I Carol? I said – *Pack a bag, I'll drive, we're leaving tonight.* And we did! *Well* – I'm like that, aren't I, Bonny, utterly impulsive. I had to cancel a job to come, but what are friends for? Carol would've gone *mad* at home, just waiting around for news! Wouldn't you, Carol?"

Carol – anxious-looking, dumpy, short mahogany-coloured hair – has been trying to get a word in all through this tirade. Now her mouth stops opening and closing like a beached fish and forms itself into a weak smile. "Yes. . ." she murmurs. "Bonny, I'm sorry, I should've phoned you, but in the rush, I forgot to scribble down your number. . ."

"S'all right," mutters Bonny. "I expect you were in shock."

"Oh, she still is, aren't you, Carol?" brays Tigger. "Utterly shocked. Who wouldn't be, being treated like that by her *own daughter*?"

"I didn't mean—"

"The *one person* who's supposed to love you most in all the world? Of course, Bonny, if you'd let *me* have your mobile number, there wouldn't've been a problem, would there, and we'd've known where to *come*. . ."

Bonny sighs. "You didn't have to come, Mum. Rich and I are sorting it out."

"Oh, listen to her. *Rich and I!* Darling – I nearly passed *out* when Carol told me you'd come up here with Richy! Honestly, Bonny – fancy not telling *Mummy*! But then you always were such a secretive little girl! Now – are you still claiming to be *just friends*, or what?"

I put my arm round Bonny's shoulders and say, "No, we're not just friends. Not any more."

The macaw-like scream which erupts from

Tigger's mouth sends a group of rooks panicking off a nearby treetop. "*Ooooh*, that's *wonderful*! Oh, *darling*! I want to hear *all* about it! D'you know – I *knew* you were made for each other." She turns on me, wags her finger in a grisly parody of playfulness. "So it really is all over with that gorgeous girl Portia, is it, you wicked boy? You finally realized that looks aren't everything?"

Her closing comment hits our ears like a slab of concrete. "I realized I liked Bonny's looks better," I say loudly. "As well as just about everything else about her."

"Oh, isn't he *gallant*? Isn't he *sweet*? What a catch, Bonny – don't you go letting *this* one get away! Now – let's all go eat somewhere. Come on, darlings – my treat. I'm *shattered*. I've just had a *huge*, long interview with Rupert – well, Carol was there too, but she was too upset to contribute much, weren't you, darling? So really it was all down to me. He seems such a sensitive, spiritual man – one had to be so careful, so delicate. As well as ask the right, penetrating questions. About poor Lizzie's welfare. *Exhausting*. Rupert asked me to stay and dine with him – between you and me, I think he was a bit taken by me! But – well, he hadn't asked Carol, too, so I thought I'd better decline, I could hardly leave her on her own in the state she was in, could I?"

There's a brief pause as Tigger recharges her lungs. "Bonny, have you seen Liz?" gulps Carol.

"Yes. She's OK. She's—"

"We saw her, just quickly. Rupert sent for her . . . Kell was there too. She told me she was fine. But she was like a *robot* – and she seemed so *scared* –"

"I know – I think she is scared."

"Kell hits her, doesn't he?"

"Now, Carol, you don't *know* that!" shrills Tigger. "Rupert was adamant that nothing like that was going on. It's just these really rather sweet ideas they have about going back to the old order of things, men being men, women being women. . ."

"I think – *maybe* – he does hit her," says Bonny. "But we're going to get her out. We're going back tomorrow – Rupert thinks we want to join up and—"

"Well, he thinks *I* do too!" squawks Tigger. "I was terribly convincing, wasn't I, Carol? Of course – I had a head start. I know all about these kinds of alternative groups – I used to be a hippy. Well, not a real hippy, I'm far too young. But when I was about sixteen I had this older lover – oh, he was *wonderful*. And he was a hippy. Fabulous long black hair. He played the guitar like an angel." She pauses, simpers. "He used to call me Stardust."

There's a short, nauseated pause. Then Bonny says, "Mum – it might be better if you stayed away tomorrow. Liz is far more likely to open up to me than she is to you."

"That's what I said—" begins poor Carol.

"Oh, Bonny, *don't* go getting all silly and possessive!" screeches Tigger, shooting her daughter a savage look. "I know this is your little *project*, sweetheart, and of course you can talk to *Liz*. But I've struck up quite a rapport with Rupert, and it would be madness to waste that—"

"Rupert's mental," I put in, bluntly. "You can strike up what you like with him, it won't mean a toss once we've got Liz to agree to leave that place."

Tigger waves a heavily-ringed hand dismissively; her toxic scarf floats up behind her head. "Oh, *Richy*. You young boys – so *one-track*. No good at seeing a subtle side to things."

"*Can* you have dinner with us?" pleads Carol, obviously expecting us to cut and run at any minute. "Then we can talk—"

"Of course they can!" interjects Tigger. "Come on, follow me. Dinner at our hotel. The George – only twenty minutes away. The food's quite acceptable really, for somewhere so far north. Passable wine list too. Drive carefully, Bonny darling." Tigger turns to me, adds, "She gets so *nervous* still – especially on the big roads."

"She's a great driver," I say.

"Oh, he's so *sweet*!" trills Tigger, and totters off in her wine-coloured suede ankle-boots to her car.

We lock ourselves in Bonny's little car and swear horribly for a minute or so, full of disbelief at how appalling

Tigger is. Then I squeeze Bon's leg and say "OK, babe – *breathe*. Breathe in and out, and let all the stuff she came out with wash away like the sewage it is."

"It's OK," she says, almost laughing. "It's OK. You know – for *once* – I was actually able to stand back from it all."

"Great. That's *great*."

"I mean – she's just horrific, isn't she?"

"Yup. And not only to you. The way she scared the shit out of poor old Carol, the way she bullied her to come up here –"

"Ironic, really. She's right about the Fellowship."

"Although now she seems to have fallen for Rupert. *Such a sensitive, spiritual man. . .*"

"*Don't* do her voice, Rich. It makes me think of *Psycho*." I laugh, and Bonny goes on, "She hasn't got the same power she had, that's what's so brilliant. You know – to make me feel like shit."

"Great. 'Cos, *boy*, was she trying."

Bonny sighs, puts the keys in the ignition. "Think you can stand having dinner with her?"

"Do we have a choice?"

"Not really. *God*. All this – it's just another chance for Mum to show off, prove how great she is. She's so excited about it all – it's sick. She doesn't give a toss about Liz."

"Or Carol. So what's new."

Bonny turns to me. "Rich – it's 'cos of you I feel OK. It's 'cos you're here."

"Well, I'd love to claim the credit," I gruff out, touched, "but it's not only 'cos of that and you know it. It's you, too. You've made the break. You're so much stronger."

"We won't stay long," says Bonny, dimpling up. God, I *love* it when her face does that. "We'll just eat, and talk to Carol, and scarper."

"You're on." I plant a big kiss on her cheek, glance up, say, "Urgh – look – the vampire's pulled out – we'd better go."

Bonny's just starting the Polo up when Tigger sticks her head out of her car and calls back, "OK, Bonny darling? You've not stalled, have you?"

Bonny's car roars angrily into life, and we're off.

The George is exactly the kind of grand, pompous place you'd expect Tigger to stay at if denied somewhere really fashionable – it's all nineteenth-century splendour and sycophantic staff. We're ushered through into the dining room immediately; drinks are ordered and brought. I scan the menu, and decide to have the most expensive steak on offer.

Carol's looking really dejected. Anyone would, I suppose, being battered at by Tigger for a whole day. She empties her wine glass almost in one go, and the waiter refills it.

"Now," says Tigger, all conspiratorial. "What are our plans for tomorrow? I've agreed to meet Rupert at eleven o'clock. I feel quite special – he's asked me to sit in on a Meditation Tuition session. One of the advanced ones – one of the ones *he* takes."

"Useful," I grunt.

"I thought so. Useful in trying to find out what the Fellowship is all about."

"Mum," says Bonny, "we're not bothered about what it's about! We just want to get Liz out!"

"Don't you think that's a little narrow, darling? To judge a place before you've understood it?"

"I've understood it," I say. "Rupert's an ego-obsessed nutter and Kell's a bastard. Liz would be far better off without the pair of them."

Tigger turns on me, mouth open ready to fire, but Carol, who's nearly emptied her second glass of wine, gets in first. "Rich – do *you* think he hits her?"

"Yes. He treats her like shit."

Carol grabs a napkin from the table, sniffles into it.

"There – see what you've done?" spits Tigger. "Ever heard of the word *tact*, Richard? It's OK, Carol darling. Don't listen to him. We don't know anything yet."

"It's her *father's* fault," wails Carol, emerging from the napkin. "It's all a reaction to him! He never had much time for her when she was little – and then the way he left home – like she didn't matter at all! He made her feel worthless!"

"Bonny's father was the same," soothes Tigger. "But luckily I managed to make up for it—"

"Girls like that – they get in relationships with

awful men! They don't think they deserve anyone good. I've been reading all about it – it's because they're insecure."

"I know, darling. I know. Bonny too. Her father was appalling. It's such a pattern."

"Dad was *not* like that, Mum!" says Bonny, fiercely. "He made me feel great. And my relationship with *Rich* is great. He's –"

"Bonny – we're not here to talk about *you*!" erupts Tigger. "We're here to talk about *Liz*!"

There's no other response to this but to burst out laughing. Which I do. Tigger glares at me, scandalized. "Something *funny*, Richard?" I shake my head, finish off my beer. "Honestly – you might *try* to be a bit more sensitive. Think of Carol!"

"I am thinking of Carol," I say. "Carol – we're going in tomorrow. We're going to get Liz out of there if it kills us."

Carol gives me a hopeful, desperate smile and sniffles, "Suppose she wants to stay?"

"Exactly!" trills Tigger. "She may be finding what she wants there, what she—"

"I really don't think she does," says Bonny to Carol. "We had dinner with her, yesterday. I think she's beginning to see Kell for what he is."

"Yeah, she is," I add. "She's also beginning to realize that the Fellowship is Planet Insanity."

Carol disappears into her napkin again. "I wish you could keep an open mind about all this!" nags

Tigger. "Some of the things Rupert was saying were *beautiful* – it would do you two good to follow them, frankly! Carol doesn't want you just railroading in there, do you, Carol? She wants you to *discuss* everything with Lizzie, *listen* to her, to find out how she really feels about the Fellowship, whether it's just a bad patch with Kell, whether it can be worked on, maybe talk with Rupert, ask his advice, he's such an inspirational man, he's—"

Carol reappears from the napkin, eyes blazing. "Oh, Tigger, for goodness' sake, *shut up*! I just want Liz *out of there*!"

For a few beautiful moments Tigger is too stunned to speak. Bonny and I exchange top-speed grins; Carol leans across the table towards us. "I'm so grateful to you two, I can't tell you. Just get her out for me!"

"We will," says Bonny.

The waiter appears at the table. "Fillet steak, please, mate," I order cheerfully. "The extra-large one, with onion rings and chips."

Chapter 42

Back at The Green Man, Bonny and I lie in each others' arms and discuss the day, laughing as we remember Tigger's face when Carol told her to shut up. "You saw how quickly she recovered, though, didn't you?" asks Bonny. "She lives in her own reality. She'll interpret it as Carol having a little outburst due to stress. She'll *forgive* her."

"God, poor Carol."

"I know, being *forgiven* by Mum – she's stressed out enough as it is. Did you see how much wine she put away?"

"I don't blame her, spending all that time with Tigger. I had three beers and we were only there for an hour."

"That's your excuse, is it? What about the huge pudding?"

"Yeah, well, I thought if your mum was paying —"

"Rich, we've *got* to get Liz on her own tomorrow."

"Trouble is, if you wander about, you break their poxy rules, and they'll ban you —"

"I know. I'm gonna have to be so careful."

"We both are. No more smooching in the shrubbery —"

"No infra-sex, or we'll be banned from dinner again —" She tightens her arms round me.

"What can I do to help?" I whisper. "Beat up Kell?"

"Just be there, Rich. If I know you're there, it's OK."

And then we're kissing, and then making love, like it's a sweet continuation, a part of the conversation we're having together. "You won't let her ruin things, will you," she murmurs. "Mum, I mean. You won't let her come between us."

"Bonny — she doesn't stand a chance against what we've got."

When we're satisfied and drowsy I make Bon laugh telling her about Quentin the long-haired weirdo and his pledge. "I think that's quite romantic," says Bonny. "In a way."

"*Romantic?*" I scoff. "Psychotic more like."

"It's like one of those old stories."

"What, Rapunzel?"

She shakes her head. "No — more like the girl who kept her lover's head in a basil pot."

"What the *hell* –?"

"Her brothers killed him, cut off his head, and she kept it, she buried it in this pot with basil growing out of it. . ."

"*Jesus*, Bon, if that's your idea of romantic, I'm not looking forward to Valentine's day."

She laughs, and we hug each other tight, and I know she's thinking, like I am, of February 14th next year, wondering how we'll celebrate it in a kind of sending-up but meaning-it-underneath way, sure we'll still be together then.

It's a great feeling.

Ten-thirty the next morning, we're back at the Fellowship. I'm put on Gardening Duty, on the potato patch, and Bonny's whisked off to the Laundry. The unspoken hope passes between us that Liz might be in the Laundry too, since she was carrying a pile of towels yesterday.

There are only three interruptions to the extreme back-breaking tedium of my potato-trench digging day:

1) 11.45 a.m.: Helena from the kitchen appears at my side, with a mug of tea, two apricot cookies, and some heavy-duty flirting, which recedes a bit when I swallow a cookie whole and then burp.

2) 1 p.m.: I get to sit with Bon over lunch and she

hisses at me that she's seen Liz. Who didn't speak but apparently did a lot of desperate signalling with her eyes. This doesn't seem much to me, but Bonny's triumphant, sure that she'll get to her tonight at dinner, sure that Liz is ready to make the dash for freedom. We get up to as much infra-sexual under-table activity as we can. It's dead erotic, a bit like making out in church.

3) 3.30 p.m.: Tigger (in flowing terracotta robes and big clanking necklace) glides by the potato patch, accompanied by Rupert. She makes a big thing out of not knowing me, and another big thing out of knowing Rupert. She has her hand looped through his arm; she's laughing extravagantly.

4) 4.45 p.m.: Frazer appears, tells me to bugger off and have a bath at the pub. Then I can return for dinner. *Success!*

"This is it, Rich," says Bonny, excitedly, as we drive back to The Green Man. "Tonight's the night. I met this really nice girl in the laundry – well, loopy as hell, but nice. And she told me that before dinner, the boys and girls get together in the dining hall annexe for drinks. Only they're not together 'cos the boys are at one end, and the girls are at the other."

"Oh, my God. All part of Rupert's New Way for the sexes?"

"You got it. The separating of male and female energies, she said – before they fuse over dinner."

"Great. So you'll see Liz then –"

"And maybe you can keep Kell occupied?"

"If I must," I groan.

While Bonny's in the shower, I lie on the bed and think about sex. I don't mean the usual physical stuff, with Bonny being naked just the other side of the door and everything. No, I'm getting philosophical. I make a revolutionary link between prudish, preachy types who deep down want to illegalize sex, and laddish, wa–hey, gimme-some-of-that-types who rent porn videos and whose idea of a brilliant career move is to become a five-shags-a-night rep on the Costa del Sleaze. And this link is: both types see sex as dirty. The prudish types hate it and the wa–hey types love it, but they both basically have the same take on it. Both of them put sex in a box, shut it away, cut it off from the normal flow of life. You can't do that to real sex, I decide. Real sex takes you over, it's there with you at breakfast, it walks alongside you, it fills your veins. It's a true, real part of you, there all the time.

Shit – where's all this come from? Does it mean I'm in love?

Chapter 43

We go back into the Fellowship like the original Twin Avengers, all charged up. I feel like I could take Kell apart with my bare hands. I tell Bonny this and she laughs, says she hopes it won't come to that.

"All right," I agree. "But tonight is definitely the night. Crunch time. And look, Bon – if Liz *has* decided she wants to stay, you've got to give up, OK?"

"I know. But she won't. You should've seen the way she *looked* at me."

"OK, this is it." We've reached the doors of the annexe, and we're immediately swept up in a tide of Beloveds, all smirking and making serious eye contact with each other. Down the middle of the annexe, separating it into two halves, is a trestle table laid out as a bar with glasses and bottles of wine. The women are heading to the right, the men to the left. I squeeze Bon's hand, mouth, "*Good luck*," and we're off on our separate paths.

I spot Kell right away, standing in the corner craning his neck to see over to the other side of the long room. Better get over there, I think, and deflect him from spotting Bonny heading for Liz. But I'll get myself a drink first – if I've got to talk to him I'll need it. At the bar I ask for a beer, but the ice-maiden serving says there is none. "Rupert directs that only wine should be provided," she drones. "It has higher and more refined energies than beer."

I choke back my response to this, settle for a glass of cheap red plonk and head over to Kell at speed. "Bet you're – you *are* – dead surprised to see *me* here, aren't you?" I ask, brightly.

He glares at me with acute distaste, karate-chopping me at the same time. "No. I saw you gardening."

"Well, aren't you going to ask what happened to change my mind? About the Fellowship?"

"I am not remotely interested. I am only surprised that Rupert permitted it."

"Permitted it? He practically *begged* us to join up. We had a long talk with him, and we *jelled*. Rupert said we were exactly the sort of people he wanted here. Especially Bonny. He reckons she's been called."

Kell snorts with disbelief, and turns away like he can't be bothered to question me further, craning his neck towards the other side of the room again. I follow his stare, and see that Bon and Liz are standing face to face. "Why are they talking?" he snarls. "I do not want that female to influence Elizabeth."

"Mate, fear not! It's Liz that's doing the influencing! Bon's really curious about the Fellowship, really drawn to it – she wants to find out all about it."

"And you?"

"Well – I'd do anything for Bon. I'm mad about her." I'd already decided to take this tack, that it was me following Bonny, 'cos I knew I couldn't quite pull off making out *I'd* had the call.

Kell's face is distorted into his favourite sneer. "You will have to change *that* balance if you come here."

"What d'you mean?"

"Rupert directs that men and women should find their true levels. The man leads; the woman follows. '*He for God only, she for God in him*.'"

"*What?*"

"That is Milton. Rupert thinks a lot of Milton. And, by the way, your conversation is riddled with connectives and if you make no effort to stop them I cannot be expected to photograph every one."

"Sorry, mate," I say humbly, trying not to laugh. "So men and women aren't equal here, then?"

"They are not *equal* anywhere. But here, the inequality is recognized. *Celebrated*. Women have their separate strengths which come out best when under the guidance of a man."

My urge to laugh is almost overwhelming now. I'm thinking what Bon would say if she was here. Or whether she'd abandon talking and just whack him one. "Sounds cool, man," I gulp. "You mean they got to do what you say?"

"It is not as simple as that," he says shortly. "The man has great responsibilities. Elizabeth has been going through a difficult readjustment period. She cannot yet see the higher way – the freedom that comes from submission."

I'm let off having to respond by the sound of an irritating little bell, rung vigorously by the ice-maiden behind the trestle-table bar. As one, the Beloveds turn and trot into the dining room. I follow, repressing a strong desire to bleat like a sheep.

As we flow into the hall, the Beloveds start to eddy around in what could almost be confusion. Everyone who is part of a couple – which is just about every-one – is seeking out their other half. Kell heads off like a heat-seeking missile to track down poor old Liz. And there's Bonny, coming straight for me.

"She wants out," she hisses.

"You sure?"

"*Yes*. She has horrible bruises right round her neck. She pulled her jumper down to show me. He tried to strangle her last night."

"Oh, *God* –"

"She was so scared she could hardly talk. She's terrified of him. He's –"

Bonny breaks off. The couple to our right have stopped eddying and are waiting pointedly for us to seat ourselves. So we do, and they sit next to us. "I've sorted it out," Bonny says. "It'll be OK to do it tonight." The woman sitting next to her karate chops her grimly; we both shut up.

Once we're all eating and the nosy couple has started chatting, Bonny hisses, "Right after dinner *he* has some special all–male meditation session. She's supposed to just go to their room. He's been locking her in."

"*What?*"

"I'm *serious*. She says there's a way in through a window. We have half an hour to get her out, and get away."

I motion with my eyes to the guy next to her, who's started listening to us again. "I think we should do that little job as soon as dinner is over, Richard," Bonny says, all casual. "That would be the best time."

Chapter 44

Bonny and I lurk about at the end of dinner, wait until Kell steers Liz out of the dining hall, then we follow them. "I just need to see which stairs to go up," whispers Bonny. "I know the way after that."

We watch Liz disappear round the top of the stairs, like she's going to the executioner's block, then we retreat until we see Kell come down and go off back to the main part of the house for his all-male meditation session.

Then we head up. "Bon, you *sure* this is the right corridor?"

"Yes. She said keep left all the way. It's second from the end. There. That's the door."

We both stand and look at it. Somehow neither of us wants to knock, just in case it's not Liz inside.

"This is so over the top," I grumble. "I mean – if she wants to get out, why didn't she just walk out, with you, before dinner? What would Kell do – what *could* he do, with everyone else there?"

"Well – I suggested that. She looked *terrified* – she couldn't do it. I don't know if it's Kell, or Rupert, or both of them together, but the only way we can get her out is like this, I promise you."

Bonny crouches down against the key-hole, hisses "Liz! *Liz!*"

There's a faint answering squeak. Bonny wrenches at the door handle; it's locked. "Shall I break it open?" I breathe.

She shakes her head. "Too much noise. Look – there's the window, at the end. Liz says there's this little balcony that goes all the way round."

"So why didn't she just get out that way?"

"'Cos this window is kept locked. Look."

The big sash window has two screw-bolt locks, but they're easy to undo. The window slides up soundlessly. I look down at the slim balcony, running underneath it. "Reckon it's safe?" I murmur.

"Yes – look at those huge plant pots it's supporting." We crane round to the right, and hear a faint "*Hello. . .*"

"Is she coming to us, or what?"

"No, she's too scared. And she told me she had two bags. I'll go along –"

"Let me go, Bon."

But Bonny shakes her head. "She's in a real state, Rich. She's like jelly. I'll be better with her."

"You sure?"

"Yeah. You stay here and if Kell comes back, deck him."

"Trust me."

She gives me a kiss and hops out through the window. I watch her inch her way along the skinny balcony with her back against the wall, then turn the corner. Then I hear some low, excited talking and the sound of scrambling, and I know she's made it into Liz's room. I head back to the bedroom door. "All right in there?" I hiss, through the keyhole.

There's no answer, but I can hear them talking together – Bonny all reassuring, and Liz shrill, weepy. It goes through my mind that if Liz is in such a state I should get in through the window too, and help take the bags while Bonny handles Liz. And that's where I make my big mistake. I press my ear to the door to hear how things are going instead of keeping my eyes glued on the corridor. That's why I don't spot Kell until it's too late. I look up just in time to see his fist heading for my face.

Chapter 45

I move, fast, but he catches my jaw. The pain jolts me back; he follows it up with a shove that sends me sprawling. By the time I'm on my feet again he's got a key in the lock, he's pushing open the door. I lurch in after him, fists hard, ready to fight. He's not facing me, though, he's facing the wide-open window on the other side of the room. Bonny's out on the balcony, clutching a small suitcase. Liz is still inside, frozen like a rabbit in headlights, her face grey with shock. Her terror fills the room; drains the anger pumping through me.

Kell makes for the window like a bullet and I'm flooded with fear. I shout, "Get back!" and Kell lunges out at Bonny like he wants to knock her off the building but she's jumped out of reach, she keeps her balance. Oh, *Jesus*. I watch her as she disappears round the corner to safety.

Cursing, Kell slams the window shut. Liz doesn't move, just flinches at the noise. I start to rush him but before I get to him his arm shoots out and grabs Liz's arm.

I stop dead. "Let go of her," I say, trying to sound calm. I feel like I'm dealing with a madman. An unexploded bomb.

He stands and stares at me, and while he's staring he twists her arm, twists it round and down until she collapses on to the floor.

Then he lets go of her arm, and steps clear away from her, still facing me. He's so sure of how scared she is. Sure she won't move. "Get out," he says. "Go and collect your girlfriend, and get out."

"We're not going without Liz," I say. I make a move towards her but Kell blocks me. "Come on, Liz, stand up. He can't hurt you when I'm here."

Kell scoffs. And Liz doesn't move. "You need help, mate," I say. I want to reach down to her but I know if I do he'll be on me. "Look what you've done to her. You're sick."

"It's the world that's sick," he spits. "You have not the slightest understanding of what is happening here – what *new order* Rupert is trying to bring about."

"And that new order includes hitting girls, does it, you bastard?"

His face jumps. "*Get out.* I don't have to explain myself to you. The lower cannot see the higher."

"Yeah? Well, in my book, you can't get much lower than hitting women. So it's you that can't see, mate. You can't see anything."

Kell takes a step towards me, fists bunched. Behind me, someone has walked into the room. I don't risk taking my eyes off Kell but I know it's Bonny. "Come on, Liz," she says. Her voice is trembling just a little. "Let's get out of here."

Liz looks up, but she doesn't move. Bonny walks towards her. And suddenly Kell lunges, and shoves Bonny back, hard. I catch her, steady her. Then I pitch myself at him, slam him back against the wall.

"*Don't you touch her*," I breathe. Our faces are almost touching. He bares his teeth like he's going to bite me, then he shoves me back. We face each other, waiting. Then I swing, a good hard one to the side of his head. He lunges at me, grabs me; we crash against a table. And he's on me like a madman. We're both flailing punches like crazy, like a frenzied playground fight, and right now he's winning. He gets my head in an armlock; I'm bucking furiously to stop his fist smashing my face. I slam my elbow into his stomach, wind him just enough to make him loosen his grip, wrench myself away.

Then we're scrambling to our feet and facing each other again. "Come on," he says, panting. "Come *on.*"

"Look, *fuck-head*, I'll fight you if you want. But nothing's going to change the fact that Liz is leaving here tonight."

"*Come on*," he roars, and rushes at me. We're smashing at each other like berserkers when somehow over the top of flesh hitting flesh and Bonny screeching at us to stop I hear, "*What on earth is going on in here?*"

And then two guys are grabbing my arms, wrestling me to the floor.

Rupert towers over me. Kell's been grabbed too. But Kell pulls his arm free from the guy on his right, who doesn't recapture it. Kell points at me, hand shaking with rage. "He broke in. Into our room."

I jerk at my arms but they're held fast. "*Let go of me!*" I shout.

"We will let go of you when we have sorted this out," proclaims Rupert. "What are you doing here? Why are you in Kell and Elizabeth's room?"

"We're getting her out of here," I say. "She wants to leave, but—"

"We have discussed this. She had her chance to leave."

"She's terrified. He beats her up." From the corner of my eye I see Kell tug his other arm free.

"What nonsense. You two have betrayed my trust. You lied your way in here. You have betrayed the Fellowship."

I get this cold, creepy feeling that something very

nasty is about to happen. And I'm pinned like a chicken.

"*Oh, for Christ's sake,*" erupts Bonny. "Liz – tell him. *Show* him." She pulls Liz over to Rupert, she tugs at the neck of her jumper, pulls it down to show the necklace of purple bruises. "*There*. He did that. And she's terrified. Look at her. She's really screwed up. She's too screwed up to just *leave*. You and Kell did that – between you, you did that. I don't know what's been going on here to make her that way – apart from getting knocked around by *that* scumbag – but I'm gonna find out. And if you know what's best for you, you'll let us go. Now."

I think, *That's done it, Bon*, and wrench at my arms again, half expecting Rupert to come at me with a syringe full of something dazing and powerful. But instead, Rupert turns his massive head to Kell.

"Did you do that?" he asks. "Those bruises?"

"You told me to be firm with her," mutters Kell. "You said she was too volatile."

There's a silence. Then Rupert makes some kind of sign with his eyes at my two jailors, who drop my arms. "OK, Bonny, get Liz," I say. "Hand me that bag. Come on."

Kell stands motionless. No one touches him.

Bonny picks up the bag; I take it from her. Then she puts her arm round Liz and steers her to the door.

I follow them. The back of my neck is prickling like crazy, but I won't let myself look back.

Then when the girls are safe through the door, I do turn back. "Don't think this is the last of it, buster," I say to Rupert.

"Those bruises are nothing to do with the Fellowship," he replies. "I abhor violence."

"Maybe, but it was here it happened. It was what goes on here that let it happen. It was the way that sick-head interpreted the crap you come out with here."

Rupert turns away; one of his lackeys shuts the bedroom door on me.

I catch up with Bonny and Liz, take Liz's other arm, and together we half steer, half carry her. All the way down the stairs, all the way through the hall. Out of the front door, all the way down the long drive, and out through the great iron gates.

Chapter 46

Inside the car, sitting in the front seat, Liz starts to cry. She cries and cries, not hysterical exactly, just like she can't stop. Bonny has her arms round her, hugging her – I'm sitting like a spare part in the back, wishing I wasn't so useless and could drive.

"Liz," murmurs Bonny, "Liz, c'mon – I want to get us back to the pub, OK?"

It's like Liz hasn't heard, though. Like she can't hear.

"Liz – back at the pub, you can sleep. C'mon. I want to put some distance between us and this place, OK?"

That seems to get through. Liz nods her head, sniffs. As Bonny frees up her hands to drive, I lean over from the back and put my hands on Liz's shoulders. Then I kind of massage her shoulders, all the way back to the pub, half to comfort her, half to keep some kind of hold on her, in case she collapses on to Bonny.

It's getting on for nine-thirty when we pull into the pub car park, although – with everything that's been going on – it feels more like three in the morning. And Liz suddenly speaks. "I don't want to see Mum," she croaks. "Not tonight. She'll get all upset and I just can't *deal* with that now. . ."

"OK," says Bonny, carefully, "but I ought to phone her, Liz, tell her we've got you out –"

"Oh, Bonny, thanks."

"I'll tell her you're OK – but knackered. I'll tell her you've gone to bed."

"Don't let her come over, will you. I can't face her tonight, not all her questions and everything. . ."

It seems like the wrong time to ask where exactly Liz is going to go to bed. We half carry her into The Green Man; I can see the proprietor peering out curiously from behind the bar as we walk through the entrance hall, and I call out, "Be down in a minute, mate, OK?" He's going to need some kind of explanation.

Once we're in our room, Bonny steers Liz on to the bed and Liz sits there, hunched, as though her stomach hurts her. "D'you want a coffee, Liz?" asks Bonny, gently.

Liz doesn't answer. She kind of twists, collapses,

on to the bed; then she's crawling towards the pillows; she pushes one into her face, and just *howls*. It's not loud, all muffled by the pillow, but it's terrible, full of grief, it hardly sounds human. Bonny climbs up next to her straight away, wraps her arms round her and just holds on.

"D'you want anything?" I hiss, trying not to sound as freaked as I feel. "Like a drink?"

Bonny nods. "Brandy," she says. "Two."

At the bar, I say, "Bit of a crisis on, I'm afraid."

"You got her out, then," the owner replies. "What happened to your face? Put up a fight, did they?"

"Something like that," I mutter. "I need two brandies for the girls."

"And another for you?"

"I'll have a beer, mate. I'll be back down for it in a minute. Look –"

"Yes?"

"All right if she crashes here tonight?"

I'm half expecting him to make trouble, insist we book another room, but he nods his head straight away. "Course it is. Poor kid."

"I'll sleep on the floor, or something."

"There's some extra bedding, top of the wardrobe."

"Thanks. I really appreciate it."

I take the brandies up to the room. I feel a bit weird about going in again, if you want the truth – scared of the state Liz'll be in. And there's something else. That room, that bed – it was precious to me and Bonny, sacrosanct. I feel almost like Liz will infect it with her misery . . . I tell myself not to be a selfish prat, and push the door open with my foot.

Miraculously, Liz has stopped crying – she's hunched on the bed with the duvet round her, a mug of coffee in her hand. Bonny's talking to her in a low voice. I put the brandies on the bedside table and leave as invisibly as I can.

The proprietor of The Green Man is very patient with me for the next hour or so. I tell him the girls are talking and he lets me sit at the bar and rant on about how deranged the Fellowship is. He even joins in the conversation a bit, in between serving people. "What's it *for*, that's what I don't get," I say. "Why on earth would you go there?"

He shrugs. "Some people are looking for a teacher. You know – for enlightenment."

"Oh, bollocks, *enlightenment*. What's that mean?"

He polishes a beer glass thoughtfully. "I've read a bit about it. There's this idea that we just sleepwalk through life – a teacher wakes you up."

"So does an alarm clock. Come on – who needs to be told how to live?"

"Not you, evidently."

"Anyway, there's no way Rupert is any sort of teacher. He's so phoney. He's a complete fake."

"I'm sure he is." He turns away, picks up a fistful of dirty glasses. "Ever heard the saying: there's only counterfeit gold because the real stuff exists?"

I'm not sure I've heard him right at first, then I think I probably have, but I'm not sure I understand what he's on about. "Cheers, mate," I say. "I'm going up. See how things are."

He smiles at me. "Good luck, lad."

When I get upstairs, the room is dark, and Liz and Bonny are asleep, stretched out side by side under the duvet. I pull the curtain back a little, let the moonlight in on their faces. Liz looks white, but oddly peaceful. Bonny looks gorgeous. I think how great she is, how strong she is, the way she's looked out for her friend and taken care of her, and I'm suddenly full of wanting to get in beside her, wanting to sleep up close against her.

There's almost room for me on her side of the bed. I strip off my jeans and top, slide under the duvet. "Mmmmph," she breathes. She twists towards me, nestles into me like even in her sleep she knows who I am. I put my arms round her, loving the warmth of her. Then very gently I reach out with one hand and shunt Liz a little further across the bed, and shuffle the two of us into the space.

Chapter 47

"*Rich!*" Bonny's hissing into my ear. "Rich – wake up!" She's propped up on one elbow, smiling down at me, smoothing the bruise over my eye with a careful finger. "You cheeky bugger, were you hoping for a threesome or something?"

"No way. Just you. You looked so lovely, I just found myself getting in beside you –"

"I thought you'd sleep on the floor!"

"Too hard, babe."

She clambers over me, ignoring my seductive efforts to pull her on top of me. "I'm going to get dressed. You get up too, Rich."

"I am up."

"Oh, *shut* up. Come on – let's get breakfast. I've got to talk to you."

"What about Liz?"

"I'm gonna leave her to sleep as long as she can. She's absolutely wiped. Now get out of there – I'm not having you lying in bed with my best mate!"

Thirty minutes later we're all showered and dressed and sitting downstairs in the sunny breakfast room at the front of the pub, with a fat teapot between us and toast on the way. And I'm gagging with curiosity. Bonny had refused to tell me anything while we got up – she said she couldn't risk Liz overhearing.

"Well?" I demand.

"*Well* – I don't know where to start. The Fellowship is sick, even worse than we thought. It has all this *power* over anyone who goes there. And Kell is the biggest bastard going. He not only hit her, he played on how scared she got, so he could control her. To make her fit in with the Fellowship. Between them they *really* messed her up."

"If it was that bad, why the *hell* didn't she just get out?"

Bonny glares at me. "Because she couldn't."

"Oh, *come* on, she could've done a runner. You telling me they had her chained up the whole time?"

"No, but . . . *OK*. You listen to what happened, and then see if you still think she could've just *done a runner*. He's *hurt* her, Rich. I mean it. She's damaged. It's going to take her ages to get over it."

"I know, I know." There's a silence, then I reach apologetically round the teapot and take Bonny's

319

hand. "Liz'll be OK, Bon. She's got you as a mate."

Bonny smiles down at the table.

"Come on – tell me what happened." I urge. "Start at the beginning."

"Well – they got there," says Bonny, taking in a deep breath, "and she hated the place straight away – all the rules and the craziness. She tried to fit in and get involved, because Kell wanted her to, but it was clear pretty soon that it suited him a lot better than it suited her. Rupert kept going on about the *progress* he was making, and taking him off for special meetings, while she got treated like a failure. They'd have the fattest arguments, and she'd talk about leaving and he'd beg her to stay. He said, *If you loved me, you'd love this place too.*"

"Wanker."

"Yeah. He didn't even consider leaving with her. He said if he left, he'd be betraying his inner being – that the Fellowship was what he'd been searching for all his life. And – you know – he had this *hold* over her. She was besotted with him. He'd talk and talk and she'd end up convinced he was right. And she'd promise to give it another go and sometimes he'd make love to her – like a kind of reward—"

"*What?*"

"One of his things, apparently, was he didn't want to have sex very often—"

"Is he queer or something?"

"No, he just thought sex should be special. Liz

said she felt she had to *earn* it."

"*Bloody* hell."

"Anyway, the next day she'd be full of good intentions, but pretty soon she'd be back to square one. . ."

"Right. Peeling half a tonne of potatoes in the kitchen and wondering what the hell she was doing there."

"The potatoes were the easy bit. It was all the meditation and readings and exercises that really screwed her up. Some days she felt part of it – some days she just wanted to run away and scream. It was an absolutely horrible time, she said – she felt desperate, confused, with no one to talk to –"

"Why didn't she ring you?"

"It was against the rules."

"Oh, bollocks. Surely she could've sneaked out and phoned you?"

"She said she thought about it. But it would have been so awful if she'd been caught. She tried discussing what she felt with some of the others but everyone had swallowed the party line. They'd tell her that fighting the Fellowship, criticizing it, was her bad, mechanical side. . . *If you question what's here, it's because you're weak, you don't want to work on yourself.*"

"God. Talk about brainwashing."

"It *is* brainwashing. See – once you're there, you cut yourself off from the world – you've given *up* the world. You've got no money – you work there, gardening and cleaning and stuff, and you get given your food. You've got to believe it's right, or what have you got left? And Liz had Kell hammering away at her, too. She said she'd have days when she felt almost mad, when it was like the only way out was to submit to it, to swallow it completely. I reckon that's how a lot of them feel."

As I ponder this, a surly girl in her early teens stomps up to the table with a rack of toast, asks if we want the "full Scottish breakfast" too.

"Full English, please, darlin'," I say, automatically. She scowls at me; Bonny kicks me under the table and says, "Yes, please."

"Him too?" snarls the girl.

"Yes, please," Bonny repeats, as charmingly as she can, and the girl stomps off. "She's gonna spit on your bacon now," she hisses at me.

"I'll swap with you, then. Go on, Bon. When did he start laying into her?"

"Well, one really bad day – when she'd been shut up in a stuffy room trying to meditate for two hours and then been told to iron hundreds of little napkins into *lotus* shapes, for the Formal Dining – she finally cracked. Or rather came to her senses. She realized it might be everything to Kell, but for her it was insane, and if she stayed much longer there wouldn't be any of the *real* her left."

"Good for her."

"She got up early the next day – Saturday – and

packed her bag. Then when he woke up she sat on the bed beside him and told him that she now understood that – whatever happened – he had to stay. And he said, 'Well done, you're learning.' And then she said, 'It's the same for me, Kell. However much I love you, I've got to *leave*.' She was crying and everything, but knowing it was the right decision, knowing they had to say goodbye. He got out of bed but he wouldn't talk to her, wouldn't say a word. I don't think he could *believe* she was going against him like that. She started to walk out of the door – and he got her by the hair and jerked her head right back – *snap*. She said it was like he'd broken her neck. Then he dragged her back into the room."

Chapter 48

Bonny's eyes are fixed on mine across the table, wanting me to be as upset as she is. "Liz said it was so vicious it made her go cold," she croaks. "She didn't want to believe it'd happened. And then he let go and started blubbing about how sorry he was, he'd been so upset at the sight of her going he couldn't control himself. So she stayed and they talked again and they both *cried* and he was saying stuff like – *If you won't stay, I can't stay, not on my own.* So she felt very hopeful – she took it as a sign that he might leave with her."

"Bad mistake."

"Yes. But she didn't *know* that, then."

The surly girl appears at the table, plonks two plates in front of us. I pick mine up and make a joke of going to swap it with Bonny's, but she doesn't laugh. We both start eating. "Go on, Bon," I say through a mouthful. "What happened next?"

"Well – they went down to breakfast together. Porridge, it was always grey gluey porridge. She thought they'd sit on their own and talk but Kell made them sit with this real poisonous couple who've been with the Fellowship for years."

"And are therefore insane."

"Exactly. Kell asked them for advice through a difficult time – when you feel you want to leave. They started on about submission bringing freedom, all the usual crap – how if you left the Fellowship it was like choosing to sleep through your life. And Kell was nodding and agreeing with them. Liz said she sat there feeling like a great stone hand had come round her neck, squeezing her to death. She knew he wouldn't leave and she knew she had to get out. She stood up so fast she knocked her chair over – she said she remembered the noise, and everyone looking round. She ran out of the room – Kell came after her. She got to the bedroom, and picked up her bag, and said – *I'm going, whether you come with me or not.* And that's when he hit her."

"Shit." I stop eating.

"He slapped her – really hard, with his hand in a fist. He was shouting – *You're not going anywhere*, stuff like that. Then he got hold of her and shook her, and she started screaming and he slammed her back against the wall and stuck his hand over her mouth and then someone started hammering on the door."

"*God*. Did they help?"

"No. This is the really nasty bit. Kell went to the door, went outside and shut it. She said she kind of slid down the wall once he'd let go of her – she was retching – she was just so *shocked* – she thought she was going to throw up. She went through to the bathroom – all the bedrooms have these little en suite bathrooms, 'cos it's in a mansion I suppose."

"Yeah – go on."

"She was kind of crouched over the bog retching still when Kell came in and just stood there, in the doorway. She said he was different – all the anger had gone, he was really cold. She pushed out past him, ran to the door, and it was locked, so she started banging on it. He got her by the arm and pulled her away. He told her to be quiet – no one was going to come to help her. He told her he'd just spoken to Rupert and Rupert had agreed to her having a period of isolation."

"*What?*"

"D'you remember Rupert going on about how the first few weeks at the Fellowship were very hard – how people fight to avoid seeing the truth about how mechanical they are and stuff, how they want to leave?"

"Yeah."

"Well, it's apparently normal for people to actually

crack up. And this was all the excuse Kell needed. He told Rupert she was having a very difficult time, got Rupert's permission for her to withdraw, do some kind of hermit contemplation thing. . ."

"Oh, shit. Only seeing Kell?"

"Only seeing the Beloved, right. This is what Kell told Liz, and even if it's a lie – even if he told Rupert she was ill or something – no one came to check on her."

"So he just locked her in that room. . ."

"Yup. He told her he loved her too much to let her destroy her chance of enlightenment by running away."

"Sick."

"Very. He said she was going to come through it – she'd see the light in the end. Which she took to mean he'd keep her locked up until she was broken."

"I don't understand why she didn't *fight* more –"

"On the first day, she smashed a window. And then he really beat her up. She said it was terrifying. He was ranting on about how she'd ruin everything, how she'd ruin his chance of awakening."

"Fucking screwball."

"He *needed* her there, you see. Couples – the Beloveds – have this high status there. If he let her go he'd slide right down the hierarchy. And he was obsessed with her – he loved her."

"Yeah. In his own sick way. Didn't the window alert anyone?"

"No – that sort of thing happens there all the time! They actually think it's a good sign – Rupert says when you really see the falseness of your existence, you react violently. Liz said there was another girl, further along the corridor, who she used to hear crying for hours at a time, and she didn't get any help, either."

There's a pause, while we both fork up the last of our breakfast, then I say, "So she really couldn't just walk out. What a horrible set-up. Anyone would've gone under."

Bonny nods. "Before she *went under* she got that postcard to me. She had to pretend to Kell she'd come around, pretend she wanted to stay, just to avoid getting beaten up. So he believed her when she told him she wanted to write to me to tell me everything was fine. She told him I'd think it was so weird if she didn't write I might come after her. He didn't want that so he gave her the postcard to send."

"And she used your old game. Meaning the opposite of what she said. Clever."

"Yeah. He didn't want her to sign off *I love you and you love me* because he said she should only love him now. But she told him it was an in-joke with us, I'd think it was odd if she didn't use it. He was pleased by what she'd written, she said. Didn't hit her once that night."

"*Jesus* Christ. Is she going to go to the police?"

"I hope so, but last night getting the police

involved wasn't exactly top of the agenda. She was just *spilling* it out – all that happened to her. She went over the same things again and again, like she was trying to come to terms with it all."

"So how long did he keep her locked up for?"

"About three days. He got her so she was too terrified to sleep. He'd lose his rag if she said one thing out of place. After three days, Rupert insisted on seeing her. But the stupid bastard let Kell be in the same room, while he talked to her. And Kell had threatened her so much beforehand she was too shit-scared to say a word out of place. She made out she was beginning to see the light, and Rupert decreed she should enter back into the life of the Fellowship once more."

"So she was let out of the room. . ."

"Yes. But Kell watched her like a hawk. And all that Fellowship crap about women being subservient to men – *led* by men – that played right along with it of course. People *expected* her to defer to him the whole time. And if she did anything wrong, he'd bring it up later in their room at night, and he'd end up hitting her. . ."

"OK, OK. I understand how messed up she was, too scared to get out and so on – and it fits, the way she was when we first saw her. What I don't understand is the way she was when we saw her for the second time. That dinner. She was all keen on the Fellowship, and all over Kell."

Bonny takes in a deep breath, pours herself some more tea. "She said after they'd seen us that morning, she was terrified he was going to take it out on her, but he took her up to their room and absolutely *wooed* her. He kept kissing her hands, telling her how great she was, how they were soul-mates and they had to stay together – how he'd hated hitting her, but he was just so scared she'd leave."

"He must've been afraid she'd do just that. With us there."

"Exactly. Anyway, the way he was – she said it made her cry – it was so good to feel his arms round her again – it was such a comfort. Even though she knew it was because of him she *needed* the bloody comfort."

"This is so weird, Bonny."

"I know. You've got to remember she was half crazy by this time. She said it was like pressing a rewind button. Pretending all the horrible things hadn't happened. They ended up making love, for the first time for absolutely ages. She said it was cosmic. The best ever."

I shake my head. "God knows what a psychiatrist would make of that."

"The way she talked about it – it was like she'd had a big hit of cocaine. She said she felt *wonderful*; everything fell into place, like she'd seen the secret of existence or something . . . Kell was wonderful, the Fellowship was wonderful. . . She says she knows, looking back, that she really was over the edge then."

"Well, that's something. If she can see that."

"And then it all turned, remember? When Kell realized she'd tricked him somehow, with the postcard to me? That was my fault, my big mouth. It was my fault she got beaten up again that night."

I reach over the table, take hold of Bonny's hand. "It wasn't your fault, Bon. Look — you stuck by her, you could've just gone away when she told you to, but you knew something was wrong. And you *got her out*. It's over, she's safe now."

"I need to go and check on her," she sniffs. "And I need to phone Carol again. I only got her off the phone last night by promising to ring again soon as Liz woke up today."

"Come on, then," I say. "Let's go up."

Chapter 49

Liz is up and in the bathroom, which Bonny says is a good sign. She disappears in there with her for a few minutes, while I lurk tactfully in the bedroom outside. When she comes out she picks up her mobile to phone Carol. "Liz has agreed to go straight over there," she says. "She says she feels better – she slept like a log."

"She realize I was in bed with her?"

"No. And I didn't tell her, either. She's had enough excitement in the last twenty-four hours."

I pull a face at her as she punches in the hotel number, then I get occupied making some coffee. But when Bonny gets off the phone she has a strange, slightly sick look on her face. "What's up, Bon?" I ask. "It's OK to go over, isn't it?"

"What? Oh, yes – Carol can't wait to see her. She was like – *incoherent* with gratitude."

"So what's up?"

"It's Mum. Carol said she went to the Fellowship last night and she – didn't come back. To the hotel."

"Oh, great. Didn't she phone?"

"No. And when Carol tried her mobile, she said it was switched off."

"Look, Bonny – don't go getting all anxious. I told you I saw Tigger dressed like some guru, clinging to Rupert's arm. She's probably just stayed the night with him."

"Oh, *Rich*! Are you trying to comfort me or freak me out completely?"

"Look, Bon, your mum is a living, breathing disaster. She – *does* those things, you have to accept that about her. She'll be back. And if she's not, I'll go in and look for her."

Bonny looks down at the ground, visibly twitching. "I ought to look for her."

"Why?"

"'Cos – she's my mum. I ought to *face* her."

"Yeah, Bon, yeah. Climb back in the washing machine again."

"What?"

"The washing machine of all your mum's . . . *crap*. Going round and round, getting all churned up and tangled up and bashed about and. . ."

"OK, Rich, don't milk it – I get the image. It's just. . ." Bonny trails off, twitches again.

"Well, I'm offering, Bon. I'll do it if you like – I can

be more, you know, *objective*. I'll check out what's happening, find out if she's all right, report back to you."

"And if she wants to see me. . ."

"Then you can make your mind up if you want to see her. God, Bonny, don't put yourself through it if you don't have to. What's the need?"

There's a pause, then she suddenly springs at me, gives me a heart-stopping kiss right on the mouth. "Dragon-slayer," she says.

I grin. "Give her till after lunch."

We check out of the pub. I insist we should act like we're leaving tonight, mission accomplished, and Bonny – a bit waveringly, because of being so worried about her monster of a mother – agrees with me. Then we drive over to The George, with Liz slumped like a zombie in the front seat. I think about putting my hands on her shoulders again, like I did the last time we were in the car, but in the end I don't.

At The George, I stay outside beside the car and once again lurk tactfully. I'm getting so good at lurking tactfully I could take it up as a career. After thirty minutes or so, Bonny runs out of the hotel. She says, "Let's go," and starts up the engine while I'm still scrambling into the front seat. As she starts to pull away, she throws something in my lap.

It's a wad of money.

"What's this?" I demand.

"From Carol. Gratitude money. *Guilt* money."

"*Shit* – there's hundreds here! Why did you take it?"

"I didn't *take* it, Rich! She shoved it at me, and then collapsed on to Liz's neck, and they both burst into tears, and when I said, '*I don't want this*,' she went off on one about how it was the very smallest token of how grateful she was. . . Oh, *look*. She's pretty loaded. I decided not to argue. In the circumstances."

I pick up the wad of money. It's almost exactly the same size as the wad Nick Hanratty shoved at me across the desk the first time I met him. "Expenses," he said, to smarten myself up to see that alcopops client, lifetimes ago, aeons ago. . .

Six months ago, that's all. I frill the notes with my thumb. It's just money. It doesn't have the old power, not a bit of it.

"Shall we go and get some lunch?" asks Bonny. "And a *drink*? We could afford somewhere posh. To celebrate."

"Anywhere, Bon," I say. "As long as I'm with you, babe." And she laughs, and I join in.

We choose a bar-restaurant, nice and airy, lilies in the corner, wide, scrubbed tables. Bonny says she wants wine. "Even if I can't drive for a while, I want wine. I *need* wine."

She's all wobbly and giggly with relief that all the drama's over, that Liz is safe. While she's telling me about Liz's reunion with her mum she downs her first glass, orders another. "I could buy a vineyard if I wanted," she gurgles, pulling the wad of money out of her pocket.

"Put that back, Bon! D'you wanna get mugged?" And then I grin.

"What?"

"I've just realized something. About money. It really is just oil, isn't it? *Lubrication.* It's not what you're actually about. It makes things easier, that's all."

"A lot easier."

"Yeah, but I could be anywhere with you now, I could be in a bus shelter, a *dugout*, it'd be just as good. . ."

"Aw, Rich, that's sweet." She puts her glass down. "I've realized something too."

"What?"

"When Liz had gone to sleep last night, I lay awake – I was thinking about you, about *us*. . ."

"Yeah?"

"It's just – I – oh, *shit*. You've been brilliant these last few days, Rich. Not just –"

"The sex," I breathe, leaning close all comedy-seductive.

"*No!* Although that was—"

"*Brilliant*."

"*Yes*. Back off Rich, that man over there's looking."

"Stuff 'im."

"It was . . . the way you just came up here with me, and the way you've – you've been such a support, you've . . . oh, *shit*. What I wanted to say was . . . look, I'm so crazy about you, all I can think about sometimes is how much it's going to hurt when we split up."

"Nice, Bon. Positive."

"I can't help it. It's horrible. Part of me's always holding back, screwing myself up, thinking *keep some back, don't get in too deep*. Well – I decided. When I was lying awake. I'm not going to pretend I can *do* that any more."

"Good."

"I'm not going to hold back any more."

"*Good*."

"Well – that's kind of what I had to tell you. I thought about what Liz went through with Kell and I thought if she can go through that, I can stop being such a coward, can't I? When you finish it I'll just have to deal with it."

"Suppose it's you who finishes it, have you thought of that?"

She shakes her head. "It won't be."

"Yeah, it could be. You're off to uni – you don't know who you'll meet. Why d'you assume I'm the inconstant fly-by-night type? It could be you." She starts to laugh, and I add, "Yeah, you heartbreaker. *Slut*. It's gonna be you who splits us up. I hate you."

We're both laughing now, and through it I say, "No, I don't, I love you."

It kind of falls on the table between us, like I'm laying down a card.

There's a pause, then she says, "D'you mean that?"

"Yes."

"I love you too," she says. "I always have."

Chapter 50

After that, of course I have to go back to the Fellowship to check on Bonny's lunatic mother. Anything less would be pathetic in the extreme. Bonny and I drink coffee until she's sure she's sober enough to drive, then we drive over to the mansion and she parks as close to the gates as she can. "Lock yourself in the car, babe," I say. "If I'm not back in half an hour, call the feds."

"Oh, shut up," she groans. Then she kisses me.

I feel like a hero as I swagger up the mansion drive. The dogs don't scare me, nothing scares me. I bang aggressively on the front door, which is opened rapidly by Frazer. I start to cross the threshold and he puts out an indignant hand out to stop me. "What are *you* doing back here –? "

"S'all right, mate, I haven't brought the police with

me. Not this time. This is personal." And I barge through his arm, making sure my shoulder knocks into his as I pass.

Halfway up the main stairs, I'm met by Rupert. "Ah, *Richard* –"

"Ah, *Rupert*. Bonny's a bit concerned about her mum. Seeing as her best mate came to such grief here. By the way, have the police been in touch yet?"

"The *police*? No, what are you –?"

"They will, they will. Now. Tigger. I have to make sure she's safe."

"Why – she is just fine. She and I were just talking." He waves a fat hand towards a grand door half open on the landing. "She was telling me – *Richard, where are you going?*"

I leg it past him, towards the open door, and through it. Tigger's standing in front of the ornate fireplace, back to the door, face reflected in the huge mirror above the mantelpiece. As I focus on her reflection a cold thrill judders through me. She looks mad, *desperate*. Her face is contorted, mouth wide open, lips curled back, like she's screaming inside at a horror beyond belief. . . She turns round. "*Richy!*" she squeals.

"Tigger – you all *right*? What's *happened*?"

"Nothing!"

"But your *face* – you looked terrified –"

Tigger flaps her hand in front of her mouth, coy and – I swear it – blushing. "Oh, how *embarrassing*.

Just my face exercises, sweetie. To keep my jawline firm. One isn't as young as one was – *you* know how it is –" She breaks off with a girlish cry as Rupert heaves himself panting into the room. "*Roopie!*"

"My Beloved," he intones, scarily. "It seems the commotion at the front door was this young man. It seems he is concerned for your welfare."

It's hard to talk through teeth that are gritted against explosive laughter. "Yeah, Tigger," I gasp. "We wondered where you were. Your phone's been switched off."

Tigger raises both arms, flips her hands like she's doing some Eastern dance. "It is not only switched off, Richard," she trills, "it has been disposed of. The Fellowship is no place for a mobile phone."

"OK," I say evenly, "what about Bonny? She's worried about you."

"Oh, dear. That child is *so* possessive . She always has been. She has to learn that – yes, I am her mother, but we each have our own paths. She must learn to let go of me, however painful that is for her. She must learn to *separate.* So we may each follow our own truths."

Tigger's complete inversion of reality leaves me too gobsmacked to reply. Bonny would *love* to hear that, I think. Meanwhile, Rupert is heading towards her, beaming proudly. "Beautifully put, as always, my dearest," he says.

"What about Carol?" I choke out. "You can't just abandon her – you drove her up here!"

Tigger shoots an indignant look at me. "Bonny has got her car, has she not?"

"Yes, but—"

"Then you can give Carol and Elizabeth a lift home, can you not? I hardly think it would be appropriate for me to share a car with Elizabeth now. Not now she has turned her face away from the truth. And anyway," she simpers, as she turns to Rupert, takes hold of his arm, "I plan to stay for a while."

Rupert pats her hand lovingly. "Tigger has so much light inside her," he gushes, "it is as though the Fellowship was created for her."

The two of them make eyeball-searing eye-contact, and I'm suddenly dead redundant in the room. "OK," I cough, "so I'm to tell Bonny—"

"Oh, tell her anything you want," snaps Tigger, with a return to her old style. "I shall stay here. I have discovered something here that I cannot turn my back on. Not without a loss to my innermost being. There is such peace here, such . . . *rightness*." She eyeballs Rupert again. "I shall stay here for as long as I feel I am in the *right space*."

Chapter 51

I don't bother to control my laughter any more as I leg it down the staircase. I let it come out in great ragged whoops that bounce off the balustrades. The front door is already open. It takes me only minutes to make it back to the car, and fling my arms round Bonny.

"*Well?*" she demands.

"*Well* – you're free. *We're* free. Tigger is very much alive and happy. She's heard the call. She's joined the Fellowship. She's in the *right space*."

"Oh, *God* –"

"Bonny, don't knock it! She's as happy as Larry. She and *Roopie*, as she calls him—"

"*Yuuuch* –"

"– have obviously got a thing going on. Just as I suspected. He calls her Beloved. That means she's top dog. Or queen bitch anyway, over the whole set-up. She'll love that. And she's swallowed the philosophy hook, line and sinker. Trust me, Bon – she's glowing. In clover."

"But I can't just go away and leave her there on her own! It's such a sick place!"

"Ah, but you must. You must each *follow your separate paths*. She said that. She also said you were too possessive of her. Unwilling to separate."

"*Whaat?*" Bonny collapses her face down on to the steering wheel.

"Looks like Carol and Liz have lost their lift, anyway." I squeeze her shoulders, hoping she'll come up laughing, not crying. She comes up doing a bit of both.

"This is so weird," she gasps. "I phoned Carol, and she said that she and Liz were standing at Pittlowrie station, waiting for a train. She said she hoped I wouldn't be upset, but they'd decided to leave without Tigger. So I said of course I understood completely. They're heading for Aberdeen, where Carol's cousin lives – big house, lots of open space. They're going to stay there – so Liz can have a good rest."

"Did you talk to Liz?"

"Yes. Yes, she was fine. Crying, but fine. *Relieved*. She said it all seemed like a bad dream, now."

"She'll get over it, Bon."

"I know she will. She's going to phone me from Aberdeen."

The car is filled with a wonderful silence, a silence full of potential. "So, Bon," I say at last. "It's just us. Let's hit the road, eh? Find somewhere nice to stay for the night?"

"I can't just leave Mum," croaks Bonny. "Can I?"

"So what do you want to do? If you go back in there she'll only say to you exactly what she said to me. Only it'll *upset* you."

"We could wait for a bit—"

"What, hang around in case she gets sick of it? Bon – she can leave any time she wants. It was Kell that kept Liz prisoner, not the Fellowship. And Tigger's got her car."

"I s'pose. . ."

"You should've *seen* her with Rupert. He's besotted. In fact it's him I'm worried about, not her." Bonny laughs, and I press on, "What it comes down to is – d'you want to waste the last bit of summer hanging around here in thrall to an insane mother who's just discovered her hippy roots and told you to get lost? Or d'you want to take off with me? We can take the long route home, Bonny. We can take days."

Bonny grins, eyes wet, turns to me, and plants a kiss squint across my mouth. Then she puts the keys in the ignition. "Fasten your seatbelt," she says.

Out now, a gripping new novel from Kate Cann. . .

Leaving
Poppy

*It's time for Amber to leave home,
get out of her sister's clutches. But what if her
new life isn't a safe place? Someone is waiting
for her there – waiting for Poppy. . .*

Then she was awake, fully awake. She heard a key turn in a lock, so close it had to be her door, even though her key was on the inside. Silence, then someone muttering *It's your fault, your fault* . . . and then, directly above her head, there was a noise, rhythmic, repetitive, wood on wood.

The rocking chair.